Lost!

Lost!

by
Charles Malato

Translated, annotated and introduced by
Michael Shreve

A Black Coat Press Book

Visit our website at www.blackcoatpress.com

ISBN 978-1-61227-670-0. First Printing. September 2017. Published by Black Coat Press, an imprint of Hollywood Comics.com, LLC, P.O. Box 17270, Encino, CA 91416. All rights reserved. Except for review purposes, no part of this book may be reproduced or transmitted in any form or by any means, electronic or mechanical, including photocopying, recording, or by any information storage and retrieval system, without permission in writing from the publisher. The stories and characters depicted in this novel are entirely fictional. Printed in the United States of America.

TABLE OF CONTENTS

Introduction

"Never surrender your conscience, your reason. Always think for yourself and you will be a man." [1]

"Forced to hide in the still unexplored regions of Morocco, the hero whose adventures Charles Malato relates is caught in the grips of the most unexpected and most extraordinary predicaments."

Thus reads the blurb on the illustrated cover of *Lost!* published c. 1915 under the original title *Perdus au Maroc* [Lost in Morocco].

The series of adventures, each one more extraordinary than the last, piling mystery upon mystery, peril upon peril, come directly out of the tradition of *the roman feuilleton*, or serial novel.

The popular novel owed its birth to newspapers where longer stories were published in installments over a series of several issues, hence the cliffhangers. These popular serial novels in the 19th century were akin to melodramas (they owed much to theater): they had the same clichés, the same sentimentality, the same intrigues, often centered on the persecution then subsequent rehabilitation of the hero, and the plots came straight out of the police blotter.

By the end of the century, the serial novel was subdivided into several categories. It could relate a police intrigue, follow a criminal hero, or even illustrate an historical drama, or, more rarely, delve into the unknown in

---

[1] All quotations are from the works of Charles Malato.

the form of the *roman scientifique*, a precursor of what is known today as science fiction. But the most popular genre was the social novel, or novel of contemporary mores; the representation of "real" people became more important and it was the workers, not just the criminal underworld, which took center stage. The adventures of the hero were meant to both entertain the reader and teach them about proper morals, mostly equivalent to middle class ideology and thus glorifying the three key values of work, family and country.

Adventure novels came out of the serials, turned into "dime novels" and eventually pulp fiction. They are basically thrillers and can include elements from mysteries, detective stories, romances, fantasy and science fiction. The best stories can be read on multiple levels where the physical travel is just as important as the inner journey where the hero will learn not only about strange new worlds, but also about himself; where the quest for power, in gold, knowledge or magical items, is the usual reason for facing such perilous adventures. In *Lost!*, that quest is basically a desire for freedom.

"[As a child] I filed away the terrible Jehovah with the bogeyman and other old-fashioned scarecrows; the god of Victor Hugo seemed too vague; I built in my heart an altar to the radiant goddess Liberty… True liberty, the liberty whose name is written on the walls and that we try constantly to reach, consists in being absolute masters of our persons and wills, the independence of each assuring naturally the independence of all."

True to the genre, Charles Malato based his novels on facts and real events; he wrote entertainment that could inform the readers; he wrote cliffhangers in a crisp, lively style to keep their attention. The action and adventure was most important, but like other anarchist authors, he turned his novels toward more democratic and liberating ideas. And although we find monsters, mutants and miscreants, we do not have the sneering super villain of melodramas. For Malato, the real villain was "centuries of oppression and poverty that have turned man into a wild animal—and it will howl, this animal, oh yes, it will howl!"

"What could the children of such beings [alcoholics, syphilitics, epileptics, idiots] be if not a race of monsters? Likewise, how many men in possession of verbal language are, like parrots, unable to understand ideas even a little complicated! In their modern suits, they remain pithecanthropus of the tertiary period, Stone Age primitives."

Malato's heroes are not stereotypes. The pariah, the outsider, criminals and vagabonds incarnate the conflict between individual and society. They cannot be classified, labeled, integrated or imprisoned. They are foreign, bringing a radically different vision of the instability of the world around them. They refuse to stagnate, always on the move, trying to escape the harsh conditions of the time in order to demystify the systems that confine the individual, both externally and internally. These heroes are not in search of power and conquest except the conquest of oneself. They are subversive, marginal figures, living on the fringes of society, escaping from society like the contemporary "anarchist" heroes of Fantômas, Arsène Lupin and the real-life Bonnot Gang.

"Freethinkers rise up in the middle of medieval theocracy, republicans amidst monarchic absolutism, socialists in the capitalist regime, anarchists forming the autonomy of the individual in the face of the despotism of the State, they were or are *prophetic species*."

In truth, if we want to look for models for Malato's hero and prototypes of his adventures we need look no further than his own life.

"On March 1, 1875, I left Brest on board the frigate *Le Var* heading for New Caledonia. My father was being deported along with 25 other communards locked in a cage under the not very kind surveillance of four or five policemen. My mother and I went with him into exile sharing the common room of paid travelers. At night a sheet was modestly lowered to separate the women's hammocks from the men's and a guard, stiff as a eunuch in the observation of his duty, made sure there was no hanky-panky. I was 17 years old, full of imagination and naïve sensitivity, and far too shy—I still am—but I had no fear of danger.

"At an age when other kids were off getting into trouble, I never went out into the street alone and I would babble for 15 minutes before daring to speak directly to anyone. I read the classical epics, then the marvelous novels of chivalry and finally Jules Verne and Captain Mayne Reid—they filled me with excitement early on. I dreamed of fighting grizzlies or cougars. During the siege of the Commune I was itching to shoot guns and constantly harassed my parents for this, but I would have died of shame rather than let any vulgar or obscene word escape my lips lest my grandmother tell me, Charles, you're talking like a man of the people!"

Charles Armand Antoine Malato de Corné (September 7, 1857-November 7, 1938) was born in Foug (Meurthe-et-Moselle) of a Sicilian father, rich, aristocratic and very traditional, and a mother from Lorraine, intelligent, sensitive, with a long line of doctors behind her. It was his father who taught him about revolution. After being sentenced to death and exile a number of times in Italy for his republican actions, he finally moved to France.

"At the time when my father with his friends (now all quieted down) fought against the masters of Italy, it was political independence alone that was at stake; industrialism had not yet posed the dreadful problem of work... But there is an anomaly that we often see among victims of a good bourgeois upbringing: My father, although fundamentally revolutionary in temperament and even in spirit, always upheld the customs of his aristocratic family and my mother, likewise raised in a less plebian environment, admired them despite her great breadth of thought and sentiment."

Malato was gifted in mathematics and science at an early age but it was literature, history and art, what spurred his imagination that really interested him. In spite of his lifelong love of books, works of rigorous scholarship as well as pure fantasy, he was much more a man of action. Along with the journalist and writer ran a militant, an insurrectional anarchist.

"The man who taught me how to think awoke in me the life of the mind. Without him what would I have been? A machine of flesh, a kind of domesticated animal... Certainly it's a very good thing to educate the people, but it would be much better to teach them to think, to allow them to have their own ideas rather than just telling them your own."

The stories he wrote are not only a reflection of his ideas, of his moral and philosophical truths, but also a play of imagination that parallels the growth of science fiction and fantasy in literature. One frequent theme that dates back to ancient myths is the descent into an underground world where the hero goes in search, willingly or not, of a secret.

From Charles de Fieux's proto-fantasy adventures in *Lamekis*[2] (1735-38) to Edgar Allan Poe's *The Narrative of Arthur Gordon Pym* (1838) to Jules Verne's *Journey to the Center of the Earth* (1864), travel in exotic lands morphed into fantastic adventures in subterranean worlds where other life (or beyond life) -forms exist, where the everyday, rational existence slipped into a strange, shadowy, hidden world, an occult world of unknown powers and riches.

There were hollow earths (Edgar Rice Burrough's *Pellucidar* novels starting in 1914), lost races (Edward Bulwer-Lytton's *The Coming Race*, 1871), lost worlds (Arthur Conan Doyle's *The Lost World*, 1912) with underground continents, strange creatures and lost civilizations set in remote and unexplored parts of the globe: deep, dark Africa, the jungles of the Amazon, islands in the Pacific or the mountains of Asia. *Lost!* is somewhat unusual for its setting in Morocco near civilization, albeit the culture was still quite alien to most Europeans. Most of the standard devices of lost world novels—a usurped throne, an enemy priest or priestess, trial by combat, precious treasures, an ill-fated romance—are found in *Lost!* but with an unusual, original twist.

If lost world novels have merged with fantasy and science fiction (because there are no more uncharted territories on this globe) then *Lost!* would fall into the dark urban fantasy genre.

"This [future] race that will be simply the *human* race, will differ from us more even than we differ from our primitive Stone Age ancestors. Nothing can put limits on progress; who can say that humanity won't acquire new senses?

---

[2] Black Coat Press ISBN 978-1-61227-003-6.

"How then, with a lot of shyness due mainly to my environment and education, was I later able to break with everything that is law, custom and convention and become one of those wild anarchists who propose very sincerely to flip society upside down like an omelet? For such a transformation one must be very disgusted with this society and very sure that the subversive ideas are superior."

Malato's father played only a minor role in the Paris Commune, so the authorities could not justifiably arrest him. However, due to his former revolutionary activities in Italy they could accuse him of being on the run. They threw him in jail, closed all his businesses and ruined the family. In the end he was convicted and deported to New Caledonia. His mother, meanwhile, was locked up in Saint-Lazare prison for ten months with prostitutes and other victims of misfortune.

Charles Malato was barely 17 years-old but ready for action. Alone he wrote up some flyers calling on the people to rise up against the Imperialist State. Just as he was posting them on Rue d'Alsace, he was arrested. He pretended to be crazy, calling himself Napoléon IV, and after ten days sharing a cell with bedbugs and fleas, he was released. He joined his mother just in time to catch the boat and bid farewell to his native land.

The crossing to New Caledonia took three and a half months. In Nouméa, the young Malato was hired into the telegraph service, a job that sent him all over the island.

"I was sent into the most remote of the new posts, to Oubatche, in the middle of tribes still independent and maybe cannibals."

Now his desire for knowledge and adventure could be fully realized. Not only did he study the geography

13

and tribes, but he liked to strip down, paint himself black and participate in the war dances of the natives.

"They're a lot less ferocious than we Europeans who went and took their land, their women, turned their way of life upside down, didn't give them our virtues but our vices, made them drunks and liars and profoundly selfish to boot… Pretending to make them civilized, we went and made them syphilized."

In 1878, he was witness to the famous Kanak Rebellion (under Chief Ataï) that killed up to 5% of the population. Although his parents' house was burned by the insurgents, they managed to escape and avoid being killed and eaten (by the cannibal Oébias for example).

In Nouméa, he lost his mother. "The burial of my mother was religious. Raised in a half-aristocratic, half-bourgeois family she had kept her spiritualist beliefs and with following strictly the letter or even the narrow spirit of the dogma, she had expressed many times the desire to be buried like all her ancestors. In the name of liberty my father and I inclined and the coffin, even though accompanied by our exiled friends, entered the church. Need I say that this anarchist today doesn't regret the respect paid not to an enemy cult but to a sentiment and a will? A few days later Louise Michel, whom we didn't know, came straight to us from the Ducos peninsula."

He and Louise Michel shared a deep and lasting interest in the language, customs, legends and hopes of freedom of the Kanak people. They were two of the only deportees who took the side of the Kanaks during the revolt of 1878 and they were alone in this interest in ethnography that would become the foundation of a lifelong friendship. Malato's recounting of the story of "The Rat and the Octopus" translated here was included in her 1885 book *Légendes et chants de gestes canaques*.

"A young man fed on Jules Verne and Mayne Reid, to go exploring this still savage 'bush', to develop relations with the last cannibals, to study in place the dialects and customs... A young imagination avid for the unexpected... I violated the graves and stole the skulls that I put on my shelves like trophies. Burning with an unfortunate penchant for anatomy, ethnology and a few other natural sciences."

There are particular scientific marks that are found in lost race fiction: a scientist hero who discovers maps and manuscripts, takes specimen samples and constructs ethnographies. Again we find these in *Lost!*, but with a difference. The hero is more like Robinson Crusoe than Allan Quatermain, a teacher rather than scientist or adventurer, and all his discoveries and observations are focused on survival instead of economic or intellectual enrichment.

"After a quick glance at the mission and nearby tribe I went to visit the grottoes that are famous on this tiny island [of Lifou], a simple atom lost in the blue immensity of the Pacific.

"There are two grottoes: one remarkable for its stalactites and columns among which swirl, when light shines in, clouds of bats. The other, much bigger, seemed, with its natural spiral staircases, to sink into the subterranean abysses. I plunged in, accompanied by a guide and armed with a torch whose light made the crystallized rock sparkle. Ulysses, Telemachus, Aeneas and all the ancient characters who, while alive, descended into underworlds certainly saw no more impressive scenery. At the bottom of the grotto stretched a thin patch of salt water: we were at the level of the sea that filters in through limestone rocks."

When Malato would later write his memoirs of this time, it read more like a serial novel than a non-fiction memoir. Not only the physical but also the mental adventure left an indelible mark. The search for truth and reason, the respect for liberty and the absence of dogma, these all pushed rebel writers like Malato toward anarchism rather than socialism. Anarchism was a weapon against prejudice, injustice and right-wing regression. To use literature was one among many ways to take part in the social struggle. To spread the ideas of liberty and equality through writing was to work for the emancipation of men and women. So, the fundamental principles of anarchism—solidarity, autonomy and liberty—are illustrated in these works of fiction.

"Life in the open air and primitive naturalism pleased me a lot. Wasn't this true liberty much more than speaking tours or bloody battles over party politics? Yes, but it's the vegetative life of mollusks, only digestion is easier under the clear blue sky. Isn't a hell where we think better than paradise where we are asleep forever?"

A utopia is a nowhere or at least a marginal place, outside of "common places" where people are normally imprisoned. All utopic literature shares this other, better vision of the world but often ends up as rigid as where it escaped from becoming the flipside of the same coin. Between Soviet communism and modern capitalism, for example, we are given no alternative. Anarchists were especially wary of this false choice and constantly warning against revolutions recreating the same vices and domination as contemporary society.

"We must not destroy superstition only to replace it with error... We must not replace one religion with another... When we want to free Humanity, we must first have the courage to free ourselves."

Utopias, therefore, were suspicious, always vulnerable to petrifying into dogma and mutating naturally into dystopias. Malato offers neither a utopia nor a dystopia but a metaphor of reality. In the degenerate subterranean race or the idyllic life in the oasis we see cloudy reflections of man and nature.

"Fifteen centuries ago a world died… State, religion, family, social bonds gone to dust. What was to come?… Christian religion based on faith, replaced the Roman society based on strength. It lasted 15 centuries. Today more death throes are in process. The throne and altar already belong to the past; kings are just living ghosts. Bizarre beings, common in times of decadence, swarm around us and sit enthroned, as masters for the day, on the dunghill of our century. It is the end."

His is not mere escapist literature like H Rider Haggard, nor socialist visions like H. G. Wells, but art as action, as a weapon. Of all the writers of fiction it was Malato's friend, Louise Michel, "the prophetess of the revolution", who was his kin.

"My father and I had a lot of trouble persuading her not to return to New Caledonia to open schools in the bush for young Kanaks. Which the missionaries would have destroyed in a flash."

She completely revamped the serial novel to snatch it out of the constraints of the genre and invent a new form that owed as much to the noir novel as the utopia. She was one of the first anarchist writers to venture into science fiction and fantasy. Other contemporaries include Michel Zévaco, Han Ryner and André Laurie.

At the turn of the century, literature was becoming democratized but the distinction between popular art for entertainment and social art as an instrument for social change was still blurry. Both, however, were opposed to the conception of art for art's sake as an end in itself. For anarchists the debate was open: should the artist be socialist, individualist or try to reconcile the two? Louise Michel, despite her eclectic tastes—she wrote utopias, social novels, "noir and pulp" fiction, non-fiction—never separated her militant anarchism from her literary work. Anarchist art must first be an art of combat. Although Malato was intent on highlighting the ills of society and showing the way to freedom, his novels were never didactic. His theories are presented at a distance, if not symbolically, metaphorically. He does not rise to the level of utopia but neither does he sink into dystopia or indulge in mere satire.

"Today people are skeptical, as if withered up, pretending to know everything and be excited about nothing. They call this progress, civilization. Well, I don't hesitate to say that it's a backwards civilization that confines the human being and makes him into a kind of thinking machine... Life would be so good for men if only they loved it!"

Amnesty was declared for the Communards, so on February 18, 1881 the father and son boarded *La Loire* and sailed back to Brest, six years after being shipped away. With the help of another deportee Malato set up an agency where he translated foreign journals and newspapers from 7 am to 11 p.m.

Soon after, he got some copying jobs and then became a reporter for the *Reveil Lyonnais*, a radical socialist newspaper. Around the same time he sold his first novel to the *Gazette du Soir* (paid with a handshake and congratulations).

"To write! To give form to thought! To shout out loud what one feels, what one believes to be true, just and beautiful! This had been my dream for a long time."

Little by little he made his living as a writer, founding newspapers, contributing to others, producing pamphlets and in 1888 publishing his *Philosophy of Anarchy*. In 1890, on the eve of the May 1 demonstrations, Malato was arrested for an article that appeared in *L'Attaque* for "inciting murder, pillage and arson," and was sentenced to 15 months in prison and a 3000-franc fine. "Found guilty of wanting to turn society topsy-turvy with our pen, we were sentenced on the spot with so hard a sentence that we earned the ardent sympathy of the female public."

He wrote two books while in Sainte-Pélagie, one a humoristic portrait of the prison with Ernest Gégout (*Prison at the End of the Century*), the other a very serious study: *Christian Revolution and Social Revolution*.

History and anthropology were two intertwining interests in Malato's writings.

"The young proletarian generation, just like the bourgeois, know nothing at all about contemporary history. They move around in a Europe that they don't know, in the midst of men and parties whose names, past, goals and connections they don't know."

Lost! gives his imagination free reign to roam through civilization, past and present, to explore humanity's progress, seek out the contradictions and question it. Imagination, yes, but based on science.

"Poets like William Morris, novelists like Wells, sociologists like Bellamy [*Looking Backward*, 1888] and Spencer tried to explore future times until such time—which will come—as the laws of history are formulated like those of chemistry and mechanics and they can predict more or less far in advance, the great movements of humanity, just like we predict celestial phenomenon."

19

Evolution is a staple subject in science fiction but for Malato it is not approached with a view to an idealized (or dismal) future but rather for a better life in the present. "Anarchists must be and are evolutionists at the same time as revolutionists."

Along with his prison term, he was sentenced to expulsion because they considered him Italian, despite being born in France and working for the government in New Caledonia. This conviction was suspended until 1892 when he and many others were condemned after the first anarchist attacks in the midst of the dynamite period. Being warned by a friend, he managed to evade the police and take refuge in London.

"If individualism must reign, it's not in economy but in the domain of thought, philosophy and art. And how can you be really yourself if you have to confine your spirit to the common rule formulated by some anonymous tyrant?"

London was the traditional refuge for outcasts of every defeated faith. The anarchists, chased like wild animals after the explosions in March 1892, followed the general example: they came to the capital to ask for work and freedom.

"I went out looking for Louise Michel and I found her. It was the same Louise Michel of Nouméa and the public meetings that I saw again, still passionate, brave in spite of all the years, prison and exile—the anarchist prophetess living her ideal to the full. Threatened with jail by the bourgeois who consider every noble idea madness, she came to live in London, waiting for the evolutionary hour to return to France."

In London, Malato made a living by giving French lessons. He also continued collaborating with different journals and he wrote plays. In 1893 in the company of

Errico Malatesta, he went to Belgium to join the fight for universal suffrage. Later that year, he was in Italy for the agrarian revolt. 1895 saw amnesty for the anarchists but Malato was barely back in France before he was arrested again. This time, however, they accepted that he was French and he could stay.

Friends called to Malato from Spain to help with the escape of the revolutionary Ramon Sempau, sentenced to death for his role at Montjuïc where anarchists were massacred for supporting worker's rights. They were betrayed and the plan failed, but Malato and his partners evaded the police and Sempau was eventually released. After this, Malato headed to Valencia and then Cartagena to support the social war but he found the efforts weak and compromised, so he went back to Paris.

This was at the time of the Dreyfus Affair during the *fin de siècle* which saw France split in two over antisemitism. He fought with written and spoken word against the anti-semite nationalists, which would rear its ugly head even more fiercely in Europe before he died in 1938.

"It's hard to imagine humanity without vices... Humanity is, in fact, a man who is always perfecting himself and never dies: man is a summary of humanity... an animal who, as unsociable as he might appear, cannot live except in society... Social equality yes! Physical and moral uniformity, no! We must not, on the pretext of strict equality, break the individual and clip the wings of genius."

At the turn of the century, the opening of the "Bibliothèque des Égaux" was announced. It was a libertarian library that was inaugurated by a conference organized by Malato on the "Crimes of civilization." In the new year, he wrote a satirical drama in two acts,

Barbapoux, an allegorical farce that was a precursor of Alfred Jarry's absurdist theater.

"As prisoners laughter was our only weapon and our only distraction." Irony in Malato is essential and his dark humor is used to reveal the horror in order to learn from it. It is a caustic, subversive sense of humor that leaves no one untouched, not even the revolutionary heroes. "Do we have to put on gloves to touch these vampires who suck the blood and life out of workers? Society is still attractive to those who look at it from afar; it's repulsive to those who see it up close!"

Then came the famous affair of Rue de Rohan in 1905. A bomb was thrown at a car carrying French President Loubet and the young king of Spain, Alfonso XIII. Malato, who had fought in support of the Cuban revolutionaries, the prisoners of Montjuïc, and the worker strikes in Barcelona, became the object of revenge. He was accused of attempted regicide along with five other anarchists and arrested. But at the trial on November 27, no proof or reliable witnesses were brought forth, so they were acquitted and released after six months in prison. The *New York Times* printed a story about it on June 3:

"Cultured Anarchist Accused of Paris Plot: Accused by French police of organizing a plot to assassinate King Alfonso of Spain… Charles Malato's political articles are remarkable for their polished literary grace. Malato himself is noted for the elaborate perfection of his manners. But in a society where words mean nothing, labels have become an illusion."

In 1908, Malato gave up full-time journalism, finding it too hard to stay independent, although he would continue to contribute articles to various socialist and radical papers. Instead he devoted himself to writing novels, scholarly books, memoirs, translations, plays, essays and children's books.

"Education, which should be of utmost importance in a democratic country," was always a primary concern of anarchists so it was natural that some writers turned their pen to children's fiction: Louise Michel and Jean Grave; Han Ryner wrote *The Human Ant*[3] (1901), Séverine *Sac-à-tout, memoirs d'un petit chien* (1903) and Charles Malato, under the pseudonym of Talamo. his *Memoirs of a Gorilla* (1901), included in this collection, as well as a *Life of Louise Michel* (1905).

Animalization played a special role in this literature for two reasons: one, since animals are considered lower than humans their voice could never become authoritative; and two, it allowed an outsider voice to critic the society of men. We see this recurring in fantastic fiction, especially with anarchists, from Louise Michel's *The Human Microbes*[4] (1887) to André Laurie's *Spiridon*[5] (1907) and on to George Orwell's *Animal Farm* (1945).

Malato plays with his gorilla narrator to denounce colonization and the treatment of minorities. He may also be reflecting the vision of a writer living amongst men but refusing their authority, assuming that his knowledge should be put to use to improve men, not to instill his own ideas in them but simply to stimulate their minds. His own thought was in constant evolution and rejected every concept of the absolute. His great ideal was the respect for life and its perpetual movement. This is what kept his philosophy from petrifying into dogma.

"If there ever were a science that attracted the anar-

---

[3] Black Coat Press, ISBN 978-1-61227-323-5.
[4] Black Coat Press, ISBN 978-1-61227-116-3.
[5] Black Coat Press, ISBN 978-1-934543-61-3.

chists (the enemies of borders, governments, religions and laws) it is astronomy. How could they believe in the sacred character of fictions accepted by the human unconscious when they see how small a place our humanity and the earth itself occupies, when they see life go on beyond us in all its constantly changing forms? The poet and the visionary are joined and that's why astronomer-poets like Flammarion so often become anarchists!"

At the outset of World War I, Malato was a supporter of the *union sacrée* and a signatory of the pro-Allies Manifesto of the Sixteen. Thus he would not protest the government during the war, which was a source of great conflict in the revolutionary movement.

"I was anguished because it seems to me that nature, where we play an integral part, is going to fall into ruins in a terrible shake-up; we feel, however, that the death of present things will give rise to new life... The earthquake that suddenly opens up abysses, the torrent of lava that erupts from a volcano and rushes down into the valleys are the results of a long series of latent actions: this work is no less catastrophic... It dislocates, pulverizes and disperses what was already shaken up."

To the end of his life Charles Malato was honest to a fault and firmly devoted to the revolutionary cause. His life was full of fierce battles, unwavering assistance, court appearances, imprisonment and exiles. Along with the man struggling to stay free we find united in him the missionary of anarchy and unrepentant agitator. In his actions and his writings his primary message was this: think for yourselves!

"The present is destroying itself and the future is being built... Everything transforms and nothing is created because nothing is destroyed—death is only the starting point of a new form... Where movement starts,

life also starts… The work is not finished, it's just beginning!"

Michel Shreve

Malato in 1890

LOST!

I. Escape

"Alerta!"

A gunshot followed the shout of alarm from the Spanish sentry of the Ceuta presidio. In the almost pitch black night surrounding the penal colony a shadow disappeared, melting into the gloom.

The soldiers, however, and the Moroccan foremen were running around. A Lieutenant cried out, "Caramba! Search everywhere! Bayonets fixed!"

The troops spread out and examined the ground as carefully as they could in the weak light of the lanterns carried on poles by the Arabs.

A cannon fired, rumbling long and muted through the mountains, announcing to the coast that a prisoner had just escaped.

At the same time inside the presidio they took roll call in the convicts' dormitory. The missing number was quickly found to be 3516, a certain Antonio Perez y Rosal.

"Demonio!" the director of the presidio muttered, "A political prisoner!"

Known now as a political prisoner the escapee aroused two very distinct feelings among the administrative and military personnel. The men in charge felt anger mixed with fear. The subordinates, however, felt a little sympathetic. They told themselves that, after all, if one of the prisoners under their guard managed to regain his freedom, it was better that it was not a murderer or a thief.

Perez, in fact, had committed no crime other than living in troubled times in a small Andalusian town and falling afoul of the mayor. With a solid education and having traveled and seen a lot, Perez had wanted to open a school in Alcala del Valle, his hometown. In Spain, education is free: a professor does as he wants as long as he does not rock the boat. On the other hand, the power of the local authorities has stayed almost dictatorial in many places, especially in Andalusia, a quasi-African land where the spirit of the Middle Ages lives on. Antonio Perez's system of education had the bad luck of displeasing the mayor who took it upon himself to close the school.

A bitter war broke out between the two men who quickly got supporters on both sides. A little later a farm workers strike broke out in the area. It was scarred by bloody confrontations. Even in Alcala there were casualties among the farmers and wounded among the police. Perez had not played even a minor role in the agitation, but the opportunity to get rid of him, the enemy, was too perfect for the mayor to ignore.

And the poor man, accused of being an instigator of the revolt, was sentenced by a war council to 20 years of hard labor!

They shipped him off to Ceuta, the biggest penal colony Spain had on the Moroccan coast. The others are Melilla, Alhucemas and the Penon de la Gomera, not to mention the prison on the Chafirinas Islands.

He spent three years in this hell amidst the worst offenders under the bludgeons of the Arab foremen who were more vicious than the prisoners and glad to be lording it over Europeans.

Perez had already seen many of his partners in misfortune die under their blows or from hardship. Besides the fact that the sweltering weather did not help the appetite much, the *rancho*, an awful liquid mush that the dogs refused and that was his daily meal, was not enough to keep up his strength. He had become terribly thin. At times he felt like a cloud was passing before his eyes, like his blood had frozen and his heart stopped beating.

"But I don't want to die here!" he repeated to himself with fierce determination.

The day after his sentencing he was obsessed with only one thing: escape!

But how?

On board the *Pelayo*, which had transported him to Ceuta, he stayed down in the hold with his fellow prisoners in the looming darkness. After getting off they had thrown him into a team repairing the buildings around the penal colony under constant, relentless surveillance. Then he had been sent from one work site to another, all of them well guarded.

Finally, after three lethal years, an opportunity to escape arose. The *capataz* or barracks boss, thinking that everyone was asleep, dozed off after one too many gulps of *anisado* and Perez, with his mind incessantly focused on the same goal, took swift advantage of it.

As supple as a snake he slipped out of the dark building and snuck past the guard on duty just when his back was turned. He had one circumstance on his side: it was the new moon and only the stars were shining in the dark sky.

Nevertheless, as careful as he was to stay close to the ground and hold his breath, he kicked over a small rock that rolled off and gave him away. He had just passed the second guardhouse at the gate in the outer wall of the presidio.

Perez jumped up like a lunatic and was out of sight in no time. The guard, dazed and confused, hesitated a moment before firing at random, not so much to hit the fugitive as to sound the alarm. Perez felt the bullet whistle by an inch over his head.

A few minutes later the fugitive was scrambling down into the town. The rhythmic march of the patrol rang in his ears. Dim lights pierced the darkness in places, glowing behind the curtains of houses or from the rare street lamps. The sound of a *guzzla*, an old fiddle, died off in the distance.

Perez hurtled through the shadows into a maze of narrow alleyways to evade the patrol entering the town, which he knew nothing about. The only thing about Ceuta he knew was the penal colony!

When the sound of the pounding boots grew dimmer the prisoner started wandering around haphazardly. Angry barking mixed with monotone and nasal singing told him that he was approaching the black-Arab quarter. Perez veered cautiously to his left. A straight, dark line stood before him. It was the ramparts of Ceuta.

A sudden thought flashed in his mind: he could not get out through the gate being guarded by sentinels. Was he condemned to be imprisoned in this city, wandering around until he was captured by a patrol and thrown back into prison, this time never to leave again?

His heart sank in despair. But no! He would rather jump off the ramparts and smash his skull in a ditch.

As he was thinking this, he tripped over something. He bent down, reached out and felt the ground. It was a rope, used during the day as a clothesline and stretched out on the ground now like a long snake. They had left it here, lying useless.

For the fugitive it was salvation. A minute later the rope was tied to a tree growing next to the rampart with the other end thrown over the wall. Perez shimmied down into the ditch and when he felt his feet touch the ground he was off again.

Still in unknown territory, more than ever in the dark, he ran as fast as he could away from Ceuta.

II. A Risky Swim

Ceuta, in Arab Sebtah, is a strongly fortified city enclosed on a peninsula. The sea and the walls built on the isthmus surround it with an impregnable barrier lined with cannons. The Spanish who took it over in 1570 have guarded it ever since, using it in their many sieges against the Moroccans. One of these sieges at the end of the 17th and beginning of the 18th century lasted 26 years!

The city is totally white with finely wrought balconies and flowery terraces. Clean, quiet, stretching out between the twin blues of the sky and the sea, Ceuta gives the impression of a calm, sweet life. In spite of the attacks that once raged around its walls you could choose it for the location of some oblivious fantasy.

But this Eden has a hell: the penal colony! There in the blazing sun, haggard, hungry and dressed in rags because the prison administration thinks that clothes are a waste of money, the poor devils from all over are herded together by the loaded rifles of sentinels, the pistols of the guards and the clubs of the Arab foremen. You can see all kinds, all characters among them: the *salteador*, the highwayman, the murderer who took justice into his own hands, the clever thief and sometimes also the innocent thrown into prison because the stars were against him.

Perez was ready to do anything to avoid getting caught and thrown back into that place of mental and physical torture.

He looked around to get his bearings. If it were daytime he would have seen the bulk of Mount Acho behind him along with the Almina Peninsula and the isle of Santa Catalina; before him the fortifications of old Ceuta. But besides the fact that he had only a vague notion of the area's topography, the escapee could not see through the curtain of darkness. He saw only 30 feet in front of him.

Suddenly he listened carefully. He was not mistaken. He heard the rumbling of the sea on both his right and left. He had not left the narrow isthmus that connected the Ceuta Peninsula to the continent. And he remembered that another fortified and guarded border should be formed across the entrance to this isthmus. At least that was what the stories of his fellow captives, the few who had failed to escape, had taught him.

Perez made a quick decision. He veered off to the left, guided by the sound of the waves that grew louder and louder. Soon the salty sea breeze was whipping his face. At the same time glowing points came and went on the dark, shifting surface, making it hard to tell the difference between the sea and the equally dark sky with its glimmering stars.

"I must be in the Madrague Bay," Perez thought. The Madrague Bay, Vina Bay and Point Zorra to the southeast and the Campo Rocks to the northwest was all that the prisoner knew about the area.

His feet suddenly felt something warm and wet. He had reached the edge of the sea. A row of lights burned in the night a long way off.

The fugitive kept walking into the sea, water up his ankles, then to his waist. Finally he made up his mind to start swimming, guided by the points of light that must surely be the coastline.

His plan was to use the sea to skirt by the obstacle that he had no hope of getting through directly. He had

33

already managed to slip out of the presidio, then get over a wall, but he could not hope to be three times lucky. That would be tempting fate. Better to reach the other coast by swimming a safe distance from Ceuta.

Perez was a good swimmer and the desire to regain his freedom boosted his strength. For 20 minutes he wheeled his vigorous arms. At about this time he realized that the lights looked just as far away and he started to feel anxious.

His clothes were soaked, sticking to his skin and soon bound to drag him down. In fact, he wore only a loose jacket, a simple shirt and gray canvas pants, plus a pair of *alpargatas* or espadrilles.

With a great deal of effort Perez managed to take off the jacket and shirt and he felt instantly relieved. Wisely he kept on his pants and espadrilles.

To catch his breath he floated on his back, still drifting toward the lit up coastline. All of a sudden something hit his head and stunned him. He was starting to sink when he felt something grab hold of his arms and legs and waist all at the same time. But it was not human hands clutching him. The squishy, cold, sticky embrace followed quickly by the feeling of suckers immediately woke him up—there was no mistaking the tentacles of an octopus!

The swimmer had bumped into a rock jutting out of the water and the shock had attracted the mollusk that had been sleeping or lying in wait for some prey. The eight tentacles, like eight different snakes, immediately attacked Perez, imprisoning him in their coils and sucking hard.

The fugitive felt his whole body tremble and revolt against the filthy feeling at the same time as his blood started pumping hard through his veins. The octopus stared at him with its phosphorescent eye and its calm, merciless glare was terrifying.

The mouth of the gelatinous monster, a weird mouth that looked like a parrot's, was already getting ready to taste his poor flesh.

Perez knew the power of the enemy he had just been trapped by. The octopus, the great hunter of crabs and lobsters, had no fear of attacking enemies such as man. It was as smart as it was ferocious: they had been seen putting a rock between the two valves of big shellfish to keep them from closing up while they fed.

To fight against this misshapen and terrible ogre of the sea Perez had no weapon. His muscles were already tired from the slaving away during the long swim and were powerless against the tentacles and their suckers. His hands struggled in vain to grab the jelly beast: the soft, slimy surface kept slipping out of his grasp.

He felt lost and could not help crying out in despair.

His cry had an answer. A voice came out of the sea speaking two words in Spanish: "Quien vive?" (Who's there?)

Immediately afterward a light shined out of the jumbled mess of a boat and in this boat was a man.

Panting, weary, half-suffocating, Perez could not see the boat well or the person inside. But the other had seen the tragic drama. With a single stroke of his oar he came straight to the two fighters and grabbed hold of Perez, who was sinking fast, along with the clinging octopus.

An instant later the fugitive was lying on the bottom of the boat. The body of the mollusk was as dead as a doornail. The head, its only vulnerable part, which the man had cut off with a knife, was lying next to it, a shapeless, slimy thing.

The savior was one of the Spanish-Arab mixes with rugged looks, a black beard and eyes that shined like rubies. Dressed simply in a sweater with bare legs but wearing a fez, he brought his lantern over to examine Perez with grim curiosity, more curiosity than pity.

Amar Beloud, the name of the man, had been a tuna fisherman since he was a kid. While lying in his boat he had heard the distress call from the struggling Spaniard. But more than anything this was a practical man and he was no fool for silly sentiments. One look at the shaved face and the fabric of the pants was enough to tell him exactly who this man was whom he had snatched from the clutches of death.

"An escaped convict," he muttered.

Now, not only was helping a convict to escape a punishable crime but a reward was given to whomever brought one of these poor men back to the presidio.

"Nice catch!" he said aloud. And he bent down to look for a rope to tie up the prisoner sent to him by fate.

Perez was coming around, heard the exclamation and understood what was happening. The fisherman had saved him from the octopus only to send him back to his jailors.

There was no time to waste. He tripped and pushed the mestizo headfirst overboard. At the same time, grabbing the oars, he sent the boat skimming over the water while his savior and enemy, stunned by the sudden attack, floundered in the waves.

When Amar realized what had happened and wanted to get his skiff back, it was already a long ways off, invisible, vanished in the darkness because Perez had blown out the lantern whose light would have given him away.

III. Pirates of the Riff

On the rocks that extend to the south of Cap Negro a half dozen men armed with rifles were crouching, watching the sea. Two of them wore the white burnous of Arabs; the others were covered in their multi-colored rags that had plenty of flair. All of them were tanned with a hooked nose and the sharp eyes of an eagle.

They looked both majestic and barbaric. They were the pirates of the Rif.

These rocks, which seem to defy both the sky and the sea, are their domain. Smugglers, looters, fishermen at times, they outdare the soldiers of both the sultan and Spain. Invulnerable in the rocks and gullies, they can, at the same time, keep an eye on the vast plain of the sea, Ceuta the Spanish town and Tangier the Arab town.

The oldest of the group concerning us wore the native costume of turban and burnous. He might have been 50 years old. "Brothers," he said, "the sultan will soon have finished the sale of this holy land of Maghreb to the Europeans. On that day guns will do the talking not just on the coastline."

"If it pleases God," one of his companions muttered.

"On that day, my brothers, you will be able to come out of hiding and like a vengeful plague ravage the cowardly inhabitants of the towns. They are the ones, lured by money, who tried to betray us to the *roumis*,"

"Curse on them!" one of the pirates grumbled. "We'll nail their heads and hands to the doors of their houses after throwing their bodies to the filthy dogs."

The elder of the group nodded in approval at the display of fine sentiments. "The Prophet," he said, "ordered war on the infidels, so…"

He was interrupted by a gunshot. Right away all the pirates jumped behind a big rock, rifles at the ready and eyes on the lookout. A few minutes passed. No sound was heard.

One of the pirates finally broke the silence, "It must have been that son of a bitch Amar Beloud whose boat we saw this morning and who is always getting in range of our rifles."

"The bastard," someone else said. "He's a spy for all the roumis. If we catch him we should skin him alive."

Just then another pirate appeared from behind a rock, walking toward them holding a rifle.

"Hey, Ahmed, was that you who fired?" one of the men asked.

"It was me."

"At Amar Bedoud?"

"No, at a roumi."

"Where'd he come from?"

"From that dog's boat that he left in the sand."

"And who was with him in the boat?"

"He was alone."

The pirates looked at each other in astonishment. They knew the tuna fisherman and knew that he would never lend his boat to anyone.

Ahmed explained the mystery in two words: "Escaped convict."

Their faces relaxed. Everything was clear. Some *presidario* had grabbed the boat and rowed off without permission from its owner. Seeing the European naked to the waist Ahmed easily guessed, even at a distance, that he had escaped. And just like his companions he could recognize Amar's boat from afar.

"Did you kill the foreign dog?" the elder pirate asked concernedly.

"No," the shooter answered. "My gun can't reach that far." This was easier on his pride than to admit that he had missed his target.

In fact, Perez had landed on this wild part of the coast because it was less dangerous for him than the civilized region where the penal colony stood. Leaving the boat in a small cove hidden by the rocks he had wandered off down the beach. His plan was to walk all the way to the Guad-el-Gelou, a river that waters the plain around Tétouan and empties into the sea. He only had to wind his way down the coast for three or four miles to reach the city. Maybe the Arabs and Jews would welcome him there. In any case, at least the Spaniards would not come looking for him there.

Tétouan, "the water springs", is a lush city perched on a 200-foot plateau and surrounded by a real forest of orange trees through which run creeks and brooks down from the craggy mountains that form a circular projection to the west. The stream (you cannot really call it a river), the Guad-el-Gelou, crosses the valley up to the Douane, a square, Arab-style, fortified building, then flows into the sea. The city, called "holy" by the faithful, is very commercial. It has a population of 30,000 including thousands of Jews who control almost all the trade.

"When I get there," Perez told himself, "I'll be able to find some work. I'll hire on doing any kind of work to earn a little money. Anything would be better than the penal colony."

The fugitive was thinking this when the bullet whistled by his ear. At the same time he heard the distant

39

sound of the gunfire. But it was useless to look around; there was nothing to see. Even the wisp of smoke from the gunshot had instantly vanished in a gust of strong wind from the sea.

Nevertheless, Perez knew that even if he could not see anyone, he himself was seen. But he decided not to protect himself. The first and most important reason was that he did not know from what direction the shot had come; then because he was brave but miserable. He had no fear of dying in the sun from a bullet to the chest. It was something different than the hell of Ceuta or the horror of his battle during the night with the octopus in the sea.

Therefore, he went on his way, calm and peaceful, which surprised the pirates. In any case, since he was coming to them alone and unarmed, they could just capture and interrogate him before killing him.

Perez was starting to feel hunger gnaw away at him. He had eaten nothing since the day before and his eventful odyssey at sea had given him a hearty appetite. Two or three times he stopped to pick up some shellfish from the hollows in the rock. He cracked them open with a stone and ate them raw.

But his hurry to get as far away from Ceuta as possible was stronger than his hunger and it spurred him on.

"The Guad-el-Gelou!" he shouted on spotting a river reflecting the sunrays and extending a white bar of foam between two flowery mountainsides.

From now on he had a definite landmark. He only had to follow the river upstream and he would reach Tétouan. "I'm saved!" he sighed with inexpressible joy.

At that very moment, the men jumped out from behind the rock and knocked him down before tying his hands behind his back. Another rope was wound around his ankles so he could only take small steps. The pirates did all this in the wink of an eye.

As Perez sat there stunned by the sudden turn of events, they yanked him to his feet and a hard blow to his back from a rifle butt snapped him back to reality.

"Get going! Walk!" the one who had hit him ordered.

The fugitive felt driven like a wisp of straw in the wind by this drama of his life that was rolling on like an avalanche. He was certainly not scared: resigned and too tired to fight, yes, and aware of his powerlessness. Oh well, he would die like a man, his head held high, even happy to finally find peace in the grave.

"Anda! Anda!" the meanest of the Riffians repeated, backing up his order with a flood of carefully selected insults in both Spanish and Arabic and even in French. These bandits were multilingual in their way.

As the abuses were accompanied by blows from the rifle butt Perez straightened up. "You cowards! Why are you torturing me? Come on, let's get it over with! Kill me!" Continuing to challenge them and believing that he could push them to finish off this tragic drama, which is what he wanted now, he added, "Revenge the owner of that boat, one of your brave partners no doubt, who I threw into the sea."

If Perez had thought he could anger the Riffians with this startling revelation he could not have been more wrong.

The tuna fisherman, as we have seen, was no friend of the pirates. Of mixed race and living a shady life between the Spaniards and the Arabs, Amar Beloud was hated by the latter. Not only had he turned in or given information to the Spanish authorities about escaped prisoners on several occasions, but they also accused him of spying on the pirates. No news, therefore, could have been more welcome to them than to hear about his death.

But was the fugitive telling the truth?

"Halt!" ordered the elder of the group, acting as chief because of his age.

Sitting down on the rocks they interrogated their prisoner in Spanish mixed with Arabic after untying his legs. Perez answered in pure Spanish using his hands to illustrate his explanation. Even though he had learned a little Arabic in the penal colony, he felt that his linguistic knowledge was not needed: his listeners understood him well enough.

He told them of his adventures including the reasons he was sent to prison. And it was weird for him to catch these savage pirates, whose heart seemed as hard as stone, showing signs of pity.

But what they liked most was the trick played on Amar Beloud, their enemy. Had he drowned? They could not dream of it without being sure. Anyway, if he had survived he would be without his boat, which was his livelihood. So, two of them went to check where Perez said he had left the skiff.

As for the prisoner, he was pleasantly surprised to see them untie all his ropes. One of the pirates even took off one of his rags that served as a coat, grabbed a bag of dates and gave them to him.

Perez was starved. But before gobbling up his unexpected meal he had the presence of mind to declare, "The prophet said that you must help the man who is at your mercy out of bad luck."

Did Mohammed ever say such a thing? Perez had absolutely no idea. But his steady nerve effected the pirates who were not well versed in Koranic studies.

"After all," Ahmed muttered, "we might end up shooting him or beheading him, so what's the point in torturing him?"

"Is it really worth killing him?" another asked. "We could sell him as a slave to some inland tribe."

This time the pirates were presenting their relatively humanitarian arguments in Riffian dialect, but the escaped convict understood that they were talking about him and the fate he would suffer at their hands. Having a personal interest in the subject he broke in with this statement, "What is written is written. If Allah wants to save me from your hands, I will be saved."

"If it pleases God, it will be so," the spiritual chief of the gang added.

"But you, being believers, won't give me over to the roumis."

A vigorous agreement ran though the pirates. Of course they were looters, murders and even torturers and never backed down from a cruel act except of becoming the smug servants of the Christian authorities they hated.

Perez had hit the target on appealing to the religious fanaticism of their race. After a long discussion the pirates decided to spare his life and keep him as a slave for the moment, whom they could sell later on.

IV. Prisoner of the Riata

The mountains of the Rif form an impenetrable range inhabited only by bandits and eagles, dominating the Moroccan coast from the Guad-el-Gelou to the west up to the Algerian border in the east.

The fearless men who made it their lair lived truly independent, not so much in tribes as in small groups constantly on alert and in action. In the narrow canyons, scattered here and there you would find the tents of a *douar* where the women without veils over their faces would be preparing the *couscous* for the warriors while the herds grazed on the green slopes. But in the crevices of the rocky walls protecting the oasis are the groups of pirates keeping watch, their eyes and rifles on the look-out.

From time to time bad weather forces a fishing boat to land on the beach in front of the apparently uninhabited cliffs. But from the heights there are invisible eyes watching the newcomers. All of a sudden gunshots ring out, leaving the unlucky sailors dead or wounded on the sand. And from all the nooks and crannies pirates jump out to attack and pillage the boat.

Perez spent a few days with the pirates. His status as slave was better, on the whole, than as a prisoner. He had to be up at dawn to fetch wood and dry peat (without wandering too far from the camp) to cook the common meal of the day, go down to fill the goatskins with water, carry the baskets of fruit and vegetables on his back when the people in the vicinity were nice enough or scared enough to give some to the Riffians—he never once saw his masters spend a single *douro*. After all this, being fed whatever leftovers they were willing to give him, he had the right to lie down on a rotten old mat and sleep under the stars.

With some plant fibers taken out of the rock crevices he made a kind of coat. One of the pirates threw the tattered shreds of his *haïk* (the native robe that is held up with knots or pins) around his shoulders.

The Riffians had their own boats, very slender, very light, that they dragged onto land and easily hid among the rocks or behind bushes. Two or three times they brought their prisoner fishing with them. It was a delight for him: since the fish were bountiful he could eat as much as wanted. Still, his companions watched his every move. The way this roumi had treated Amar Beloud, even though they liked it, it made them think.

At this point a new Riffian arrived from Ceuta. He was a pirate too and used to go off sometimes to gather information. Among the news he brought back was that of the resurrection of the tuna fisherman. The mongrel had managed to swim to land. Furious and shouting that he was ruined by the loss of his boat, he had got a job as foreman at the presidio as compensation.

"Why didn't you hit him over the head with the oar while he was splashing around in the sea?" the Riffians asked the fugitive.

He saw the disappointment written on their savage faces. They thought they had got rid of a man whom they hated and believing this they had spared their prisoner's life. Now the enemy was back. Their trust had been broken, so did they not have the right to avenge themselves?

Perez could feel this and once again was expecting to die.

However, even the pirates hesitated to kill a man whose life they had spared and with whom they had lived for a while. Besides, the death of Perez was of no use to them.

One fine morning the escaped convict was kindly woken up by a kick in the ribs and the raspy voice of one of his guards yelled, "Get up! We're going to sell you to the Riata."

As stoic and as prepared as he was to face all the blows of fate, he felt his heart gripped with anguish. After his life was spared he still had hope of someday escaping to Tétouan. There he would find civilization and his freedom. But instead of this his bad luck was sending him to new masters.

What the Riffians were on the rocks overlooking the Mediterranean coast, the Riata were in the mountains that ran between Fez and Tlemcen. Fiercely independent they recognized no god, no sultan and no chief. Their women, far from being passive recluses like other Arab women, went with them on their expeditions. Tall and strong, their faces covered, their skirts hiked up over their knees, you could see them fraternizing with the men. Sometimes they slung a rifle over their shoulders and were just as fearless in battle.

A rope tied Perez' hands behind his back. The end of the rope was held by one of the Riffians who ordered the prisoner, "Walk!"

One of the pirates started off toward the sierras that stretched out to the south. Perez and his guard followed; another fell in behind them.

They walked all day long, making no stops except at noon under a thin stand of pine trees to eat a few dates. Shortly before sundown they saw the hide tents of a douar set up next to a stream in a narrow valley where tall ferns flourished.

Then one of the Riffians let out a long, earsplitting whistle three times in a row. Two long, inflected whistles answered. Then they saw ten men come out from the tents, all carrying rifles. It was the Riata.

At first sight Berber blood seemed to flow through the veins of these warriors much more than pure Arab blood. Their skin color was like slightly tanned Europeans. Most of them had blond hair with reddish tints. When they got closer Perez could see that many of them had green eyes, not black.

"Who knows," the fugitive wondered, "if they aren't the last descendants of those Vandals who ravaged Spain in the 5th century before crossing the Mediterranean and invading Africa."

The Riata and Riffians were talking. Long negotiations were taking place. At the same time signaling whistles echoed everywhere; and were answered. Men, women and children came out in groups. There were already more than 60 people around. Only a third of them barely showed traces of pure Arab blood.

The women came and went freely and really looked like old shrews. Very few of them, even the young ones, were pretty. Moreover, many of them were hideously ugly.

However, Perez noticed one, well past her prime, who was watching him out of the corner of her eye with a strange look of sympathy.

"Would she show me some pity?" he wondered.

The Riffians and Riata, squatting down with rifles between their legs, kept up their negotiations. Once in a while the captive managed to catch a few words: hadjar (rock), djebel (mountain), chaaba (ravine), which told him nothing. So, he gave up trying to understand, surrendered to his fate for the moment, waiting to see what would come.

Finally the Riffians stood up. One of them untied his hands; another took off his rags. A circle of Riata gathered around him, examining him like an animal at the fair, lifting his arms, squeezing his muscles, opening his mouth.

One of the mountain dwellers made a sign to get him dressed. Some women brought out two baskets full of figs, a couffin (a small bag of woven sedge) full of rice and a half dozen mats that they placed in front of the pirates who in turn examined the objects before wrapping up the baskets and couffin in two mats each, thus making three packages that they picked up. Then they left.

Perez remained standing in the middle of the Riata. He had just been sold for the price of goods that was worth less than 30 francs[6]!

---

[6] Around five dollars.

V. Marina

The more masters an individual has, the more un-
happy he is, obviously. One is brutal, another fickle, another stupid or elegantly cruel. The best are neutral.

It took no time for Perez to experience this.

The clan (you could hardly call it a tribe) to which
he had been sold cheaply led a more active life than the
pirates in the sense that it practiced a little farming and
trade along with pasturing its herds. Perez quickly became a slave-of-all-trades.

Not only the warriors but the women and children
were proud to have a European to boss around, doing all
they could to pile useless orders on him, always backed
up by insults.

Perez was unhappier than with the Riffians. Only
one hope kept him going: on getting closer to Tétouan he
might get the chance to escape. The Riata would go there
to sell the milk from their herds and sometimes even a
few head of cattle. They came back with cloth, powder
and also some *maya*, an alcohol distilled from grapes—
see, they did not give a damn about the prohibitions of
the Koran, so the only reason they did not have many
fermented drinks was because they only drank them on
rare occasions.

Twice Perez saw a caravan from Beni-Coudia heading across the mountains to the holy city, carrying bundles of merchandise on scrawny donkeys. He saw them
come back with the results of their swaps. But he was
never lucky enough to go with them. He was always left
to work his idle tasks under the guard of an old Riata

with a venerable face who had shaken his rifle and told him, "Listen dog, don't try to run away. My bullets are a lot faster than my legs."

Perez got this more from the old man's expression than from his words, even though he was starting to speak and understand the Riata's dialect, which was closer to pure Arabic than the Riffians'.

The escaped convict had been with the Beni-Coudia for eight days when one blazing afternoon while his masters were having their siesta and he was watching over a herd of sheep he heard a voice whispering behind him in Spanish, "Hombre!"

Perez jumped up as if jolted by an electric current. Behind a curtain of leaves he saw the mysterious woman, a finger to her lips, who had looked on him with pity when he first arrived. When she came out, looking worried, he asked in Spanish, "Who are you?"

She answered in the same language, "I'm Spanish, born in Estepona in the province of Málaga." The woman stopped for a moment, as if time had wiped out her memories or had made her forget her native language.

Perez looked at her in amazement. So, this woman whom he, a prisoner, was meeting in the middle of the Moroccan mountains was a fellow Spaniard!

She continued, "I was young when my parents came to Morocco. They were poor... very poor. My father was called Solar and mother Vichea. Me, they called... Marina."

Again she broke off, obviously worn out from making the effort to remember or from talking in a language that she had not spoken for a long time.

Perez watched her with unspeakable compassion. This woman must have suffered a thousand times more than he, separated from everything she loved and living amidst these barbarians.

"Lady," he squeezed her hands, "how long have you been with them?"

She tried to think of a specific date but failed, having lost all notion of how much time had passed. "It was after the war between the Spanish and the Moors," she finally answered, "because I remember them talking about a big battle that took place in the past[7] and a roumi General…"

"O'Donnell," Perez said.

"O'Donnell, that's it. My parents ran a small plantation for a rich *youdi*[8] merchant."

"Where was that?"

"I don't know… between the sea and the mountains… over there." Marina's hand pointed to the northwest. She went on, "One day the Moors massacred the youdis and the roumis. My parents were killed… and I was kidnapped."

"Was it the Beni-Coudia who took you?"

"No, others. And then they sold me to some mountain people. Later on they sold me to the Riata. I was still a girl. I became an Arab woman."

Hearing this story Perez felt his heart ache more and more. He asked, "And you never tried to save yourself, to go back to the Europeans?"

Marina shrugged her shoulders. "What for?" Since her fellow Spaniard looked lost in thought she continued, "What was left for me over there? Poverty. Here I'm a workhorse, it's true, but I'm alive. I eat and sleep

---

[7] In 1860.
[8] Jewish.

51

in a tent. Over there I'd have to work even harder for the roumis and besides would they even want me?"

She was speaking more fluently now. It was as if her Spanish were thawing out, but sprinkled with native expressions.

"You see," she concluded, "it was better for me to stay here, but it's not the same for you."

"I don't want to live as a slave," he said.

Right after saying this he was sorry. Was Marina the type of woman to betray him or at least let his secret thoughts slip out by mistake? But no! The woman's face showed real compassion as well as subtle intelligence.

"I'll help you," she said.

The convict almost jumped with joy before thinking out loud, "Poor woman! If I save myself and leave you here they'll figure out that you helped me and they'll kill you."

Marina shook her head. "They won't figure anything out. We're smarter than them. They think I've forgotten everything about Spain and the roumis because I never talk about it. They don't worry about me at all... But enough talking for today. We don't want to wake anybody up. After tomorrow, if we get the chance, we'll talk again."

She went away the same way she had come, without a sound and her finger to her lips.

VI. Between a rock and a hard place

Perez stood there both dazed but delighted. After casting him down into the abyss the wheel of fortune was turning again and pulling him up to freedom.

Actually his joy was mixed with bitterness: the thought of leaving poor, kind Marina with the Beni-Coudia made him sad. But he realized how impossible it was to bring her with him, to make her share a life of hardship and maybe fatal adventures in the deserted or wild regions that he would have to cross before reaching a civilized city.

Besides, she was right. She was no longer young and she had nothing. Would her life be better among her fellow Spaniards, if she even survived the journey, than with the Riata in the mountains?

All day long Perez was lost in thought, but he did his best to hide the joy in his heart from his masters. The next day rolled by without seeing Marina. No doubt she was being cautious and pretending not to care about her compatriot. Moreover, the Riata believed that since she was kidnapped so young she had become completely Arab in her manners and her heart, if not in her blood. They treated her no differently than the other women.

One day later, as she had promised, she showed up again while Perez was guarding the flock. She was carrying a bundle of cloth that she threw at his feet. "That's a burnous," she said. "I took it from the tent of Taleb el Akhbar because he's not here. You pull the hood down to cover your head completely. And in the satchel is some greasy powder: it's henna mixed with resin. Rub it on your face and body and you'll turn brown. Here's a little bag of figs. Dates would be better but they don't grow around here and we rarely get them in these mountains. I don't have any weapon to give you but you can find a good heavy stick on the way and tie a big rock to it. Here's some gut string and some halfah. You'll make good use of them."

Perez stood there stunned by the abrupt finale but he managed to ask, "When do you think I should leave? Tonight?"

"No, right now. The Beni-Coudia are taking their siesta. At night they're on the lookout."

The two of them stared at each other in silence.

"Don't waste any time." Marina finally said. "You should go that way," she pointed to the south. "At sunset you'll reach a dried up riverbed where three paths branch off. Take the middle one and walk all night. Tomorrow at daybreak you'll be in sight of the Tétouan plain. Farewell."

Before Perez had a chance to say goodbye Marina had left, vanishing into the bushes and ferns. The Spaniard stared after her for a time, then decided to take her advice without further delay. He started by unwrapping the bundle and rubbing the henna on his face, hands and legs. He slipped the burnous over his rags, pulled the hood down over his head, threw the bag of figs over his shoulder and started on his way.

He walked fast through the sparse undergrowth scattered across the land that was almost always dry and rocky. There was no path! In front of him stretched the blue shadows of the sierras, mingling with the horizon of the dark blue sky.

Several times he stopped to look back to see if the Beni-Coudia were coming after him. No, they were still taking their siesta or lost in a cloud of drowsiness. They would not notice that Perez was gone until sunset when the flock usually returned. Then, for sure, they would chase after him, but they would not know in what direction he had gone and they had no horses.

One thing that worried Perez was that he had no weapon to defend his life and liberty in case they caught up to him. Then, remembering Marina's advice, when he saw a tree with strong, straight branches he broke one off to use as both a walking stick and a club.

He badly wanted to have a knife. Unfortunately the Beni-Coudia had never left a shred of iron lying around him and Marina did not think of it or did not have the opportunity to grab one.

But he almost jumped with joy when he saw a big piece of flint, almost square with sharp edges, lying on the ground. Why not make a hammer and axe? Primitive man had no other tools for work and for war.

Perez picked up the stone. Immediately he tied it tightly to the end of his stick with the halfah rope. He smiled and said to himself, "Now I'm just like our prehistoric ancestors!"

Moreover, the only dangerous animal he feared to encounter in this region was man, meaning the Riata. Lions and panthers were once all over the mountains but had now become almost as rare as in Algeria. On the other hand, he could find plenty of one of the most harmless animals—rabbits.

"If my trip takes too long," he thought, "I'll make a bow and some arrows to hunt some prey, feathered or furry. What am I saying? I'll be in Tétouan tomorrow."

He kept walking. The sun was sinking on the horizon and the riverbed mentioned by Marina was still not in sight. Was it possible that he had taken the wrong way? No! Despite the lack of roads he was sure that he was walking in the right direction.

He pressed on and hurried his step. All of a sudden he thought he heard the distant sound of rushing water.

"It sounds like a river," he thought aloud. "But no… the river is supposed to be dried up."

At the same time he saw something beyond words. It was like a veil of fog rising in the distance, one or one and a half miles away, drifting over the ground in a straight line.

Perez froze in amazement. A swirl of black dots was crossing the sky. Some of these black dots were pelting the ground while the others continued their flight. Intrigued and forgetting any possible (even probable) danger, he rushed forward.

The sound became more and more distinct. It was the sound of explosions, one after another. The black dots turned into big, soaring birds.

The convict understood right away: two tribes were fighting. The explosions were gunfire, the veil of fog hiding the river was the gun smoke and the birds were vultures awaiting their prey. His spirits fell and cramped up. The battle in front of him was barring his way to Tétouan and from behind the Beni-Coudia were certainly coming after him.

Doesn't matter! The fighters might be less dangerous than the Beni Coudia. Besides, they would be too busy killing each other to pay any attention to him.

He stopped for a moment, uncertain of what to do. Instinctively he turned his head to look behind him and a shiver ran down his spine.

The land sloped down evenly toward the river. From the high ground that he had just left, around 300 or 400 yards back, Perez saw a chaotic throng coming fast toward him, which he could not mistake. The Beni-Coudia!

He let out a desperate cry. To think he was saved only to fall back into the hands of his enemies.

He made a mad dash forward, preferring to die by the bullets of the fighters rather than those of his former masters. And the battle was raging now. The air vibrated from all the gunfire and the ground was bouncing from the galloping horses.

More gunfire rang out from the opposite direction. Some bullets whizzed by the fugitive's ears. The Beni-Coudia had seen him and were shooting at him.

Perez felt lost.

All of a sudden he shouted. 30 yards in front of him an Arab was lying dead on the ground, his eyes glazed over, his head smashed in, and still holding his unsheathed sword. A little farther ahead his harnessed horse was struggling unsuccessfully to shake its reins free of a tangled bush.

In the blink of an eye Perez grabbed the sword and the reins , jumped on the horse and sped off, veering neatly between the fighters, who had not seen him, and the Beni-Coudia, who were chasing after him.

VII. An oasis in the mountains

Perez spurred on the Arab's horse with only one thought in mind: to get far away as quickly as possible from this treacherous place where he would run into danger both in front of and behind him.

The horse flew like the wind. Within no time the fugitive had gone around the fighters and was out of sight of the Beni-Coudia who had no horses and could only fire a few harmless bullets in crippled rage.

But when Perez was out of danger he suddenly remembered that he had missed the path leading to Tétouan. This was serious. The sun was setting and since they were in the time of the new moon the night was going to be pitch black. It was urgent not to get any farther away.

In the saddlebags Perez found two long Arab pistols, richly decorated and, even better, they were loaded. As a precaution he stuffed them into a belt that he made by tearing his undergarment. The pistols and the sword were enough for his defense, so he tossed aside the walking stick aka stone axe.

The escapee tied the horse to a puny bush and slept under the stars after eating a few of the figs that Marina had packed for him.

The adventures on his flight had exhausted him. The sun was already high in the sky when he woke up. The horse was grazing next to him, not on grass, which did not grow here, but on the bark of the bush he was tied to.

"Good boy," Perez patted his rump. "Tomorrow you'll get water and feed."

However: man desires but destiny decides. Perez flattered himself thinking he could find the way to Tétouan and arrive in the city on the same day.

After untying the horse he had barely mounted him when it took off in a mad gallop. In spite of the reputation for restraint in his Arab brethren, the horse was hungry, thirsty and even worse it did not recognize his master. Furthermore, Perez was no expert horseman. All he could do was try to stay in the saddle.

The rapid pace would have been nothing to worry about if it was heading for Tétouan. Unfortunately, at this dizzying speed Perez could not tell what direction he was going. He thought that maybe the horse was rushing back to its douar.

Perez was wrong. The animal pulled up short in front of a row of bushes behind which was the sound of running water. Without the rider holding him back this time the horse stepped forward, stretched out its long neck toward the clear water and began lapping it up.

"What great instincts!" the fugitive marveled. Since he was also thirsty he jumped down to get a drink, naturally approaching the bank of the stream.

Events took a dramatic turn. Hardly had the horse seen its new master take a few steps upstream when it wailed out and bolted off at breakneck speed. Hunger, thirst, it forgot everything. All it saw was its freedom!

A minute later the silhouette of the proud equine was disappearing over the horizon. Perez stood there in a daze. He braced himself against despair and when the first shock had passed he tried to orient himself.

He was on the plateau, over a mile high, the northern foothills of the High Atlas that separated the Mediterranean side from the Atlantic side. Now, without really realizing it, he was 50 miles to the south of Tétouan.

After thinking about it the fugitive decided to give up, at least for the moment, on any hope of reaching Tétouan. He could wander for days on end in this desolate region without roads and get captured again by the Riata or die of hunger.

On the other hand, using the sun's position, he could head southwest and in 24 hours probably get out of this desert into the low, fertile country that rolls out to the Atlantic.

"Let's hit the road!" he said.

With sword in hand, pistols in belt, the bag of fruit over his shoulder, he started off.

The desert must have been bigger than the traveler imagined because at sunset he was still walking on granite. Here and there a scraggy bush or shrub. That was all. Life seemed to have cleared out of this desolate country forever.

However, between the rocky mountains there were green valleys and oases where cactus and figs grew near clear streams, and even some ksour[9] of settlers, shepherds and farmers. The only problem was that you had to know where to find these valleys, oases and ksour, hidden as they were in the mountains.

Perez settled down for the night in a rock crevice that he barricaded with a few big stones. No troubling incident woke him up during the night. The next morning he started walking again toward the southwest.

In spite of his perilous situation he ended up breathing freely. The penal colony, guards and foremen were far away! The Riffians and Riata were also long gone! His heart swelled with the hope of reaching some hospitable region.

---

[9] Arab villages.

Thanks to Marina's figs he could fend off hunger. But his throat was dry from thirst and he was sorry he did not or could not take a little water from the stream where the horse had stopped the day before, only to leave him behind so... cavalierly.

Around the middle of the afternoon the land started to change. The ground became darker and softer. Greenery was growing in places so water should not have been far. Thicker shrubs, less dust, a few green bushes definitely indicated a source of water.

Finally, just as he was starting to roast in the blazing sun and his bloody feet (despite the espadrilles) felt like they would fall off, Perez shouted for joy. Less than 300 yards in front of him was a dark blue forest that had been hidden by the sloping land. The forest, or rather the woods because it was not much more than half a mile wide and less than two miles long, seemed to be divided down the middle by a shadowy line formed by a gap in the trees. The traveler guessed that this gap must have been a stream.

He rushed forward, no longer feeling tired. In a few minutes he reached the first trees: argan trees, gnarled and thorny, bearing fruit as fat as apples. Perez did not stop to munch on any of these fruits that he did not know but in which he would have found a nut containing an oily almond. His impatience pushed him into the middle of the woods where he guessed there was some water.

He stepped through a thick tangle of vines, not without difficulty, causing a flock of scared, wild pigeons to soar off into the sky.

"Damn, this would be a great place to hunt," he figured.

Then there were cacti with wide, thorny leaves, followed by cork oaks proudly stretching out their thick branches. In the middle of these trees, what gave life and cooled the air was a fast flowing, rippling stream.

Perez dropped to his knees on the bank and took a long, cool drink before washing his hands and face. Then he soaked his bruised feet. Now he felt energized and could think clearly.

"In fact," he mused, "why am I in such a hurry to reach the coast? Is it better for me there than here where I'm free? I doubt it. These woods are lovely, cool, full of game to boot." Then he thought, "Yes, these woods are full of game but what can I hunt it with?"

He had a sword and two big, loaded pistols, which were excellent weapons for defense but quite useless for hunting. An idea popped into his head: why not make a bow and some arrows?

There were plenty of raw materials and he could use the sword to cut the bow and sharpen the arrows. He went to work immediately.

A stick, both strong and flexible, formed a good bow. The ball of dried gut that Marina had given him made the string. All he needed were arrows. After a long search Perez ended up finding, on the banks of the stream, some reeds that were thin, straight and firm enough. But that was not everything. He needed the arrows to have a sharp head.

Perez got the idea of using the resin that was seeping out of certain trees to glue the thickest, strongest thorns he could find from the argan trees to the end of the reeds. Thus, he got barbed arrows that might not kill but at least would badly cripple any unlucky birds he ran into.

While crafting his weapons he could not help wondering about this cruel law of nature that forces creatures to kill each other to live.

"Poor birds!" he said to himself, sticking a thorn into his last arrow. "They have their families and feelings and fun and I'm coming like a barbarian to destroy everything in one fell swoop. Ach! They destroy life, too, when they attack insects. Come on, the battle of the species is inevitable. The only real problem is when it happens between men!"

He stood up, leaving his now useless and cumbersome sword on the ground. In the basket of figs, which he still carried over his shoulder, like in a quiver, were eleven of his arrows. He held the twelfth in his right hand, the bow in his left.

The woods, as he called them, were bountiful. When the pigeons got scared of Perez they went cooing up into the branches of the trees. The fugitive set the arrow to the bow, pulled back the string, aimed at one of the feathered fowl and let it fly. The arrow shot through the leafy dome, causing the birds to flutter away, and fell harmlessly in a bush.

"I'm such a klutz," he grumbled.

He went to fetch the arrow because he did not want to waste his weapons. To his great surprise he saw the arrow shaking as if it were stuck in something that moved. He snuck up carefully and saw the arrow sticking out of the back of a small, four-legged animal that was thrashing about.

The animal was just a big rat. On falling straight down out of the air the arrowhead had stabbed it like a fork. The harpooning would not have been enough to keep the rodent from scurrying off if the other end of the arrow had not got caught in the bush.

Feathers or fur, it was still game. Perez grabbed the rat and strangled it, paying no mind to its scratching claws.

Five minutes later the animal was skinned, gutted and eaten raw because the fugitive had nothing to light a fire with. Nevertheless, he found the meal delicious, all the while thinking, "I shot at a bird and hit a rat. The world is full of contradictions."

VIII. The Mysterious Grotto

After getting some rest and relaxation Perez decided to start exploring the oasis. He walked up alongside the stream that seemed to cut the woods into two equal parts. It ran over the rocks made of magnesium silicate, then after half a mile or so became a narrow brook, disappearing into the ground under a block of sandstone.

"Let's see what's downstream," Perez said to himself.

He traced back his steps and found the mica schist rocks again, then the reeds that he made into arrows. He kept walking.

Something suddenly struck him: the current of the stream was getting faster. Did it run down into a waterfall? What might support this idea was that the once quiet murmur of the stream was getting louder, turning into a kind of muffled roar.

To the right and left grew high grass. All of a sudden Perez was facing the entrance to a grotto. The stream rushed furiously inside, hollowing out a narrow bed in the middle of the rock.

For a minute the fugitive stood there, not knowing what to do. The cave seemed wide enough to enter if he bent over a little. But it looked dimly lit inside and perhaps it became utterly dark. It might be the lair of some dangerous animal.

"But still," the explorer thought, "if could be a lair for me. If only I had a torch."

His eyes gradually adjusted to the semi-darkness. He even thought he glimpsed some kind of faint light farther in. He lacked a torch but he had his weapons. He made up his mind. With the sword in his right hand and holding out his left to protect his head from any sudden, unseen projection of rock, stepping cautiously, he boldly continued his exploration.

While walking he could not help thinking of those Arab legends that say that in grottoes like this are treasures guarded by monsters. But no enemy jumped out of the shadows to attack him. There were no monsters and apparently no treasures!

Perez walked slowly for what seemed a long time and the roar of the stream got louder and louder, which meant a steep slope. Staying close to the walls he sometimes felt the water getting close to him, depending on whether the grotto got bigger and smaller. At these times he could see the strength of the current.

Little by little the darkness dissipated. Perez found himself in a cave almost ten feet wide but that went on and on forever. A kind of huge tunnel carved out by nature. Being a tremendous architecture, nature had even thought of providing the tunnel with something like air vents. Looking up the fugitive saw an almost circular hole where the dim light he had seen from afar filtered into the grotto.

This hole was probably a "rift" that a geological disruption had dug out of the rocks at ground level. A rift that had then been filled in, but not completely, by other movements of the earth and by plants growing and dying to form the levels of humus.

Now Perez could see that on either side of the stream, which kept flowing down a slope of 30 to 40 degrees, ran a wide and totally dry embankment. The grotto rose up to an average height of ten feet and the walls were still mica schist.

Continuing beyond the zone of light the fugitive went another 100 feet into the grotto without finding an end. All of a sudden he slipped down a slope that was so steep he barely had time to reach out his left hand and grab a rock jutting out from the wall, which saved him from a drop that might very well have been into some bottomless pit.

He was careful going back. That was what Perez did, but with the promise that he would return with torches.

He had plenty of resin. He had seen it seeping out of the trees. All that was left was one crucial element: how to get fire?

Perez tried the traditional way of primitives. After piling up some brush and branches and dried leaves he took two pieces of wood, one pretty wide and the other pointed. Then he carved out a notch in the first with the tip of his sword and sticking the end of the second in the notch started rubbing, twirling the stick faster and faster. He was able to heat up the wood but not get it burning.

"Maybe with a spark from some flint, I'd be better off."

There was no shortage of flint around him. On the riverbank Perez picked up a fat, long rock that looked like a flint stone otherwise called gunflint. Holding the rock in one hand above his tinder he started striking the side of his sword.

Suddenly he cried out in pain, followed immediately by a shout of joy. After hitting the rock the sword had slipped and cut his hand. But at the same time a spark had set the dry leaves on fire and now a flame was growing, crackling merrily and brightly along.

On seeing the flame Perez forgot about his wound, which was luckily just a small cut. The most important thing was to keep the fire going since it was no easy task to start. He also had to make sure that he contained it within a safe space. He had no desire to burn down the whole forest.

He threw a few big, green branches on the flames that should burn slowly. Then he dug in the ground with his sword, honorably transformed into a shovel, to make a wide, deep hole. Into this hole he threw some rocks and burning wood. Over the wood he laid down a very thin layer of dirt mixed with some ashes from the flames.

Certain now that he a good fireplace and that even if the fire went out he could start a new one with some flint and his sword, the fugitive remembered that he wanted to explore the rest of the underground grotto. It might hold a few surprises.

He quickly gathered a half-dozen leafy ferns and wove the stalks together of each one, which he then covered with resinous gum. In this way he got six torches. He put five of them into his fig basket, which had already been used as a quiver, and lit the sixth.

Then he headed back to the mysterious grotto.

IX. In search of a sword

When Perez had first entered the dark subterranean cavern he had thought of those fabulous caves of legend, but when he carried the torch inside he really believed he was transported back into the *Arabian Nights*.

The light from the torch reflected off the mica-studded walls and made them sparkle like a rain of gold frozen in the rock. After going through the grotto in dark shadows, he was now going through in dazzling light.

But he did not stop. Eager to get to the end of his exploration and convinced that the cave was sheltering no dangerous animal, he hurried along carrying the torch in his left hand and the sword in his right.

When the first torch was almost entirely used up, Perez threw it in front of him after lighting a second. This one was still burning when he arrived at the place where the slope took a dizzying drop. It was here that he had stopped his first exploration after almost tumbling into the void.

He looked around and was overwhelmed by a sensation of both terror and admiration. The tunnel turned into a waterfall that dove into the bowels of the earth at an angle of around 50 degrees. At first he could see only a black hole where the water howled down. But at the far end he could make out a circle of faint light.

In what kind of geological disaster had this subterranean passage opened up to the fresh air? Did it go all the way to the bottom of some huge, natural funnel?

The second torch was burning out. It would be reckless to continue with the other four on an exploration that might present unexpected—maybe even insurmountable— difficulties. If he wanted to go on, he would have to get a lot more torches, a rope and some food because he might find himself stuck somewhere for more than a day.

But really, as strange as this grotto was, even admitting that it was like Fingal's or Mammoth Cave, geological wonders of the world, what was the point of wasting time and effort exploring it?

The sun was just setting when Perez came back to the cave opening. A blue glow enveloped the forest. In the heavens a thin crescent moon was shining and the stars glittered. Not a sound, except for the murmur of the stream, disturbed the calm of night.

"How beautiful it is!" Perez muttered, admiring the impressive scene in its wild simplicity.

It was really the first nice night that he had spent since his escape. The two previous nights had been much less comfortable. Now he had a stream to quench his thirst, a forest that provided him with game, a grotto to shelter him and plants aplenty to make a bed.

Perez only had to take a few steps to get armfuls of grass and dried reeds that he spread out on the ground inside the grotto, not far from the entrance, and he was soon sleeping fitfully, the sword lying in arm's reach.

#

When he woke up it was daybreak. After the blue glow of twilight came the full light of the sun turning the sky purple with a violet red that would soon turn to azure.

The Spaniard's first move was to dip his face in the clear water. Right after this he was struck dumb: his sword was missing!

It would be impossible to describe his state of mind when he realized it was gone. Was the oasis, therefore, inhabited and inhabited by men? Nothing so far had hinted at their presence. But the sword did not walk away on its own. Certainly whoever took it could not have been too savage, otherwise with Perez asleep it would have been easy for them to kill him or at least tie him up and make him their slave. Furthermore, why did they take his sword but not his pistols?

Perez racked his brains but could not find an answer. Maybe during his sleep he had turned over and pushed the weapon into the stream whose current carried it away.

"But no! It's not possible," he mumbled. "The sword is too heavy and the ground isn't steep enough here for it to roll down."

However, seeing that there was no other possible or rather plausible explanation, Perez ended up sticking with this one. And since the sword was of primary importance he resolved to search for it down where the stream must have washed it away.

It would no doubt be a more difficult exploration than the last. So, it was necessary to take things that would be indispensable for such an undertaking.

First of all, Perez ran to the fire that he had prepared the day before. Under the ashes he uncovered two big embers that had not yet burned up—a precious find since he could now create sparks with the flint and his sword. He quickly got the fire started again and threw on the fat trunk of a bush that he had pulled up.

After this he thought about hunting. Birdsongs were rising in the clear morning, proving that the forest was inhabited by animals that were still not scared by the presence of a man. In short time two fat pigeons and three blackbirds were felled by his arrows.

After plucking and opening (with his fingernails!) and gutting his catch, Perez roasted the birds by poking a long stick through them and hanging it over the fire. He ate two of the blackbirds and despite the lack of seasoning he felt a gourmet's delight in chewing the well-cooked, tasty meat.

The other blackbird and the pigeons were put in the basket next to the last of the figs.

After preparing the food, Perez thought about a rope. A plant similar to halfa and that grew at the edge of the forest made a very thick, very solid cord, a good dozen yards long, that he wrapped around his waist.

All that was left was to get enough torches. He made them quickly, adding a little wood so he could light a fire at some point if need be. Since kindling was rather bulky, the traveler made another basket to hold it.

Finally everything was ready. After lighting one of the torches Perez, for the third time, entered the grotto.

The fugitive knew the layout now. He walked so quickly that he lit the second torch only at the threshold of the long drop. While walking he scrutinized the streambed but he did not see this sword. The current must have carried it farther down.

When he got to the dizzying drop he held out his torch and could see the circle of light at the bottom of an unfathomable distance. The stream jumped down the waterfall, over the banks to spray the rock walls. Slipping on the rock, which was worn smooth by the water, could plunge the traveler into the abyss.

Perez tied his rope around an outcrop of rock and used it to climb down, or rather slide down five or six yards. Bracing himself against the wall he yanked the rope free and started again. Doing the same thing several times he ended up at a less steep part of the descent. By now he was on his fourth torch and as it was sputtering out Perez reached the end of the cave. Daylight—still a very dim light—blinded him an instant. And fresh air lashed his face. The fugitive looked up.

He was at the very bottom of a crevasse whose walls were around 20 feet apart and rose straight up at least 500 feet. It was impossible, even for the bravest acrobat, to think of climbing on either side of such a wall. The air and the light came from above, dwindling in the stupendous drop.

Something weird here: another cave opened across from this one and looked like a continuation of it. What gigantic terrestrial spasm had split the underground tunnel like this?

Perez did not hesitate. He lit a fifth torch and stepped into the second cave.

The ground continued to slope down but much less steep. At the same time the tunnel got higher and wider. The air felt less heavy. All of a sudden the Spaniard saw an arm pop up and start waving his sword in the air.

He had already given the sword up for lost and now he almost fainted from astonishment. What human being could be living so deep underground?

Perez wondered if he were not dreaming or if the old tales of mysterious caves guarded by legendary beings, giants or gnomes, were not telling the truth.

But he had seen only the sword and an arm. Then the creature attached to the arm let out a shrieking, beastly howl and jumped up, unbelievably, onto a rock ten feet above. What kind of man could be such an acrobat?

"Amigo," Perez shouted in any case, lifting his torch and trying to see the face of this creature whose body and limbs were completely naked. And he repeated two or three times the same word, finally adding "bueno".

The creature answered his calls for friendship with only a series of inarticulate shrieks.

"But it's not a man!" Perez was astounded but laughing. "It can only be a monkey."

Reassured by this idea he grabbed one of the pistols from his belt, aimed at the simian and fired.

The bullet did not hit the target, but the sound of the gunshot, echoing loudly through the cave, was deafening. The monkey got scared, leaped off and disappeared behind the rocks, dropping the sword on the way. Perez shouted for joy and went to pick it up. It was in perfect shape. Sliding it into his belt he promised never to let it out of his sight.

Still, he thought he heard other noises, a distant chaotic clamor from the depths of the cave, which seemed to go deeper for some indefinite distance. The ceiling was now at least 30 feet high. Perez could not help admiring the dimensions of this crypt where the stream emptied into a big lake. Then his burning fingers shook him out of his reverie—the sixth torch had just burned out in his hand.

But almost immediately the explorer forgot about the physical pain in the midst of the totally unexpected sight that struck his eyes: even though he had not lit another torch, he could see!

Not like in broad daylight, of course, but well enough. A kind of white air floated high up in the crypt. Perez believed it was due to electro-chemical radiation produced by certain unknown bodies that must have been embedded into the rock walls. This discovery was a great relief to him. Until now he had been pretty worried, torn between his desire to push his exploration to the very end of the mysterious grotto and the more cautious decision telling him to go back before he ran out of light. Now he could continue his journey.

How could this crypt be inhabited, seeing that the monkey he had shot at was obviously not alone—the commotion he had heard could only come from a group? Above all, how was it that these agile animals, who used extraordinary acrobatics to clamber back up to the surface and into the forest, had not left the underground for good? The question seemed inscrutable.

Perez, whose eyes had adjusted to the dim light in the crypt, noticed that it went on and on, higher and wider. Granite blocks rose up hundreds of feet; the interior lake turned into a sea; and suddenly the traveler noticed that he was walking on plants. Colorless grass was growing in the dirt along with weird plants: leafy cryptograms like ferns up above, moss, lichen, mushrooms… and finally real shrubs with fan-like leaves resembling palm trees and bearing fruit and flowers. But the flowers had no color or smell and the fruit looked unappetizing.

Perez was curious enough to pick one and taste it. The fruit, as big as an egg, had a bland pulp that was more sour than sweet. The heat of the sun, which nothing can replace, was needed when ripening.

The fugitive understood that he just walked into not a simple cave but an entire subterranean word, unknown and maybe immense, that spread out under the world that humans lived in.

"Well, why not stay down here a little longer? I might discover… scientific treasures!"

X. In a strange world

The look of the hypogeum, i.e. the catacomb, made this hope feasible. Generations of creatures had come before him: it is very rare that where plants and fruit flourished, animal life does not show up.

It was essential, therefore, without further delay, to find out what resources this subterranean realm could provide. Since monkeys lived there, why couldn't a man find enough to live on?

There was plenty of light and since it did not come from a wandering star it should be continual, with no periods of day and night. There was kindle for fire naturally provided by the plants but how to set it aflame? Was there flint underground here?

Perez was soon happy to find some and make a shower of sparks fly off the steel of his sword. Now he was confident: he would have enough fire just like the light. But a more sensational discovery was awaiting him.

As he walked along the lake on the ground covered with pebbles, one of them caught his attention. It was a small cube, perfectly formed, two inches per side and silver white. Picking it up Perez was surprised by how light it was. He also noticed that the pebble seemed to be covered with a kind of varnish.

"That's weird," he muttered.

Then, automatically, he threw it away. The pebble bounced off a rock and fell into the lake. At the same time something strange happened: the water started boiling and a little flame jumped up, only to go out a few seconds later. And despite the explosion being so abrupt,

Perez saw some shadowy forms come up under the rippling water. They were probably fish attracted by the flash of light.

"So, the lake is inhabited," the thought happily. "I won't be forced to eat only the plants."

Then he became obsessed by the phenomenon he had just witnessed. What was the material that caught fire on contact with water?

Perez knew that potassium produces this particular effect. But potassium is not found in its natural state because the oxygen, a gas it craves, in the air or water would immediately decompose it either into potassium oxide or potassium hydroxide. That is why it has to be kept in a substance that is impermeable to air and water, like naphtha oil. So, was the varnish coating the surface of the pebble a kind of insulation? An insulation that shattered or crumbled when he threw it against the rock so that the potassium caught fire when it hit the water?

"Yes, that must be it," he mumbled.

If he could find some more potassium cubes he would have another way to make fire. His wish came true: Perez found four more little potassium cubes. Lining them up to examine them more closely he was startled. The cubes were exactly alike in size and weight. It was as if they had come out of the same mold.

The fugitive was amazed. Didn't this uniformity prove that they were manmade? But how? The unknown chemist who knew how to preserve this simple but terribly unstable material that was first isolated by Davy in the early 19th century could rival the best of contemporary chemists. But what era and what race did he belong to?

Perez sat there struck with admiration. All his fear had washed away. He now had all the elements necessary for life: air, light, water, fire, plants and fish to eat, since he could surely use fibers from the plants growing in the crypt to make a solid net. And then this idea came back to him: why go look for shelter elsewhere when this grotto was open to him and could sustain for as long as he wanted?

Was the society of men really so attractive to him that he would face new and unknown dangers trying to get back to it? Some of those men, civilized men, had made him, an innocent man, into a convict. Others, barbaric men, had made him, the fugitive, their slave.

"My mind's made up," he muttered. "I'm staying here. Robinson Crusoe lived on his island—I'll live in this cave!"

Once his mind was made up Perez felt relieved. Besides, when he got tired of living underground he could always try to retrace his steps.

He was hungry and thirsty. He went to the edge of the lake, cupped some water in his hands and brought it to his lips. Straightaway he spit it out, disgusted. It was salt water. Not as salty as the sea but enough to deepen his thirst instead of quenching it.

"That's weird because the stream feeding it has fresh water."

It was important to clarify this point. Perez headed back, tasting the lake water as he went and finding it briny every time. But when he got to the waterfall he mumbled to himself in satisfaction: the water was fresh and delicious. He took a long, pleasant drink.

There was only one reasonable explanation: on flowing into the lake in the crypt the fresh water must have run over a bed containing huge amounts of sodium chloride and other salts. Who knows? Maybe the lake, like any number of African chotts (dry salt lakes) had once been linked to the sea.

Everything that Perez saw became extremely interesting to him. In a good mood he started walking back and passed the point where he had stopped earlier. The lake got bigger, forming an angle. Perez, standing at the tip of this angle, could not see where it ended. Maybe it was true that the glowing steam that lit the cave and was drifting over the lake like a white cloud 200 yards in front of him was hiding the other end.

He continued and reached a small beach of fine sand strewn with broken shells. He was no longer thirsty but he was starting to feel hungry. He sat down, took the pigeon out of his bag and cut it in two with his sword, which was now transformed into a simple kitchen knife. He was about to eat one of the halves when a long, sad meow made him shiver. Shudder would be a better word.

Perez, who feared no danger and not even death, felt an indescribable emotion when he heard the voice of a living creature rise up in this solitude. He had already forgotten about the monkeys. The presence of a cat, a domesticated animal, was far more exciting than the sight of a wild monkey in spite of its physical resemblance to a human being.

He saw the feline coming out from behind a bush, creeping up to him, arching its back. A dirty gray cat, terribly thin, watching him with its glowing eyes. Maybe the animal was tame. Or maybe it had never seen a man and this was why it was not very scared.

The fugitive called it by meowing back. The cat kept coming forward but what it was looking at most of all was the pigeon Perez was holding in his hand. Obviously the smell had told it there was a meal at hand.

"The poor thing is starved," Perez thought out loud.

After taking a few bites he generously offered the carcass to the cat. It stepped up, purring, and snatched it out of his hand. Then it bounded off, carrying the prey farther away, and started tearing off pieces with great care.

"What's this cat and its pals been eating down here?" he wondered.

His question was soon answered. The feline was coming back, working up its appetite. But seeing that its gracious host was offering no more gifts, it scampered off growling. Creeping along the lake it stopped once in a while as if it were examining the still water. Its behavior intrigued Perez.

"Well now, it looks like it wants to go fishing."

If only he knew how right he was.

When the cat got to a small creek it jumped into the water, then came out holding a wriggling fish in its mouth.

"A cat that fishes!" Perez marveled.

It was, however, not so incredible. Although the timid household cat is afraid of touching water, cats in the wild, out of necessity, have been known to catch fish in streams. There is even a street in Paris next to the Seine that has the colorful name of Rue du Chat-Qui-Peche (Fishing Cat Street).

This one that had just shown up in the cave was calmly eating its fish and Perez saw other cats coming out from the bushes and heading for the lake. But a tragedy was in the making.

One of the cats, hungrier or more reckless than the others, was swimming away and diving into the water. All of a sudden Perez saw the water bubbling. The head of the cat popped up, turned toward the shore and its front paws started paddling frantically to swim back in. But the animal did not have time: something parted the waters and lunged at the cat, whose body disappeared into its filthy mouth. A desperate, agonized, almost human cry echoed through the cave and froze the blood of the fugitive while the water of the lake turned red.

Wild animals were living in the cave, but the subterranean sea had monsters!

XI. Four-handed enemies

The pitiful end of the fisher-cat had made the other cats flee in terror. Perez felt truly sorry for the victim. Still, since he had planned to take a bath in the apparently calm lake, he was glad to know where he stood.

What species of aquatic animal was it that devoured the poor cat? Probably a shark, which run from the simple dogfish all the way to whale sharks. Unless it was some giant eel. As for the idea that the carnivore might be a crocodile, it was highly unlikely. Although crocodiles are known to swim up to certain river mouths, they live in fresh water and not in salt water.

Whatever it was, he kept his distance from the beach not so much out of caution but because the tragedy he had just witnessed left a foul taste in his mouth. Is it necessary for a victim to be human to arouse our pity? Isn't it logical that the groans and death rattles of lesser creatures made of flesh and blood like us affect our nerves?

He needed to find cover, not from the night since there could be no night in this cave where the light never went out, but at least to sleep. And the cats could come back to pillage his provisions. Any crevice in the rock that Perez could block off with rocks until he woke up would do the trick.

The fugitive turned away from the lake and started walking toward the rocks. Behind the thickets and shrubs granite blocks were scattered over the ground. Stalactites hung from the ceiling; stalagmites stuck out of the earth.

Suddenly Perez stopped and gasped. In front of him, on a rock, there was an engraved inscription: ANN D.

"Uhh," he stammered, confused and nervous. "What dead city has fate brought me to?"

ANN D—the letters seemed to blaze like they were on fire. It was like a resurrection from the past, rising from a grave 10 or 20 centuries old.

"ANN D has to mean Anno Dei," he muttered. "So, I'm in an ancient Roman city. But that's impossible. They wouldn't have built a city this deep underground. Besides, I'd find other remains, the ruins of temples and houses."

Anno Dei, he kept musing, 'in the year of God', which means a time after the birth of Christianity. Could this inscription be the work of some hermit meditating in a solitary retreat?

A few feet farther on the wall began. A narrow opening was hollowed out, a kind of niche, ten feet high and six feet deep.

"Here's my bedroom," he said. "I just need a door... Okay, there are two blocks that I can pile on top of each other and I'll have plenty of air to breath."

Settled in after barricading the opening, he slept. After such a full day a good rest was warranted. Perez was soon snoring soundly.

While snoring he dreamed that he was whisked away to an Oriental city in the reign of the glorious caliph Harun al-Rashid (of Arabian Nights fame) who put him at the head of his armies to conquer the land of Eldorado from the 'negritos' in the center of the Earth. A dream in which, obviously, reality was mixed with fantasy. The conquering army started out for the depths of the earth and marched through caves full of jasper columns sparkling with rubies and diamonds. The ground suddenly opened up under their feet. Perez stood there alone until a crowd of soot-colored dwarves rushed at him.

"Back off!" he yelled, flailing his arms.

He opened his eyes and wondered if he was still dreaming. A bunch of naked, hairy, little men had grabbed him in his dream and were holding him down by his hands and feet.

Little men... that was his first impression. But after a few seconds, instead of the incredibly agile dwarves, with all the shrieking and yapping, Perez knew that they were monkeys!

Monkeys that were not at all like the ones you could see behind bars in cages. These had gray skin instead of black, were almost five feet tall and had well-proportioned, skinny limbs. But what was most striking was their face: the facial angle was around 70 degrees, the nose was barely flat and under the thick eyebrows glimmered very thoughtful eyes. And then their cries, poorly pronounced of course but with clear differences in intonation—was it not a real language?

Perez felt right away that he was in the hands of exceptionally developed monkeys, you might even say *humanized*.

Was his situation any better for this? He very much doubted it.

The four-handed primates must have been watching him since he entered the crypt. They had seen him enter his shelter and barricade it. Through the cracks they saw him fall asleep and then they broke down the barricade and jumped on him. There were around 20 of them. Some had taken his supplies, others his weapons.

Perez trembled in fear when he saw one of his capturers holding one of the pistols and stepping forward. The animal pressed the barrel of the gun against the prisoner's chest. He twisted desperately to escape their clutches but they held him tight. The shot fired... or rather a spark flew out when the flint hammer struck down. It was the pistol that Perez had already fired on the monkey who stole his sword.

I scraped by this time, the prisoner thought.

The primates looked surprised. They had heard the frightening explosion when Perez had pulled the trigger and now all they got was a little spark. So, the troop started walking. Ten monkeys carried their prisoner over the ground holding him by his arms and legs.

"Where are they taking me?" the captive wondered.

They stopped at a big, square rock about three feet square, which looked like it covered some kind of pit. With a great deal of effort four monkeys lifted the cover and right away the acrid stench of death filled the air just as Perez saw the gaping black hole of a bottomless pit.

All of a sudden he got it: this revolting abyss was a cemetery where the monkeys threw their corpses and probably the bodies of other animals in the crypt so that they would not pollute the air. And this was where they were going to throw him... alive!

The unlucky traveler screamed and howled in fear. He was brave, as he had proven on more than one occasion, but he felt his courage draining away and all his blood freeze at the thought of being thrown into this black pit on top of piles of rotting corpses.

His desperate cry must have aroused some compassion in one of the monkeys who started talking, obviously trying to discourage his companions from their plans. But the simian eloquence did not seem to have much effect. Most of the monkeys, as far as he could tell, were all for burying him, while only two or three seemed undecided.

Perez was lost if something did not happen soon to turn the situation around.

One of the kidnappers who was holding the second pistol but not paying attention or not caring started playing with the trigger. This pistol was loaded. It fired and one of the monkeys wanting to bury the prisoner was hit squarely in the chest. The animal was struck dead, toppled over and fell into the pit.

All the other monkeys howled out and their heartrending lament echoed through the crypt. The ones holding Perez had let go of their captive. The others had dropped all of his belongings. Perez jumped to his feet. His first move was to grab his sword lying on the ground; the second move was to split open the head of one of the monkeys. He was going to keep it up but the troop broke up and leapt away.

XII. Are these humans?

After a scare like this Perez had no more desire to sleep. Filled with overwhelming horror he fled the macabre scene. While striding away he could not help feeling, amidst all his agitated thoughts, both surprise and awe at the monkeys' intelligence. All of this indicated a capacity for reasoning that was above even the most developed simians.

With their high forehead, their gray skin, their arms barely reaching their knees, they could be linked to the chimpanzees who were much more intelligent and lived in the African forests bordering Morocco. Why was it surprising that a family of them, maybe chased by hunters, had hidden in this crypt and their descendants had adapted to it?

They were dangerous neighbors and for a moment Perez had the vague desire to go back up the stream and live out in the open in the forest. But besides the climb, which would be a lot harder than the descent, he was ashamed to be a man retreating from monkeys. In the meantime, a new surprise was awaiting him.

He walked for a long time, trampling the strange ground. In the high grass tangled with spiny plants he found rocks that looked like they had been worked by hands: flint shards sharpened by a knife or axe and polished stones that could have been a mortar and pestle.

"I'm not dreaming. Humans lived here."

A weird sound overhead snapped him out of his reverie. It sounded like the beating of wings, big wings. Perez looked up and gasped: a huge, dark shape was flying 20 feet above him.

A bird? He could not say for sure because the loping flight was not, strictly speaking, like the swift inhabitants of the air. Some kind of giant bat, perhaps? As the winged creature was flying in concentric circles around Perez, he could clearly see the bare skin, a membrane and not feathers on the wings, but also a beak. A real beak, straight and pointed, not the muzzle of a bat.

"A pterodactyl!' he wanted to cry out.

In spite of all the surprises he had already had, this one still left him speechless. The thought of seeing an animal, whose race went extinct millions of years ago up on the surface of the earth, living and flying down here in this cave.

The pterodactyl seemed more curious than frightened by the presence of the intruder. But all of a sudden it soared off and disappeared behind a small grove of trees with gray leaves.

The traveler felt exhausted and sat on the ground to rest for a little while. Sleep is a more powerful tyrant than hunger or thirst. Perez had barely plopped down before he was stretched out on the ground and despite the monkeys, cats and pterodactyls he fell into a deep sleep.

How long did he sleep? It was hard to say because there was nothing around him whereby he could measure time. Still, he woke up refreshed, fit, and, the best of all, free. This time the monkeys who had taken advantage of his last sleep, had not attacked. Perez had slept well. And yet he remembered a hazy vision of a moving, human-like shape.

"Another dream," he figured.

The fugitive felt hunger coming on. But before breaking into his supplies it would be wise to restock them. The fruit he had tasted when he first came into the crypt and were no doubt the base of the monkeys' diet, was not appetizing. It would do in a pinch but the lake looked more promising.

Seeing that this subterranean lake had sharks and there was no way sharks would have turned into vegetarians, the lake must also contain edible fish. There was nothing easier than making a net with some fiber from the plants growing all around. Perez got to work.

Only when he had finished the work after a rather long time did he take the liberty of finishing off the other half of the pigeon that he kept in reserve. And he did not just eat the meat. He broke the bones into tiny little pieces that he threw into the lake. A matter of fish bait.

Ripples on the surface of the water showed him that hungry fish were swimming around and fighting over his scraps. Walking into the water up his knees he threw out his net, weighted down with pebbles and the opening fitted with floats made of bark. After what seemed a long time he saw the floaters bounce up and down. He started pulling in the net, slowly, then when he felt some resistance he yanked it hard.

An eel at least five feet long was caught in it and wriggling around furiously. Perez cut short its agony by severing the head with his sword. Then he gutted it and sliced up the body.

"Now," he mused, "everything's all right. I just have to smoke it and I'll have food for a few days."

He piled some tree branches together and put a crumbled potassium cube on top. Cupping a little water in his hands he sprinkled it on the metal, which flamed up right away. Then the branches caught fire. On the fire Perez laid the eel slices that were threaded on his sword. The noble weapon of destruction was now transformed into a skewer.

"Meow!"

"Skissi!"

"Oume!"

A concert of frightening meows, squeals and indescribable sounds echoed under the granite roof as the smell of fish and the smoke from the fire started wafting through the air. Perez shivered down to the marrow in his bones.

The 'meows' came from the cats creeping out of everywhere; the 'skissis' squeezed out of the throats of the monkeys who showed up as if they had fallen from the rocky roof like out of the sky; but who was whimpering those other cries, those deep, clearly pronounced, pitiful 'oumes'? What throats did they come from?

There was no possible doubt—they were human throats!

Perez remembered his dream... not a dream but a vision. Clearing up his memory, which was hazy at first, he saw again a slim, skinny shadow, a child, probably a girl to judge by her long hair.

They were coming! From everywhere! A strange army of excited creatures was moving toward him: cats, monkeys and human beings!

Wild-eyed and bewildered Perez saw only the latter. Were they really human beings, these gaunt, naked, pitiful creatures?

The fugitive from the penal colony, once a prisoner of pirates and slave of the Beni-Coudia, saw that these creatures were more miserable than he. He wanted to shout out a few words of welcome and encouragement, but he couldn't.

At first sight, before even seeing their dull, colorless eyes, he felt that these creatures walking towards him with the cats and monkeys, guided like them by voracious hunger gnawing at their guts, were fallen beyond repair. Physically they might look human but mentally they had regressed to the level of animals. There was also a disturbing difference: the monkeys had not only supported the conditions of life underground but maybe as a result of being close to beings who were once superior to them they had been humanized; the humans, on the other hand, had been animalized.

Oh, Perez felt a real horror and fear that he had only felt once before: when the monkeys wanted to throw him into the gravel pit. The degeneration of his own species made his blood freeze. He abandoned all his dreams: exploring the cave and discovering the mysteries it held. He wanted to run away.

He took a few steps back but the bizarre army—with four feet, four hands and two of each—was surrounding him. And all of them, animals and men, had turned their begging eyes on him. In the eyes of the cats and humans (if you could really call them this) was hunger, a fierce hunger that was crushing them. But in the eyes of the monkeys, who obviously fared a little better, there was something different. It was respect, veneration, a religious zeal.

The four-handed primates had seen one of their own struck dead when they were about to throw Perez into the pit. They had seen the sword wielded lethally in the hands of this strange being who was now creating this fantastic, incomprehensible new element: fire. Apparently they had concluded that the stranger was a supernatural master before whom they must bow.

Certainly their first cousin, man, was not unfamiliar to them, but the examples they had seen so far in the crypt had not given them much of an idea about the human race. Perez had the clear impression that he was dealing with the evolution of a simian species on the rise and the devolution of a human species on the decline.

One of the monkeys stopped in front of him and… bowed deeply. All the others did the same.

"What do you know, now I'm God!" the fugitive was astounded.

Without thinking, he patted the head of the first monkey who straightened up with a look of unutterable pride. All his fellow monkeys also straightened up and surrounded him, showing their delirious excitement with shrieks and howls. Apparently the placing of his hand on the monkey's head had, in their eyes, bestowed on the creature a sacred character.

"And now he's the pope or grand lama," the fugitive muttered.

The men, however, did not gush with signs of worship; they focused their desperate eyes on the slices of fish. The Spaniard counted the wretched creatures: there were 25 of them, 12 men, 8 women, both of undefined age, and 5 children. One of them was a girl around seven years old, skinny and naked like the others but her face looked normal and her eyes sparkled with a glimmer of intelligence. Perez shivered. This was the little girl he had seen in his half sleep when he thought he was dreaming.

He cut his fish slices into 25 equal pieces and with a heavy heart handed them out to the poor things who gobbled up the unexpected, paltry meal.

The cats were whining like mad. There were 20 more of them but they would have to be satisfied with the bones. When they saw that there was nothing left for them they scurried off, prowling around the lake, and some of them started to fish.

Perez was surprised by the friendly relations between the hungry men and the animals that they did not think of killing and eating. He was also surprised that since hunger seemed to be a chronic condition for the inhabitants of the crypt, except for maybe the monkeys who were less picky about a plant diet, they did not think of leaving this place.

So, did these slow-witted men not know that they could go back up the stream and find an exit? Or did the climb look too hard to them? Had they become incapable of the effort?

The fugitive figured that he had nothing to fear from such wretched creatures. The monkeys would respect him from now on and the cats were not very dangerous enemies. Why, then, would he give in to his first impression and run away?

Maybe there was a rescue mission to accomplish here. And he who had been imprisoned for trying to enlighten his fellow man, was it right for him to recoil before this new task, a noble and brotherly task, as hard as it might be?

Plus, the intelligent look of this child, lost in the crypt among degenerates and beasts, awoke in him a sense of pity. If it is true that our thoughts are reflected in our faces, this little girl was a backward human. But she could be saved.

He would stay!

XIII. Sta!

The fisher-cats had disappeared. The monkeys kept at a respectable distance, glancing at the stranger from time to time, but mostly they listened to what seemed to be a speech by the one that Perez had unwittingly baptized and called the "grand lama".

As for the "animalized"—because he dared not called them humans—most of them went away after their hunger was sated. Only a few stayed there, squatting, motionless, with an empty look in their eyes.

Nothing in them showed any sign of conscious life! Not even curiosity or acknowledgment of the individual who had supplied them with an unforeseen meal. But no, nothing at all! There was only the little girl who was watching Perez with big eyes, following every move he made.

"That girl really has a soul," he thought, imagining the true meaning of the word "soul".

And he named the girl Luz, meaning "light" in Spanish.

"Luz!" he called, waving the girl over.

The young girl hesitated a moment, then took a step forward but at the same time one of the animalized grabbed her hand and held her back.

"Her father?" he wondered.

He made a friendly gesture to both of them, doubting that any words would be understood. The little girl looked at the man still holding her back. She opened her mouth and seemed to be asking him to let her go. His only response was one word that was pronounced loud enough for Perez to hear: "Sta!"

The fugitive was shocked. From the moment he had slipped out of the hands of the Beni-Coudia, this was the first time he had heard a human voice. Moreover, the word revealed the race that these troglodytes belonged to: "Sta" could only be the imperative of the Italian "stare", stay or stop, which came from the same Latin word.

Perez blushed with joy. He spoke Italian well enough so he could talk with these men!

"Amico!" he shouted, "Non temere. Stama fratelli." (Friend! Don't be afraid. We're brothers.)

His joy was crushed right away. The man squinted and shook his head, showing that he did not understand. Then he went away, dragging little Luz after him, not violently but firmly. She obeyed him but reluctantly. Several times she looked back at Perez and her eyes showed signs of some kind of connection.

The other animalized also went away. They headed for the depths of the crypt and Perez saw that there were tunnels opened in the rock. For a second he almost wanted to follow them but he was afraid of scaring them off. So, he stayed there, did not move a muscle, telling himself that with the lake nearby, either curiosity or hunger would bring them back.

He no longer thought about leaving now that his initial horror had dissipated. The dwellers of the crypt, except for the sharks in the lake, were not dangerous and probably able to be tamed.

"We can tame wild animals! Why not men?" he pondered.

Furthermore, he had to start talking with the animalized, as impossible as it might seem, to get the key to the mysteries surrounding him.

Was it possible that it was simply by chance that they used a word that meant the same thing in Latin and Italian? No, by their skin color and facial features these humans were not Arabs. They must be descendants from a Latin race. The characteristics of this line of descent were especially apparent in little Luz, in her oval, balanced face framed in wavy black hair. Maybe in one of the tunnels where the animalized were holed up Perez would find some clues to this mystery. He knew that his exploration was not over yet. Maybe it had just begun.

But before setting out for new discoveries he had to deal with the present ones. Since he had given away all his fish he had to prepare new provisions, so he cast his net in the lake again.

At the same time he thought that one of the pins holding up the haïk that he wore under his burnous, because it was already curved, might be used as a big hook. He quickly made a fishing line out of plant fiber. Two long, fairly straight branches would do for poles, one for his net and the other for his line. All he had to do was wait for the fish to bite or to get caught in the net.

XIV. The manuscript

Perez had baited his line with a few scraps from the head of the eel. He pulled it in three times without catching even the smallest minnow. But the fourth time he felt resistance, something heavy, and he was afraid that the line would break. And yet, his catch was not thrashing around.

"Did I hook the dead body of a shark?" the fisherman was intrigued.

He finally managed to reel in his line and he stood there stupefied. What he had caught was not a fish but a small box, around eight inches square and made of metal that was entirely rusted. The hook had stuck in some shapeless thing that was probably once a lock.

Perez shook himself and had a big smile. The box might contain some object that would shed some light on the mystery of the crypt.

Two seconds later it was in his hands. After turning it around and examining it on all sides he saw that it was oxidized everywhere and resisted every effort he made to open it. Then an idea came to him: he could break it with a big rock.

One hard strike cut a gash in the box. He stuck his sword in it and using it like scissors, running the risk of breaking the precious weapon, he started prying it open.

Perez had completely forgotten about his net. Automatically he looked up and glanced over the lake. The net was jumping out of the water. He rushed over and pulled it in. Two small eels were tangled up, which he speedily beheaded and sliced up.

But as important as this catch was, it meant little to him compared to his new find. He went back to the box in a fury and with one more blow from the rock the metal gave way, crushed into rusted shards.

With a victory shout Perez picked up a carefully folded parchment covered in greenish letters that were faded and partly erased. His heart was pounding before he took a closer look. If the letters that would undoubtedly reveal the mystery of the cave were written in an unknown language, he would be frustrated and disappointed.

But no! Trembling with joy he read: *Anno Domini nostri DXXVII Justiniano imperatore...* Meaning: "In the year of our Lord 527 under Emperor Justinian...

Perez remembered enough Latin to be able, with some effort, to read this manuscript that had been written with some unknown ink and preserved over the long centuries thanks to the hermetic seal of the metal. This is what he read:

"In the year of our Lord 527, under Emperor Justinian, as the Vandals are taking over Africa, the little church of Sancta Mater, built on the high plains of Mauretania Tingitana..."

Now being occupied by the Riata, Perez thought as he continued reading:

"...within the diocese of Spain, was forced to flee before the Barbarians. Heaven opened the land before them and they found shelter in this crypt. The community consists of 35 believers, 18 men, 12 women and 5 children. The pastor is Nestor Milesius who piously carried the sacred vessels in their flight.

"So that these Christians be not alone in their exile God sent animals to accompany them: a couple of big monkeys that look like men in their exterior form but lacking an immortal soul, and a couple of wild cats. And he did not send harmful animals, such as lions, bears or panthers.

"In this crypt the refugees found miraculous resources and they lived praising the Lord after taking a vow to renounce the outside world.

"Milesius died at the age of 100 years old after leading this new church and multiplying its resources thanks to many miracles. But the men of the third generation grew weary of living in the depths and they left this sanctuary. God punished them by making them fall prey to the Barbarians who feed on human flesh sprinkled with water and worship two false gods: Allah and Mahom.

"Only two couples returned to the refuge and they vowed that neither they nor their descendants would ever leave again. As they were pledging their word the ground rose up and closed off the mouth of the cave forever.

"The crypt was repopulated with a race of men for generation after generation. But the anger of heaven weighed heavily on them because they were tormented with the desire to return to the earthly things that their ancestors had spoken of and that they knew not. Everything worsened for them. The trees bore fruit only rarely, the water of the lake refused its fish and the planted ground gave no more seeds.

"I, Petrus Faustulus, was born in this crypt in the ninth generation after the flight of the Sancta Mater Church, in the sixth generation after the escape from the worshippers of Allah and Mahom. With me are 25 men, 20 women and 12 children.

"God has granted to keep me in his grace. But I predict a sad future for the descendants of this flock of fishermen. Already my brothers know not the name of the Lord. They care nothing about what is not of the body. They have even forgotten the language of their fathers. I alone still possess ancient knowledge: the art of transmuting and preserving rocks so that they can make fire; the art of weaving fibers; the art of perpetuating thought through writing. But after me what will become of these poor people? Perhaps one day God will send some messenger of his will to find the last vestiges of these people.

"I write these lines in obedience to his will. Whoever reads this, pray for our souls."

When he had finished the difficult job of reading the manuscript Perez thought long and hard. In this story that mixed naïve mysticism with the truth he was finally seeing the explanation he was searching for.

Yes, the degenerate creatures he had seen, sunk to the level of simple animals, were the descendants of the Christian community of Sancta Mater, which had escaped the Vandals and found refuge in this crypt. They were the remains of this community that had escaped 100 years later from the Arab invasion and a later geological upheaval had apparently walled them in. Later still another movement of the earth had opened up an exit that they could have used to escape if sloth and decay had not already rooted them to where they were. Only the nimble monkeys, already developing a more active mind, could go back upstream and see the light of day. But they took very few trips. They were used to the crypt, felt comfortable here and chose to stay.

Perez wondered about the difference in evolution between the monkeys and the men, the former only needing to perfect a clearly articulated language to become human and the latter, passive and pitiful, only had to forget the few final words they still barked out to become animals for good.

This difference must have come from two causes: a diet that was insufficient for humans but good enough for monkeys and the mental anxiety among the refugees produced by mysticism, memories and hopes—an anxiety that had ended up snapping their nerves and drowning their intelligence.

But maybe in the midst of the human herd that continued to degenerate there might rise up, once in a while, a superior individual, an atavistic awakening, and maybe Luz was an example. But what torture it must be for this thinking creature to live among brutes who were incapable of understanding her!

Would it be possible to fire up some spark in their brains that seemed to hold nothing but the ashes of past centuries?

He did not think so. For that, at the very least, they would have to leave the tomb in which their mystic ancestors had been buried. He would have to bring them up into the outside world, full of activity and thought, onto farms made fertile by hard work and into cities bustling with industry. Could he, a fugitive, do this?

He had only one chance. The language that these men spoke must be based on Latin. A deformed Latin, reduced to its most simple expressions, but that he could easily understand and learn to speak.

Obviously the troglodytes must know nothing at all about the outside world. The words for the arts and sciences certainly held no meaning for them, but whatever signified the necessary, natural acts must have survived, probably in a very different form.

The humans would be back. They would need to drink and they could only do so from the stream that emptied into the lake. Unless there was another source that filtered down through the walls and was accessible farther away. In any case, he would find out tomorrow, meaning after his next sleep.

Without a sun or moon it was impossible to tell time with any precision. He smiled at the confidence of Petrus Faustulus in stating that his venerable predecessor Milesius had died at the age of 100. Nevertheless, to have some approximation he decided to use his sleep as a period of measure. Because he felt like he was sleeping normally, it should be more or less equal to 24 hours. Since he first came into the crypt he had slept twice. Therefore, it must be the third day of his underground life. With the point of his sword he carved three notches in the bark of a shrub.

His eyelids were starting to feel heavy again, but before surrendering to sleep Perez wanted to keep everything he had as safe as possible. He bundled it up in his burnous and tied it to the trunk of a bush with enough complicated knots that Gordian's ghost would turn green with envy. The monkeys would not be able to untie if they wanted to. Neither could he for that matter but like a new Alexander he could resort to cutting it with his sword.

Then, after tying the hilt of the sword to his wrist, he slept soundly on the beach. He dreamed of the escaping Christians, of their Pasteur Milesius, of Petrus Faustulus, of Vandals and Arabs.

But he did not see the small human form come to spy on him again. It was Luz. But a hushed voice grunted and the child went back into the shadowy tunnels where she had come from, stopping to look back at the sleeping stranger.

XV. Lost in the depths!

When he awoke Perez cut the knot of his bundle, threw it over his shoulder and with the faithful sword at his side he went off to explore the cave. The tunnels might lead to new grottos. He would undoubtedly find other traces of the ancient inhabitants, some remains of their workmanship and also their bones. Unless the humans, like the monkeys, had the habit of throwing their dead into some abyss. Who knows, maybe the primates watched the human practice and started imitating it.

Perez turned away from the lake. The crypt before him got wider and the walls in places formed jutting angles. There was also water seeping out of the walls, trickling down here and there only to be soaked up by the ground.

The fugitive went through a big opening, 20 feet high by 10 feet wide. The dusky light got a little dimmer and Perez paused. But stepping closer to the wall to feel it, he saw right away that it gave off a faint phosphorescence.

"Great!" he figured, "Now I won't need matches and I can save the torches."

In the faint glow some letters appeared engraved in the rock. Perez read:

NESTOR MILESIVS
Santae Matri ecclesiae episcopus

"Nestor Milesius, bishop of the church of Sancta Mater," he translated. "This is a well-preserved inscription from antiquity. The tunnels must have a bunch more."

He kept walking, step by step, staying close to the wall. Other inscriptions were, in fact, carved into the wall: Epontius, Valerius, Domitia, Fausta... Names of men and women who were cloistered in this subterranean prison and had wanted to leave on the rock some lasting trace of their obscure existence.

All of a sudden his hand felt a rusted metal surface in the wall. He traced the worn engraving with his fingers and could barely decipher the letters: "P x aet na."

"Pax aeterna," he figured. "Eternal peace. Could this be the entrance to a cemetery... or a tomb?"

Perez rubbed the glowing wall until it grew a little brighter. He saw a narrow iron door, eaten away by rust, encased in the rock. A cross was carved in it crudely. "I was right," he mumbled. But all his efforts to break it down were useless. Obviously it had been sealed shut for centuries.

Perez continued his exploration. His mind got lost in reverie about everything he had seen these past three days. Then all of a sudden he realized that he was engulfed in shadow. He rubbed the wall feverishly but this time it did not glow. He went a few steps farther and rubbed again, hoping to find some phosphorescent rock. Nothing!

Perez felt his heart freeze. He turned back, keeping one hand on the wall, trying to find the iron door. Nothing! Rock! Just Rock!

Did he take a wrong turn while daydreaming? To make sure he went back again, still feeling the wall. Still nothing! No metal door, no phosphorescence. Without realizing it he must have followed a side tunnel.

Perez stumbled and staggered. He escaped one tragedy and horror only to fall into another situation even more tragic and horrible. Here he was, in complete darkness, lost in an underground cave, alone, without any possible help. Worn out and hopeless, he dropped to the ground. Without a thread to follow he would wander around blindly, drive himself crazy with fear and anxiety, until hunger and thirst and exhaustion finally got the better of him.

He had no idea how long he lay on the ground but the beating of wings finally woke him up. He opened his eyes and saw a beak pecking his forehead. Perez screamed and when he shot his hands up to his head, he felt something warm and wet. Then even more alarming, other wings came beating around him.

The fugitive remembered the pterodactyl. Obviously it was not the only one of its kind in the crypt. These precursors of modern bats must have been like them—nocturnal hunters. And without a doubt they were also carnivores and figured Perez was good prey.

Several times the unlucky explorer felt the filthy wings brush against him. With his left hand protecting his eyes, he swung his sword in his right hand, slicing through empty air. And he screamed at the top of lungs to frighten the predators away.

It went on forever.

Suddenly Perez felt a small hand touch him. Trembling, he lowered his left arm and felt around in the darkness. He recognized the small body.

"Luz!" he cried in desperate hope.

"Essi," said the soft voice.

The child's hand grabbed his and dragged him away. With hope pumping through his heart Perez followed his guide without saying a word, afraid that he would make the apparition vanish or that he would bring the humans who would separate them.

Luz led him through the dark maze without a moment's hesitation. Perez surmised that she was a nyctalope, had night vision, developed out of habit and from an atavism of seeing in the dark tunnels where her ancestors had lived.

Finally he saw the gray light that looked bright white to him now because his eyes were already getting used to the dark. When he got back to the entrance to the cave he was blinded as if he were staring into the sun.

"Gracias," he said. Thanks sounded the same in Spanish and in Latin. But no sound came in response.

Perez quickly pulled himself together and realized that his hand was holding nothing. Luz had disappeared.

XVI. Strange singers

The exploration he had started in the tunnels of the crypt had almost ended in tragedy, so the fugitive was in no hurry to go back. If Luz had not suddenly appeared he could have wandered from one tunnel to another, getting farther and farther away from the center of the cave and ended up dropping dead in the darkness.

The eyes of the other inhabitants of this subterranean world must have adapted to seeing in the dark. All of them, men and animals, were probably nyctalopes.

Two days, or rather two periods of sleep, had passed. Perez had built near the lake an unshapely shack out of blocks of stone, some clay and dry branches covered with leaves. His burnous was used to screen the opening. But neither the monkeys nor the wild cats tried to get into his dwelling.

Perez now knew two words of the animalized language: "Sta", which meant stop and "Essi", meaning yes. This last word was obviously a corruption of "etiam". He figured that the idiom of the degenerates came from an altered, shortened Latin, reduced to one and two syllable words for easier speaking.

While exploring around the lake he had discovered a burial mound. Digging it up with his sword he found charred dust in the shape of a human skeleton. Next to it was a silver vase, a priceless treasure not for the value of the metal but for its usefulness. So far, every time he got thirsty he had to go to the stream. Now he could keep a little supply of drinking water, about a pint's worth.

The discovery of the skeleton-shaped ash proved that the dwellers in the crypt had, at some time, burned their dead. Not at first, since they were still under the influence of Christian traditions that forbid cremation, but later. Then they must have looked for easier and easier ways, finally just throwing the dead into pits that they covered over so that the noxious stench would not poison the air they breathed. Their example was later imitated by the monkeys.

Equipped now with a container for some fresh water Perez would be ready to carry out a project that was less dangerous and maybe more useful than exploring the rock tunnels. He could go along the lake that he had so far only followed for a mile or so without seeing the end. With a pint of water he could easily live for two days. He figured that his round-trip exploration could not last longer than this.

As for food, there was plenty of that. Despite having run out of pigeons, blackbirds and figs, he still had a good supply of fish, which he had preserved by boiling them in the silver vase, even better than smoking them.

So, the vase was filled with drinking water and corked with a tight bundle of leaves, while the fish were put in a basket with some fruits from the cave and the five potassium cubes that remained. Thus equipped he got on his way.

This time he was not afraid of getting lost. His itinerary was as simple as possible: stay next to the lake at all times, both going and coming back.

He walked for a long time, finding a few undeniable traces of men in the sand on the beach: pottery shards, unfortunately unusable, and broken rosaries made of coral. All of a sudden he almost cried out in joy when he saw something gray that looked like a scrap of parchment. But when he turned it over in his hands he could not see even the faintest lettering. He finally decided that he was holding a strip of bark that had been prepared for writing but was abandoned. Still, just in case, he put it in his basket.

Parallel to the lake ran a thick forest of those trees with tasteless but edible fruit. The traveler was not surprised that the monkeys and even the men had found enough to eat in the cave. Every tree must have had at least 60 fruits.

After walking for an even longer time, when he finally stopped to eat and rest he was struck dumb with amazement, not for the first time but no less profound. He was not dreaming—he heard singing!

A song, not a bird's—which would not have been an exceptional phenomenon because other species than pterodactyls could be in the cave—but a song of human voices. It sounded like a chant in a minor key, very pleasant.

Was it possible that these humans who seemed so wretched, so animalized, almost mute, could find their voices to sing! And to sing a song so perfectly sweet! Of all the characteristics of the species that they had lost, did song alone remain to them?

Perez was right. The voices were human. Inching closer he could make out the words: "Lumen coeli".

"Lumen coeli, the light of heaven," he shivered with indescribable compassion. "See, I was wrong. The poor creatures haven't completely degenerated. As weak as their minds might be, they've held onto some scraps of tradition, this image of heaven that their ancestors had recognized and come together to worship or mourn. It was the isolation that made them savage, which is the only reason they don't not want to talk to me."

Among the singers of the sweet and melancholy air, he naturally pictured Luz, the child who had first grabbed his attention and later had saved his life. To prove that he was a friend, he sang out in Latin in the same rhythm as the other voices: "Luminem coeli vederunt patres vostres…" [Your fathers have seen the light of heaven]

The sound of splashes, things diving into the water made him stop. Perez ran over and saw what was disappearing into the lake… not men but incredibly strange creatures.

Imagine, if you can, the head of a giant lizard on a neck as long as a snake on top of a seal's body ending in a short, thick tail; smooth black skin covered around the chest only with a kind of armor; around six and half feet long from nose to tail.

At first sight Perez recognized the species of animal it belonged to: Plesiosaurs, truly a lot smaller than its contemporaries, the ichthyosaurs and pterodactyls that abounded on the earth a few million years before the appearance of humans.

But singing plesiosaurs! And singing in Latin!

The fugitive felt his mind slipping away at the thought of this fantastic phenomenon. He thought his head would explode.

But he still tried to think clearly. Articulate language was not the exclusive monopoly of humans. The parrot and other birds also possessed it and repeated words taught to them. Why could not other animals, on earth and in the sea, enjoy the same privilege? Haven't seals been heard to say "Papa" and "Mama"?

Now, the plesiosaur resembles a seal, except for its extremely long neck, but its neck might be the very thing that favored the development of a larynx. Sure, but why did these animals speak or rather sing in Latin? And

110

even a much more correct Latin than the human dwellers in the crypt!

"Yes, but they were just repeating the same words, lumen coeli," Perez pondered. "And they repeated without understanding... like a lot of two-legged creatures do."

Obviously someone must have taught them the song. It could not have been the humans here now who speak a less pure Latin, a simple dialect, in which noun cases were not expressed. Moreover, they do not seem to have kept any memory of the light of heaven.

"Was it possible that these animals I just saw were hundreds of years old? Were they tamed and educated by the men who lived here centuries ago? It is possible because we have no idea how long the plesiosaurs can live. Or else... no, that would be too crazy."

For the first time since entering the cave Perez broke out in uncontrollable laughter. He was thinking that the men of old who still spoke a pure Latin had taught these two words and maybe others to the plesiosaurs who in turn had taught them like a natural call to their offspring.

Whatever the case, it was weird and poignant to think that under the vaults of this crypt the animals themselves seemed to lament the lost light of heaven.

XVII. A lesson in bad Latin

We saw that Perez had laughed out loud. Without a doubt this was the first time in centuries that laughter had echoed through the crypt. And it had an extraordinary effect. The heads of the giant lizards poked out of the water and the fugitive saw the plesiosaurs, the amazing mimics, open their mouths and laugh with their jaws wide open.

Then untranslatable sounds, shrieks and cackles, came from the forest. It was the monkeys coming to join the concert of fun. Finally the bushes parted and the poor animalized humans, shy and scared, stepped out. There were 20 of them, including Luz who right away waved awkwardly to her friend.

"Ave," Perez said hello in Latin to his fellow men—if you could call them that.

One of the animalized shook his head, not understanding. Apparently he could not find the words to tell him.

"Amici," Perez said 'friends' very slowly.

"Ami-ci," the biped repeated, but it was clear that the word meant nothing to him.

Luz, however, ran up to Perez who picked her up and hugged her with inexpressible tenderness. The animalized cried out in terror. They must have imagined that this creature who was as different from them as they were from the monkeys was going to eat the child.

One of them, fighting back his fear, stepped forward and said, "So até."

Perez understood the gesture and this helped him to understand the words. He immediately understood "Sum pater" meaning "I am the father".

"Até?" he repeated as a question.

"Essi."

Conversation was now opened. Perez knew about the regressive development of Latin from a dialect of primitive Melanesians. Words were shortened, initial or final consonants cut off. "So" for "sum" and "até" for "pater".

He put Luz down so that the others could see that he did not mean to hurt her or even keep her against her will. He patted her head gently and petted her beautiful black hair, although it was a tangled mess that neither comb nor scissors had ever touched.

"Apou," the animalized father said, which Perez immediately translated as "caput", head.

Then he held up his arm and got the response "akio". He mimicked sleeping: "omi" several humans cried out at the same time as the one who had dared to break the ice. The gestures of eating and drinking were answered with "oume" and "vive". Then he pointed to a rock, a tree and the water in the lake. "Lapi", "abo" and "aqua" were shouted out. The first two were barely changed: "lapi" for "lapus" and "abo" for "arbor". The third was not changed at all—it sounded the same in the mouths of these poor creatures as it had in the ancient contemporaries of Caesar.

Perez was delighted to be able to understand them like this without too much trouble. But they were only simple words, not complete sentences or complex thoughts. Thoughts! He did not know if the animalized were even capable of forming them. Moreover, when he tried to express one himself, he saw that even by deforming and simplifying his Latin he was not understood.

Luz seemed much more intelligent and the fugitive felt that this little flame was destined to go out in such an environment. The refined race of her ancestors seemed to be resurrected in her. But alas, what a life she would have!

After years of suffering in the Ceuta penal colony followed by a cruel slavery Perez felt the need to love a living creature, even a dog, and to be loved by it. Destiny had led him to meet Luz and right away he felt a paternal affection for her. He told himself that he had to pull her out of the horror of this animal life. Meanwhile it was she who had saved him.

Perez knew that first of all he had to win the confidence of the animalized. The best way to do this was to give them something to eat like he had already done. But he could not touch his food supply because it would run out in no time if he had to share with them. But did he have a choice?

He threw his net into the lake, then his fishing line after baiting it with a little piece of fruit. Men and monkeys (since they had come closer) watched his every move, the former with indifference, the latter with keen interest. Luz remained by his side, also watching what he did. She seemed to understand.

"Cape pici," she said. After a moment she added, "Oume pici."

Perez translated "Capere piscem" (catch fish) "Comere piscem (eat fish). He answered in the affirmative, "Essi."

Obviously the child was intelligent. She wanted to ask questions and be taught. The other animalized were lying on the beach, waiting for they knew not what.

Luz called to them, "Omo dabi pici."

The fugitive understood these three words very easily: "Homo dabit piscem" (the man will give fish). He nodded his head.

In spite of the satisfaction that he felt in understanding without any prior study, he could not help regretting what had become of the beautifully strong Latin language, which had once been the universal language of Europe, in the mouths of these degenerates. Perez wanted to see if there were some trace remaining that could still resonate. In a loud voice he started reciting a beautiful ode of Horace:

"Justum ac tenacem propositi virum." (A man upright and firm of purpose)

But after this first line he stopped. The humans looked stunned, then stopped listening to him. Luz, however, furrowed her brow, looked distracted, lulled by these powerful words like by an unknown chant that meant nothing to her.

Perez felt ashamed of his species because only the monkeys seemed to make an effort to understand what he said. But it was clear that their mentality was not yet able to comprehend that nothing could shake the firm soul of a just and determined man.

However, between one man and a monkey a weird conversation started up in which the human spoke only a few words and the primate only a few inarticulate sounds. What the discussion was about Perez had no idea, but to his great surprise he saw the monkey stand up on his two feet and hit the man on his lower back, with more mockery than brutality.

The fugitive was confused. Then he felt indignant. Was it possible that his own species had lowered themselves to such a state? And all of a sudden he straightened up, angry, and was about to march over to the monkey to help the man. But the latter had accepted it without making a sound and Perez figured that a being whose dignity was so completely degraded did not deserve any help. Would the wretch even understand the meaning of the intervention on his behalf?

Perez remembered that in the immortal Don Quixote of his fellow countryman Cervantes the prisoners threw rocks at the brave knight errant who had freed them. Besides, the man and monkey seemed to have made up. They were sitting next to each other, with no anger, their attitude proving that the incident that had just happened held no importance and in their relationship as neighbors the humans were used to being treated as an inferior race by the primates.

"Pici," Luz touched his arm and pointed to the floater that was bobbing in the water.

Perez yanked his fishing pole. A good-sized fish was wriggling on the hook. It was the girl who expertly removed the struggling prisoner, even though she had never seen it done before.

A quiver ran through the apathetic animalized when they saw the fish lying on the ground in its final death spasms. The same word came out of all their mouths, "Oume." (Eat)

But what did this one pound fish mean for all of them? There were a few more than the first time: 18 men, 12 women and 5 children, including Luz. Perez figured that this was all that remained of the human population in the cave. In a few years the derelict race would be gone forever.

They would have devoured the fish raw if the fugitive had not waved them off, which Luz translated in a firm voice: "Epea!"

"Expectere" (Wait), "Sperare" (Hope)—which of these two verbs did the word spoken by the little girl come from? Maybe both. Even among modern peoples "hope" was often used for "wait". No doubt because waiting should always be accompanied by some hope.

The lake must have been full of fish despite the sharks because on lifting the net Perez found a big tuna-like fish flapping around. It was a good catch. Again the animalized were suddenly shaken out of their indifference. They all started shouting with joy and waving their arms in a frenzy, eager to satisfy their hunger immediately, repeating, "Oume! Oume!'

With begging eyes they surrounded the fisherman, who was like a supernatural being to them. Two minutes later, thanks to a potassium cube, a fire was blazing and the two fish were roasting in front of the greedy eyes of the hungry. They had fallen so low that they could barely even look at this element that the monkeys, on the other hand, were watching avidly: Fire.

XVIII. Luz

Perez was a believer in the thoroughly modern idea that life, especially physical life but also mental life—the two, in fact, being one—develop through the absorption and digestion of the substances that are necessary for the organism. On the contrary, undernourishment or deficiency in the diet is a cause of degeneration.

Along with their isolation and the damage done by mysticism, the lack of a healthy variety of food had driven the descendants of Sancta Mater back to a primitive animal nature. Hunger gets the best of the strongest minds.

If any recovery was possible it could only come from first of all improving their diet, then a complete change of environment.

Perez sliced the fish into 35 pieces, as equal as possible. The famished humans jumped on this manna from the sea. He was pleased to note that no fight broke out among them. Other humans could easily become violent, even turn into cannibals, when goaded by hunger. These here had only become apathetic. Apparently the feelings of community and also of fatalism that had swelled the breasts of their ancestors had also steered the successive generations along a path that was totally opposed to violence and cannibalism.

Perez had kept little Luz by his side and was watching her with more attention, admiring the symmetry of her sweet and intelligent face. Her arms and legs were slender, like her chest, but likely to develop. This young thing who had been able to keep her human features intact in such a barren environment could also, in other circumstances, become a beautiful, thoughtful creature.

At the same time he looked over the poor animalized who called himself her father and he wondered how this creature could have produced such a child. He had all the characteristics of degeneration: stunted growth, scrawny face and dull eyes.

"Até?" he asked Luz, pointing to the brute.

"Essi," the girl answered.

Maybe her mother had been stronger and smarter? And yet among the dozen females—he did not dare call them women—who were there, quiet and mute, eating their share of fish, there was not one who showed the least bit of intelligence, strength or beauty. All of them looked pathetic and who knew how old.

"Maté?" he asked by chance, pointing them out to the child.

He had noticed that the letter "m" remained in the language of these humans but the letter "r", on the contrary, had disappeared. If "até" meant "pater" (father) then "maté" should mean "mater" (mother).

Luz shook her head, pointed to the ground and closed her eyes, folding her arms under her head and pronouncing the single word, "omi".

"She's sleeping in the ground," Perez translated, meaning that she was dead. It might just be for the best.

Why did that last thought come to him?

It was because he knew that his only chance of saving this child was to take her away from her tribe and get out of the cave. As for the others, the longer he looked at them, the more he realized that any attempt to take them back to a human life would be in vain. Even the four other children were past saving. Skinny, with low foreheads and dull eyes, yapping voices, they seemed even more degenerate than their parents, if that was possible.

Of course, if the escaped convict were in any other situation he could make a firm decision to save them all. But the more he thought about it, the stronger he felt that he would have to fight them, their ignorance and their foolishness, and that he would inevitably lose this fight. Besides, supposing that he did succeed in dragging them out of the cave, what then? How would they survive in a world they knew nothing about?

No, they had fallen too low to be able to live anywhere else but in this subterranean world that was their cradle and would be their grave as it was for their ancestors.

This idea, therefore, grew stronger and stronger in him: take little Luz and escape with her. But he would have felt bad about taking her away from her mother. Maternal love, which is present in all animals, was perhaps the only sentiment that survived among the degenerated race in the crypt.

But Luz's mother was dead, which solved this problem, and the father was not overflowing with paternal love. An apathetic brute like the others! It was impossible to catch the slightest hint of tenderness when he spoke to the child. Under such conditions Perez made up his mind. Just because this degraded being had given life to the girl was no reason for her to become his property until death, especially when it ran counter to her well-being.

Furthermore, the ex-convict told himself that after escaping with Luz and settling in a country where he would be safe, there was nothing to stop him from telling the world about the grotto and thus launching a scientific exploration to come and get these last human cave-dwellers.

Meanwhile, he did not forget his own desire to explore the entire lake. He thought that Luz and her companions might serve as guides or at least give him some information. Using gestures he struggled to explain to them what he wanted. But for some unknown reason or maybe because they did not care to make any effort to thank the man who had just fed them, they sat silent and uninterested.

Luz shook her head and went back to her father's side.

"So that's that," Perez mumbled, a little annoyed. "Well, my good friends, since we only see each other when it's time to eat, I'll go alone."

He ate a slice of fish, drank some water and packing up his supplies he walked off.

XIX. An earlier explorer

On the sandy beach and in the forest were piles of rocks thrown on top of each other as if by the hand of a giant. The lake stretched on between the assorted blocks of stone. Additionally, it seemed that the once calm water was being stirred up by a hidden current and that a faint rumble, like the sound of a distant sea, could be heard now and then.

Exhausted by the long walk, the explorer stopped in the middle of a bunch of rocks and slept. When he woke up he examined the rocks more closely: they were black and hard, like basalt. Suddenly he jumped. Carved into the side of the rock, still legible, was the date "1525" and underneath it the name "José Venandez".

Perez, who believed that he had experienced all possible emotions, was shocked like never before.

So, a man, a Spaniard like himself, less than 400 years ago, had been in the crypt and seen its mysteries, all the dwellers holed up here. This José Venandez had seen the prehistoric animals and the animalized human.

But how was this discovery not known? What happened to Venandez? How was it that Perez, an educated man, had never heard of him?

He had to blame that era: 1525. A huge revival was transforming old Europe. In Italy, Germany, France, England and Flanders they were turning out bold thinkers. And in adventurous Spain they were launching themselves heart and soul into great voyages and discoveries. But on the peninsula most people were ignorant. (Pizarro, the conqueror of Peru, did not know how to read). The king and his monks, to keep a monopoly over the discoveries, allowed no publication describing them. Maybe that was the reason why the name of Venandez was unknown.

But there could have been another reason. He had entered the cave, yes, but did he leave?

At this very moment Perez remembered the manuscript fragment that he had found the day before but that was blank. He took it out of his basket and looked more closely at it. Although he could not make out any real lettering, he thought he could see some light scratches, as if a dried out quill had scored the surface.

Perez knew what a "palimpsest" was: an old manuscript whose writing was scraped off so it could be re-used. He knew that wiping it with some water mixed with a little Prussian red (potassium ferricyanide) and hydrochloric acid you could make the original writing reappear. He also knew that letters written in invisible ink would come out when heated up. Just in case, he decided to combine the two processes.

He had no chemical reagent, no Prussian Red or hydrochloric acid, but the lake water, full of sodium chloride, could, to a certain extent, take its place.

Perez took the piece of manuscript and went to soak it in the water. He was surprised: the temperature of the water was higher than in other parts of the cave. Not hot but warm. What hot spring was bubbling out of the earth to end up here?

"It doesn't matter," he mused, "but if it gets any hotter and spreads all over the lake the sharks and eels will be in big trouble!"

Nevertheless, the wash brought out some faint bluish lines on the manuscript, unfortunately still unreadable. Perez took out his potassium cubes and since flint was all around him he lit a fire and put the fragment over the flame. When heated the blue marks turned brown and started forming letters. The traveler could read:

"Yo José Venandez y Rial de V...ladol... un d.los com...eros qu Padi... luch.... P.. la lib... y quedar.. derrot.... En V..lal.. Fug...vo a Marr...os encu..tresilio tra los M..os de las sier... Busc... una via natur... cub.. esa cue.. en don.. viven homb... monos semej... a lost encuentra por et navig... cartag... Hann... en su fam... perp... No se si podr. Sal.. de es.abism."

The rest was missing. It was easy for Perez to piece together the text:

"V...ladol" obviously meant Valladolid; "com...eros" comuneros; "Padil..." Padilla and "V...lal" Villalar. It only took a little knowledge of 16th century Spanish history to figure it out.

Valladolid was one of the cities that the comuneros took, fighting with their chief Padilla against the tyranny of Charles V and eventually crushed in the battle of Villalar in 1521. Perez used a stick to write in the sand:

"I, José Venandez y Rial from Valladolid, was one of the comuneros who fought with Padilla for liberty and was beaten at Villalar. I escaped to Morocco and found refuge among the Moors in the mountains. Searching for a natural route between the Mediterranean Sea and the Ocean I discovered this grotto where monkey-men are living, like the ones encountered by the Carthaginian explorer Hannon on his famous journey and whom he called "gorillas"... I don't know if I will ever get out of this abyss..."

This last sentence was disturbing. "I don't know if I'll ever get out of this abyss," Venandez had written. Apparently he did not get out. Perez could picture him, worn out by hunger and despair, his body thrown into the death pit by the monkeys while he was still gasping his last breaths.

And what hideous fate was lying in wait for him?

"No," he made up his mind, "I'm getting out of this crypt!"

XX. An awful alternative

Perez walked for a long time without making a great deal of progress. More and more rocks piled higher and higher stopped him. To his right the lake stretched on, made choppy in places by strange currents. To his left grew the lean thickets of wild plants. The walls of the cave, which were so far apart before that he could hardly see them, closed in. The lake here was no more than three or four hundred yards wide. The sound of the water got louder, becoming a clear rumble, as if a waterfall were nearby. At the same time, the roof of the cave was considerably lower.

"I've reached the back of the crypt," he figured. "I'll have to turn back. But where does the lake empty into? Is there a series of abysses?"

Then he thought of Venandez. What had happened to the old comunero? Did he leave other traces of his journey? Perez kept an eye on all the rocks in the hope of finding a new inscription.

The rumble got louder, turned into a roar. He threw a broken branch into the lake and was surprised to see it swept away on a strong current.

"Damn," he mumbled, "better be careful of…"

He did not finish his thought. Slipping on a rock he had just fallen into the lake and was immediately swept away. Even though the water was only up to his belly, all his efforts to get a footing were in vain. If his sword were not attached to his wrist and the burnous with his supplies not tied around his shoulders he would have lost everything he had.

While the current carried him downstream, he saw an engraving in a rock that was sticking out of the water at the edge of the lake. The inscription began: "José Ven…" A second later he had sailed past it without being able to grab on. But as quickly as he had shot past, he could still tell that the message had not been finished. No doubt that while Venandez was carving he had made a wrong move and had slipped and been dragged by the current that ran into a waterfall.

Perez had no time to picture his predecessor flung into a deadly pit or swallowed by sharks. He himself, being pushed and pulled by invisible hands, was reaching the edge of the waterfall. A couple more seconds and he would be lost!

Then he felt a solid body towering up before him. Automatically he grabbed it and held on with all his might. The current was still racing past but not carrying him away. He looked at what he had latched onto. An unthinkable phenomenon: it was a tree rising 20 feet over his head but growing upside down, with its roots in the rocky ceiling of the crypt and its top almost touching the water.

It must have been an old tree, probably dead, because it had no flowers or leaves and Perez was worried that the top of the trunk he was desperately clinging to would snap under the weight of body being battered by the current.

All of a sudden he heard a slapping sound behind him. Shuddering at the thought of a new danger he turned his head and what did he see: under the surface of the clear water, a monster was swimming toward him. Not a shark nor an eel but a gruesome animal somewhere between the two. Picture a smooth body, silvery white, an eight-foot long tube like a snake, a huge, round head or in fact oval like a dogfish.

Perez knew that he was lost. If he did not move, stayed latched to the tree, he would be snatched by the monster. If he let go he would be dragged into the abyss.

Then an idea suddenly came to him. He stiffened his body, gripped stronger than ever and started shimmying to the bottom of the tree, meaning upward. The monster was less than three feet away. All of a sudden a terrifying commotion erupted: the noise of thunder or an avalanche.

It was, in fact, an avalanche. The dilapidated tree, eroded by time, had finally given way and was falling into the lake with Perez hanging on. But as it was coming out of the ground in which it had taken root it opened up a gaping hole. A flood of dirt, rocks and blocks of stone came raining down, crashing into the water and creating waves.

Surprised and scared, the monster swam away. But in its confusion it had stopped swimming sideways between two currents and was caught, doomed, despite its size, and dragged away toward the waterfall.

Perez had fallen next to a block of stone and instinctively grabbed on, watching the giant fish hurl past him. It was close enough to snap at him but the monster did not scare him anymore. He himself had fallen prey to the torrent that was trying to drive him into an unknown abyss.

By some miracle no rocks tumbling down from the top of the cave had crushed the fugitive. He was almost buried in dirt but this was no concern. He did not even feel his bruises. And the avalanche had saved him by diverting the current and throwing him onto this rock, which was only six feet from the embankment. Perez climbed on top and breathed heavily, knowing he was safe from a watery grave.

A minute later he jumped over to the shore and collapsed, losing consciousness right away.

XXI. The starry sky

When the fugitive woke up he had a weird feeling. It felt like fresh air was fanning his face and a kind of tear had been made in the glowing clouds that lit the crypt. Perez looked closely at the breach in the roof that the tree had made. And he cried out in amazement.

A kind of vertical tunnel opened up above him, a tunnel with slanting walls like a huge funnel, and far, far off in the distance appeared the star-studded sky!

Perez was stunned by the spectacle. A moment earlier he was lost in the bowels of the earth in the middle of an unknown cave that was lit by a twilight glow. Now he could see the heavens.

Apparently the tunnel had existed for centuries but piles of rubble had covered the opening and out of the rubble a tree had grown, upside down. The strange tree had grown and then died of old age, stretching out its branches and its head toward the surface of the water without quite reaching it. By hanging on to it Perez had uprooted it and this caused the ground to collapse and the rocks filling the opening to drop down. As often happens, small causes have big effects.

The fugitive was gawking, enraptured, at the dark blue sky and its stars shining like golden specks when he felt something warm touch him. At the same time a faint breath followed by a whisper of awe. He looked down: Luz was there, next to him, dazed by the starry sky that she was seeing for the first time.

"You're here!" he said.

Perez had seen too many extraordinary things to be too easily astonished. However, he was not expecting to

see the little girl in this place. She might not have understood his words, but she got his meaning.

"Até omi," she said softly, first putting her head in
her open hands, then pointing to the ground.

"Your father is sleeping... He's dead!" Perez translated. "So, poor little girl, you won't be leaving my
side."

But Luz still wanted to explain something. "Simi,"
she said.

"Simi? Oh sure, simius. The monkeys?"

His translation was correct. Perez saw by the signs
the girl was making that she meant the frisky rascals.

"Well, what did the monkeys do? Simi?"

"Simi capé me."

"The monkeys wanted to take you!" he exclaimed.

He felt rage burn through him, angry at knowing
that this child for whom he had started to feel an almost
paternal love had almost been made a prisoner of the
primates. And angry, too, at the thought of these animals
abusing the degradation of a human race.

He was fed up now with the crypt and its inhabitants and since Luz was an orphan he would not waste
one more second to bring her with him. He pointed up at
the huge telescope that the tunnel formed and the sky
with all its stars. "Tell me," he said, stroking her hair,
"you want to go up there?"

The child guessed right and without hesitating answered, "Essi."

"Well then," Perez said, "let's get to it."

He took Luz's hand and was about to head up the
lake, going back the way he had come two days ago, but
the child pulled back.

"What's wrong?" Perez was surprised.

"Simi."

131

"The monkeys! What? You're afraid of those filthy beasts? Nothing to worry about, you're with me."

"Simi... omo-omo."

"The men too! You're afraid of the monkeys and the men. Who knows, maybe you're right."

Under other circumstances Perez would have admired this way of forming plurals of nouns with a simple repetition: "omo", man; "omo-omo", men. But this was no time for philology and the fugitive was much more interested in the fear Luz was showing.

Yes, she must be right. Men and monkeys were getting together to stop him from snatching away one of the cave dwellers. If this was so, what could he do?

What was the point of being brave, of having a higher intelligence than his enemies, of holding a sword whose fatal effects the primates had seen, if they attacked him all together?

He had counted 35 animalized, including Luz and her father. The monkeys were probably about the same number. Could he ever fight off so many attackers and keep them from taking back the child?

She looked like she was reading his mind. As her friend let out a sigh of discouragement, Luz grabbed his hand and pointed to the hole in the starry sky.

"That way!" he cried out. "Yes, you're right, it'd be better. It'll be a tough climb but... it doesn't matter."

XXII. A battle

They started climbing immediately.

Perez had not been wrong when he said that it would be tough. After five minutes they had barely gone more than 50 feet. The dirt on the walls, which were more vertical than slanted, crumbled under his weight and he had to use all his strength and agility not to slide down with the dirt into the lake that would have swallowed him up this time.

Luz surprised him. The little girl climbed the rocky wall with amazing skill. Her hands found the tiniest holds; her bare feet were placed securely on the smallest bumps. She passed him, showed him the way and encouraged him with whispered calls as if she were afraid that hidden ears were listening. More than once she had to scurry back down to keep him from falling by grabbing his hand or the edge of his haïk.

Finally, having passed the part broken off by the tree, they reached a big rock that they could sit down on to take a rest. Perez was out of breath and amazed by the child's resilience despite looking frail like all the humans in the cave. Instead of strong muscles she had a keen eye, firm feet and sure hands, developed over years of climbing the rocks and running around the dark tunnels.

All of a sudden she flinched and seemed to be listening to some distant sound. Her friend shot her a questioning look.

"Simi, omo-omo," she whispered, waving her hand so they could get back on their way.

Perez listened but heard nothing. Still, he did not doubt that Luz had heard something troubling since her hearing was better trained than his. They were on the way again.

Climbing up the steep walls for 30 yards had been a daring feat, but scaling up at least 20 times this distance, with almost no footholds, was terrifying. As far as he could tell just by looking there were around 700 yards separating them from the opening of the funnel.

Suddenly he heard a commotion. "They're coming!" he whispered and he tried to hurry up.

The noise got louder, could be heard clearly, then stopped all of a sudden. They were there, humans and monkeys, 30 yards below the runaways, but they were not looking at them. For the first time in their lives they were seeing the starry sky over their heads, or at least a circle of sky a few feet round. A dark blue circle that looked dotted with gold.

Faced with this unexpected sight they were in a daze, especially the men because there were some monkeys who, by some acrobatic miracle, had followed the stream up to the entrance of the grotto. From there they could have felt fresh air wafting over their hairy faces and even without wanting to risk entering they could have seen the forest and above the tops of the trees the cloudy blue skies. No doubt they talked about these things in their language.

But the men! They had never suspected that another sky existed outside the rocky ceiling of the crypt.

For a while they all stood mystified by the sight and this allowed the fugitives to climb a little higher. Then the humans and monkeys, really just the latter, started talking about the opening. The men threw out some inarticulate shouts now and again before going back to stare in silent wonder.

"How did they track us?" Perez mumbled. "And if they are following us, how come they don't see us?"

Luz did not understand what he said. And yet, either because she made a guess or purely by coincidence, she held up her index finger and then put it to her nose.

"That's right," the fugitive agreed, "they followed me like game, by my smell."

The idea hurt his self-esteem because as far as the situation allowed he had tried to stay clean. Even though he did not take a bath in the lake because of the sharks, he had still squatted at the edge and washed himself. Whereas the animalized did not care at all about any kind of cleanliness. They were offensive to the eyes and to the nose. Even Luz, he had to admit, was not innocent of this fault.

But Perez knew that every human emitted its own particular scent, which came from its body secretions evaporating in the air and creating a kind of invisible aura. The scent, for example, of a white, black or yellow man was as different as that of a carnivorous beast from a domesticated herbivore. He had his scent, therefore, undetected by his own sense of smell but pungent to the animalized and the monkeys who could track him down by it.

However, they seemed to have lost his scent at the lakeside. The hunters were turning every which way, clearing sniffing around, but they could find nothing. Some looked like they wanted to keep going all the way to the waterfall. Others were backing away in fear.

All of a sudden a loud shriek revealed that Perez and Luz were spotted. The sharp eye of a monkey had seen them climbing like two little blotches moving up the wall. Afterward came a flood of angry, outraged and pleading howls. Humans and monkeys crying out together.

"Ya! Ya matou! Eni!"

"Skiss psuy, dzii!"

The humans wailed and whined. This girl was one of theirs, trying to abandon them when there were already fewer women than men among them, which could mean the beginning of the end of their race.

The monkeys were furious but for a completely different reason. Living side by side with the animalized, they watched them from high up, mocked their stupidity and seeing a waning race felt that they were the chosen ones. Undoubtedly they had kept some vague memory of a time when men had power over monkeys, but now the roles were reversed and it was their turn to dominate. One thing was still holding back their claim to superiority: the lack of an articulate language. Of course their idiom was already richer than the men's, who had lost more than a sixtieth of their words and barely understood many they used since they referred to ideas that had faded away. The simian tongue, on the other hand, could not be translated into the letters of the human alphabet since there were more than 100 inarticulate words, true, but by changing pitch and lengthening sounds it had created as many intelligible words. Anyway, just living so close to each other the two species could be understood.

Up until today the monkeys had let the humans die out without having to attack them. When they lost their motivation to bury their dead it was the monkeys who became gravediggers. Not out of sentimentality but because they did not want the air in the crypt where they lived to became poisoned with lethal toxins.

But now they saw Luz as a higher specimen of her race and they figured that she would belong to the noble species of monkey someday. As soon as the child lost her father they jumped on her and without hurting her in the least had taken her away. The apathetic humans had let them do it.

Luz later told her savior that she was not at all thrilled to become the companion of monkeys, so she ran away from them and they came snarling to get her back. When she was not found among the humans, all the cave dwellers figured that she had gone to Perez. The men got angry. For a moment they were shaken out of their apathy. What! This stranger who looked like one of them but was so different from them could have taken the child? The monkeys were one thing but him!

They started the search right away, accompanied by the primates who under other circumstances would not have attacked Perez, since they looked upon him as a god and held him in respect. But the disappearance of Luz changed things. The child belonged to them; she had been raised to the glorious level of monkeykind. They had to find her at all costs and get her back. If the god got in their way, too bad for him! They would rise up against his divinity.

That was the opinion—which won the day—of some of them, more tainted perhaps with skepticism. The monkey whom Perez called the grand lama had immediately sided with this idea. Both from fear of being overpowered if he resisted and also because he wanted Luz for himself.

The army of men and monkeys numbered around 60 individuals. They started off, guided by the scent, following the trail of the fugitives. When they caught up to them the animalized became sad and forlorn but the monkeys became furious. The former called out pitifully to the child, begging her to come back. The latter, not so dispirited, sent an ultimatum in the form of threatening shrieks and rocks. Luckily the rocks did not reach the couple. They hit 15 or 20 yards below them before they splashed down into the lake.

"Still," Perez determined, "it'd be better to get as much distance as possible between us and the brutes."

He did not need to push Luz. She was still climbing, so agilely that it was hard for him to keep up.

The primates saw that the fugitives were going to escape. Boldly they jumped into the funnel. Luz saw them and alerted Perez, "Simi eni!" (Monkeys coming!)

The Spaniard looked down and shuddered. He could see the heads of the attackers growing bigger in a hurry. The frisky creatures were going to reach them.

"Stop!" Perez yelled so fiercely that Luz, without knowing the meaning of the word, froze.

If they were bound to be caught, what was the point of continuing the arduous ascent? It would be better to stop on a ledge where they would have sure-footing and could defend themselves to the death.

Perez already had his sword out. He would make his body a shield for Luz. After that, overwhelmed by the greater number of monkeys, their only hope to escape capture would be to jump into the abyss.

"Maybe," he was desperate, "it'd be better to kill her now and put an end to her suffering. I can kill myself after!"

They both stopped on a rock ledge barely three feet wide, hanging over the pit. Smaller rocks were sticking out of the wall. The sight was a ray of light for Perez. Moving very carefully so as not to lose his footing he broke off one of the stone blocks and dropped it on the group of attackers. A savage, frantic cry filled the funnel, telling him that the projectile had hit a target.

Luz had cried out, too, either in terror or in pity. Leaning over the edge she warned, "Omo-omo eto!"

"Homines retro," (Men retreating) she wanted to say in good Latin. Then turning to Perez, "Simi Malou! Feli simi! No feli omo-omo!"

The fugitive understood what she meant: "The monkeys are bad! Hit the monkeys! Don't hit the men!"

Unfortunately, in such a dire situation it was hard to tell the difference. He could only hope that the humans were less bold than the primates and would let them scale the funnel alone, thereby only getting splashed a little. Because he did not stop bombarding the attackers. Luz also saw that this was their only means of defense and her little hands were wrenching rocks out of the wall to hand them to her friend.

Every shot hit a target and caused a concert of howling. Not just howls of anger but of pain and agony. The monkeys could not keep up their attack for long at this deadly rate. Every rock ricocheted off the walls and hit at least one or two of them, sometimes three or four. A dozen of them had already been picked off, their heads crushed by the heavy projectiles or smashed against the rocks in their fall. And yet they kept climbing, slower now but relentlessly, and Perez had run out of ammunition.

He was lost anyway. Lost despite his desperate defense, which only made his enemies angrier.

Above him, around 50 or 60 feet, another rocky ledge was jutting out, a little wider than the one they were on. Nearby it, in arm's reach, the wall looked encrusted with rocks as big as a child's head. There was new and precious ammunition. The trick was to get there before the monkeys.

"Let's go!" Perez shouted.

It was only to himself that he gave this order. Luz did not need to be told; she was already scrambling up and it was she who stretched out her hand to help haul her friend onto the ledge.

Perez was on his knees, about to stand up, when he felt something grab his foot. He kicked hard and shook free. A second later he was standing up on the narrow ledge, sword in hand. At that very moment, right in front of him, a monkey jumped up.

With a big build, an expression both sly and threatening on his face framed by a gray beard, Perez recognized the grand lama right away. The primate was ferociously angry but he had no weapon. With a strong swipe of his sword, in a desperate rage, the fugitive split his head in two. The grand lama gasped, dropped his long arms and fell backward into the abyss.

Another monkey had followed him but when he saw the fate of his fellow primate he did not wait for the deadly weapon to hit him. He jumped away, shrieking horribly, clamped onto the wall and scampered down at dizzying speed.

On seeing their chief fall dead into the abyss the other monkeys gave up. They were quickly thrown into a mad panic. Perez stirred up the fiasco with a rain of rocks that found even more victims. For the monkeys it was by far the most terrible disaster they had ever experienced in the crypt.

Would they ever get over it? Would their race, for a moment raised above the degenerate remains of humanity, drop down again, wearied and wasted, even lower than the creatures that it had scorned? Would the survivors perish in the crypt or after being vanquished and humiliated would they leave this subterranean world and try to adapt to life in the open? Who knows if the last of them might not guard the memory of some terrible, vengeful divinity who had punished the reckless monkey who had dared to attack it!

XXIII. A pause in the pit

Perez and Luz had got rid of the monkey hunters but they still had to get through their ordeal to be out of danger. They had only just begun to climb up. Barely 200 feet had been covered, which was less than one tenth of the total height of the funnel.

Crawling up this steep, almost vertical wall, the slightest dizziness or a tiny slip of the foot could cast them into the abyss. After his heroic and prodigious effort Perez was worn out. His arms had lost their strength and his legs refused to carry him. He wanted to lie on the ledge and rest for a while, but he was sure that a rest would be tormented by fear of falling asleep and rolling off the ledge. What a terrible awakening that would be!

He desperately mustered all his courage and started climbing again. Luz was a few feet in front of him. His legs trembled. He almost slipped off more than once. He thought that if he could not reach some platform or some crevice big enough to rest in safety before fatigue got the better of him, he would be lost. And in this case what would become of Luz?

Above him the opening of the pit did not seem to be getting any closer. He felt as if, despite all his efforts to get higher, he stayed in the same place.

Below him was a black, gaping chasm.

Perez was hanging between two abysses: an abyss on high and an abyss into the depths.

He thought he would never get to the end of the wall sloping steeply, endlessly before him. Wouldn't it be better to go back down and risk falling or fighting again with the monkeys or men, try to reach the other exit by going all the way back through the crypt?

Perez was falling into this abyss of uncertainty and perplexity when a shout of joy from Luz gave him courage. The child was walking in front of him and had just disappeared behind some tall rocks. Electrified by hope, the fugitive shimmied up to where she was and panted with relief like a castaway falling drained but saved on a beach.

There were three rocks sticking out of the wall with a few square feet of space. There was a kind of fence around it, as tall as a man, so they might not be able to stretch out but they could at least take a rest without fear of falling off.

Perez collapsed in the cramped space. He was exhausted by the constant exertion of energy. It was only after a relatively long time that he felt the need to get back some strength by something other than rest. Even after his fall into the lake, his arduous climb and the battle with the monkeys he had not lost his burnous, tied securely around his shoulder. Well, the burnous held his supply of fish and fresh water. In truth it was doubtful that any water remained in the vase, as tightly as it was closed. With all the shaking and swinging Perez must have spilled every last drop.

Imagine the joy and surprise he felt when he saw that the vase was still half-full. By instinct he brought it up to his lips but stopped, just as quickly, held himself back, and offered it to Luz. Did she understand the sacrifice that her friend had just made? She started to drink but after only one swallow she stopped.

"Po ti," she uttered.

As much as the two words her gesture with them meant, "for you".

Perez drank a little before closing the vase carefully with tightly bound leaves. There were still 6 or 7 ounces left, about one glass full. This glass of water, shared between the two of them, might mean their lives.

Thanks to the refreshing liquid running through his body he felt some life come back into his veins. His appetite as well. He ate a slice of fish after giving one to Luz.

"Vonou," she said, being as hungry as he was.

Vonou, malou: good, bad. These two adjectives were natural corruptions of "bonum" and "malum". Perez was sure that after two or three days he would be talking fluently with Luz. What a pleasure for him to be awakening this young intelligence!

In the meantime, he needed to sleep. "Omi," he said to the child. And in no time he was sound asleep.

He would have slept for a long time if her little hand had not shaken him to wake him up.

"What is it?" he asked. He wondered if the monkeys might not be trying another assault.

No. The child was pointing to the sky. Then he saw what was causing Luz to be so worried and amazed at the same time. In the dark sky a silver crescent was shining.

"The moon," he laughed.

It was true, she was seeing this star for the first time. He signed to her that the celestial body was harmless and went back to sleep while the little girl, still intrigued, sat up staring and thinking about the heavens. In the end she, too, fell asleep.

What kind of confused dream would her young mind concoct, barely out of the gloomy life in the subterranean world and arriving on the cusp of a new life?

XXIV. Deliverance!

When they woke up Perez and his companion felt ready to go. The sky was a hazy blue over their heads. The fugitive figured that it was broad daylight and the light was blanketing the earth with a golden veil that would darken before hitting the bottom of the pit.

He ate and fed Luz because they had to keep up their strength to finish the climb in 12 hours. This day would be the crucial one.

"Let's go!" he said once their meal was finished.

And for the first time in a long while—in years—he started humming a happy marching tune. The astonished child struggled to repeat the song but it was too hard for her, not knowing the words and with no idea of music. In a rhythm that barely matched her companion's she droned out the only chant she knew, the one she had learned in the crypt listening to the plesiosaurs sing: "Lumen coeli!"

"You're finally seeing the heavenly light, little girl," Perez whispered tenderly while thinking how prophetic the words were.

What a rough day of climbing it was! More than twice the height of the Eiffel Tower, that giant world monument, climbing up a 60-degree slope. They stopped 20 times, exhausted, agonizing over how far they still had to go to reach what seemed to get no closer. But they did not lose hope: Perez because he felt that he only had to fight against passive nature, far less terrible than against living creatures; and Luz because she trusted her friend.

After around three hours of this wearying march they took a break. The opening of the pit looked wider. It was circular when they saw it from the bottom but now it was an irregular shape, jagged and rough. And the climbers were still at least 400 yards from the top.

Two more hours of ascent cut the distance in half. But the slope was becoming much steeper.

"Hang in there," he mumbled, "we'll get there before nightfall."

Where were they going to get? Would it be in the middle of a peaceful douar where they would be treated hospitably? Or in the middle of the desert? For the first time Perez started thinking about how critical their situation was. In the cave they were so eager to leave at least they had food and shelter and except for the attempt to bury him too soon he had nothing to fear. Was it going to be the same now?

Nevertheless, he reckoned that he should not be too far from the city of Fez, probably between there and Taza. If this was true, he might chance upon a caravan. After escaping so many dangers he was not afraid for himself. But Luz was something else. She made him worry a lot. How was this puny child, without even rags to protect her body, going to deal with a hike through mountains and forests?

The sun was getting lower on the horizon when the two adventurers got near the opening of the pit. Luz let out a cry of awe and surprise. From their vantage point, i.e. almost at the level of the other wall, they could see a distant chain of mountains cut across the sky that was ablaze with the fires of the setting sun. Hypnotized, the girl gazed at the golden orb wrapped gloriously in a cloak of purple clouds. A warm breeze with the scent of wild plants, very different from the stale air of the crypt, caressed their faces.

"It's beautiful, isn't it?" Perez commented enthusiastically.

He felt drunk with joy at seeing the land, the sky and freedom within reach. What did he care about the risks he would run for freedom: lions, panthers and barbarians. Maybe he would have to fight again but he would be fighting in broad daylight and not in a cave.

A minute later his bliss crashed and his heart was crushed. He noticed that at the very moment when they were about to leave the crypt, one final obstacle stood before them: a wall. Not too slanted or steep but unforgivingly smooth, with nothing to hold onto, no footholds, rising up over 60 feet to the mouth of the pit.

60 feet! To be so close to their goal, separated only by this ridiculous distance, and not be able to make it after climbing over 2,300! It was enough to drive a person crazy!

He examined this last part of the wall to no avail: there was not even a bump. Luz, in spite of being as light and agile as a goat, could not get up it. The fugitive let out a sorrowful, sinister laugh. He wondered whether he would throw himself into the abyss headfirst and finally put an end to all this. Only the thought of Luz held him back. He was the one who had brought her out of the crypt. He had no right to kill himself and leave her alone to deal with the dizzying heights that would sooner or later get the better of her. The abyss really did not want its captives to escape…

What to do?

Perez sat on the ledge at the foot of this wall, the supreme obstacle. Luz came to sit next to him. The two of them just sat there, sad and silent. To have been so happy a moment before and then to see all their dreams, all their hopes crushed!

Suddenly the fugitive jumped up. "Why not," he mumbled, "let's give it a try!"

His left hand felt around the rock to test how hard it was. His right hand was still holding the sword, the instrument of death that had saved his life so many times already.

With great care so as not to break it he put the point of the sword into the wall. It was, of course, not soft dirt but it was not hard granite either. With a little difficulty Perez dug a slot about three feet up, then a second one halfway higher. Hanging onto this second one with his left hand he dug out a third. He was only about six feet up but he already felt like he had to give up. It took all his strength to hang on and dig at the same time.

"Me!" Luz suddenly shouted.

Perez did not understand. He looked down at the little girl without saying a word. Bravely she scrambled up the steps and in a second was on her friend's shoulders. She shook her hand for him to give her the sword.

"What? You want to try, poor child? But it's too hard for you. You'll never make it."

Nevertheless, as it was their last hope of salvation, he handed her the sword after taking care to attach a longer rope to the handle since dropping it would be an unforgivable loss.

With determined strength that seemed impossible to expect from her the girl dug out five new slots. When she finished one Perez climbed up one step at a time, holding on with both hands. Luz straddled his shoulders, her legs crossed over his chest, and with her hands free she wasted no time. She held the sword in her right hand to dig into the wall and with her left she shoveled out the dirt.

At the fifth step she started to get tired, but she did not stop working. She just changed hands and dug out three more. Now they had a ladder around 15 feet high, a quarter of the distance they needed.

But what should they do? They could not stay hanging onto the wall like this. Perez was feeling his muscles go stiff, tired from all the effort to keep his balance. Luz's arms were numb. If they stayed like this for much longer they would end up losing their grip and falling into the abyss.

In a desperate fury the fugitive climbed back down, still carrying Luz on his shoulders, all the way to the narrow ledge where he had started to dig the steps. Just in time! As soon as his foot hit the ground his legs gave way and he almost fell off. They needed to rest. And eat, too. They had to regain their strength to cover the final distance.

"Let's eat the last of our food," he muttered.

They still had some fish left but they were almost out of water. Six ounces to share between the two of them. Perez first thought of giving it all to her but he realized that for both their sakes he, too, had to get his strength back. After eating almost all their fish they drank the little water that they had left.

The sun was just setting. The purple sky quickly turned dark blue because the closer one is to the tropical zone, the shorter the time of twilight and dawn.

Luz sat in a daze, marveling at the changes in light and shadow. Little balls were flickering on and off in the depths of a sky that was no longer gray and rocky but immaterial and infinite. She had never imagined such a thing!

Watching her rapturous awe Perez almost forgot about his cruel disappointment. The ledge on which they were sitting and that ran along the wall formed the ridge of a 45-degree slope. As long as they were careful they would not slide off and if the moon was bright they could keep digging their ladder during the night. If need be, they could move up a few feet and come back down to rest, over and over until the work was done. It would be painstaking work but the only way to get out of their precarious position. It was especially important not to break their precious sword, the only tool of salvation they had right now.

Suddenly Luz cried out in shock. "Aqua!" And she pointed to the sky.

Indeed, a raincloud had just passed overhead and some drops of water had fallen on the child's naked body. As for Perez, wearing his haïk, he had not felt it.

Luz had no idea what rain was. Dew had never formed under the rocky ceiling of the crypt. She had only seen water in the underground river and lake.

"Poor kid, she's going to get soaked," the fugitive grumbled. He swiftly unfolded the burnous and covered both Luz and himself.

The rain started. After running out of water it felt wonderful to have the rain falling on their faces. The girl was a little scared at first but soon was enjoying it, letting out little yelps.

It started as just a shower, then bigger drops came down harder and faster. Soon it was a deluge. A bright light lit up the sky, then a long rumble ended in a clap of thunder. This time Luz cried out in fear and Perez felt her little body trembling. At the same time it was pouring on their heads. The vase next to them was filled up in no time. They drank it down because they were thirsty, and a minute later it was full again. Perez hurried to dig a little hole in the wet ground to stick it in, otherwise it would be swept over the edge by the water running down the slope.

The burnous was thick, which meant that the two climbers were only slightly soaked by the downpour instead of being drenched to the bone. Still, they were in a sorry situation: not only were they unprotected from the rain but if it continued it threatened to destroy all the work they had struggled so hard to complete.

Perez got worried. He stood up, putting Luz back on his shoulders, and climbed back up the ladder with the rain still coming down. He reached the last step and started digging again with the sword. Luckily, since it was wet, the work was easier. The rain was not so bad after all!

15 more feet were quickly dug out. They were halfway up the wall now and the rain was stopping. Hope buoyed his spirits. All of a sudden he slipped and almost fell into the abyss. He managed to hold on thanks to Luz who grabbed something hard that was sticking out of the wall a few inches below the last step. Then he heard a noise that was as hair-raising as it was unexpected: the roar of a lion.

There was no mistaking it. The hoarse growl was not the sound of thunder. Perez recognized the voice of the king of beasts right away. In truth, the roar was a little far off. Obviously the animal had not yet caught scent of the two bipeds getting closer to it. But lions generally only attacked humans if they were starving. He had to hope that this lion was not hungry. But just having it nearby was cause for worry.

Luz showed no fear. She had just heard thunder for the first time and probably imagined that this roar was the same thing. Perez did not try to set her straight. What was the use of worrying her? Besides, how could he explain to her the idea of a lion?

When the initial shock had worn off, he got back to work. Yes, they were in a terrible situation. But as long as they were not out of the pit, even meeting this fierce feline was better than staying any longer in the abyss.

The upper part of the wall was easier to work than the lower. Four more steps were hollowed out. Only six feet to go!

Perez was just getting on the next step when an avalanche of dirt and rocks poured over him. He reeled and lost his footing. But just as he was about to fall into the void, his hand felt something solid and he grabbed on. It was a rock jutting out, which had been covered a second before and was now freed by the avalanche. It was the sword that had caused the downpour when it struck the deeper layers of earth. The result: a crack split down the wall, putting the top of it in easy reach.

A giant, wild leap and the ex-convict was at the edge. He let loose a cry of freedom and hugged Luz. Then the two of them collapsed on the ground, exhausted.

XXV. In the desert bush

Neither the lack of safety or shelter nor even the nearby lion (attested by the roar) could overcome the invincible need for rest that nailed Perez to the ground. He lay there as still as a corpse. Next to him Luz was also sleeping, less tired from the hard work than drunk, in a way, on the change of air.

Early in the morning Perez woke up. His head felt heavy and he started shivering. "I've got a fever!" he muttered. The thought was depressing. He now had another soul to take care of. What would happen to Luz if he died?

The child was still asleep. A smile on her lips. No doubt she was dreaming of the wonders of this new, completely foreign world she was in. Perez watched her fondly, then he looked around to get his bearings.

He did not see the forest or the river that ran underground into the cave. He must have left them far behind, 50 miles or more, hidden from sight by the chain of mountains. The ground on which they landed formed a vast plain, full of cracks and fissures. Towards the west, around a mile and half away, stretched a wide field of brush surrounding a few clumps of trees here and there.

When Luz woke up the rising sunlight blinded her eyes, which were used to the faint, subterranean light. She smiled to her companion and with a inquiring look pointed to the daystar.

"Sun," Perez said.

He felt really sick. All the effort and fatigue had taken its toll on his body and now that he no longer had to exert himself, he was paying the dues.

Luz saw his pale face and with a worried voice said, "Ti no omi!" meaning You don't sleep, i.e. die.

"No, my girl," the fugitive answered, talking to himself more than his companion. "I don't want to die… at least not before I save you."

He suddenly thought of the burnous and his meager supplies: potassium cubes, net, fishing line and the silver vase—all his possessions! The sword was still in his hand and the pistols in his belt. Unfortunately all these things were sitting 60 feet below them, buried no doubt under the landslide that had opened the way for him and the child. After so much trouble hauling himself up to the surface, was he going to have to go back down to get them?

Just looking at his face Luz understood what was troubling his mind. She grabbed his arm and pointed to the rope that was tied around his waist. It was crudely, loosely woven but it was solid and wound several times around his haïk.

"Me," she said.

"You!" he replied.

He understood what she meant. Go to the edge of the pit and lower her down, attached to the rope. But Luz had no idea—could have no idea—of the exact distance. The rope being used as a belt for Perez was only about 15 feet long.

He shook his head slowly. The child was surprised and walked to the edge. He heard her shout something incomprehensible, then he saw her disappear. Crying out in fear he ran to the pit and then shouted again, but this time in joy.

In the landslide the dirt had formed a ramp, not too steep, that went all the way to the bottom of the wall. Luz was already at the bottom digging in the rubble and unearthing their things: first the burnous, then the silver vase, and finally the net and fishing line. As for the potassium cubes, they were lost for good.

Perez was soon at her side and both of them picked up their belongings. Then they went back up and out of the pit.

There was only one point, in the middle of the desolate plateau, toward which they could head: the stretch of brush where they might find some meager resources. They started off.

The night spent without shelter, without blankets, on the wet ground, had been fatal to Perez. Shivering and feverish he had to muster all his strength not to fall down.

Luz watched him with tears in her eyes. Squeezing his hand she said, "Ti até." (You are father).

The ex-convict's heart was filled with inexpressible tenderness. The child was reacting to her feeling for a good man who was in torment, who wanted to give his affection to another human being. She had guessed what was going on inside him. A wonderful intuition because what did she, the daughter of an animalized, know about a father's love?

Her tender observation gave Perez strength. They got to the thickets growing out of the dry, burned-looking ground. Red berries, like small wild strawberries, were hanging from the bushes. Perez picked a few and tasted them. Luz imitated him.

"Vonou," she said.

Indeed, the fruit was good and to her it must have been exquisite, a tangy, sugary taste. Perez even felt like it was calming his fever a little. A few argan trees were scattered around, sparse and thin. The Spaniard saw something sparkling in their shade. It was a trickle of water, not running water but water that had fallen into the rocky cracks during the last rain. No find could have been more precious. Perez filled the vase right away and there was enough left to fill it three more times.

"As long as there's enough water here," he thought aloud, "I'll either die or get back on my feet."

It was better to stop here, as arid as it looked. By surrounding the trunk of the argan tree with a pile of dry branches, they could make a temporary shelter. Which they did immediately. In the meantime, the muddy burnous was hung on the upper branches to dry in the sun. With Luz's help Perez gathered up some dry plants to make two bunks inside their shanty. He worked fast because he felt his fever burning hotter.

When the burnous was completely dry the fugitive cleaned it as best he could and then cut it in two with his sword. Now there was enough to cover Luz from chest to knees like a smock, tied with some rope. It was crude clothing but necessary. The child let him do it without understanding why her friend wanted to dress her. Did they wear any clothes in the crypt where humans lived like animals?

There was enough material left for Perez to cover himself from neck to mid-thigh. The shortened clothing had a weird shape. For the formless child's dress he wanted to add a hat and sandals, indispensable accessories since Luz was not used to sunlight and could get sunstroke while her feet could get torn up by the brambles that did not exist in the crypt. Unfortunately, he did not have the strength. He drifted off into a deep slumber.

When he opened his eyes again the sun was already low on the horizon. Luz was squatting next to him, watching him attentively. "Como vale?" she asked worriedly.

Perez forced himself to smile and made a sign that he felt better. In truth he felt nailed to the bed of dried grass and could barely move his arms.

What an awful situation! He was out of the crypt, in the open air, with the sun shining bright like he had desired so ardently. The lake monsters and the subterranean creatures were no longer a threat, but he was lost in a desert, knocked down by fever, with no resources, with no aide but a little savage girl who did not know his language and who was watching over him!

What would happen to her if he died? He dared not think of it!

"No," he mumbled, "no! I can't die!

But even if he were not sick, hunger would certainly bring a tragic end. They had no more food and only a little water.

Luz had just gone away. After about ten minutes she came back carrying in her skirt a bunch of red berries. In her fist she held a lizard that was wriggling desperately trying to escape.

Perez lifted his hand attached to the sword. Luz understood. She took the weapon and cut the head off the harmless little saurian whose body shook with one final death rattle.

"At least she'll eat," the sick man concluded.

He himself swallowed a handful of fruit that she held out to him. Maybe—who knows!—the berries might have an anti-fever effect. Anyway, they could not be poisonous since both of them had already eaten some with no bad effects.

Now they just had to make a fire to cook the lizard. Perez did not have his potassium cubes but he still had two pieces of flint in his pistols.

"Eba seca," he told Luz, pointing to the dried grass of the bunks.

The girl understood. She went away and a minute later was back with an armful of kindle. She was about to put it down next to Perez but he waved to her to put it farther away. All he needed right now was for a spark to set fire to the shelter and burn it down with him inside, unable to get up.

He motioned to Luz to put everything down a few feet outside their shelter. He crawled and dragged himself over with all his strength. At his directions Luz took a pistol and the sword and handed them to him. He struck the flint with the steel blade over the kindling. Sparks flew off and lit the grass.

The girl yelped with awe and wonder. She had already seen Perez make fire twice but with the potassium cubes. She did not know that this element could jump out of a rock being hit with metal. Moreover, before meeting this extraordinary man, whom she worshipped almost religiously, she had never touched a piece of metal.

The lizard was roasted over the fire and Luz ate all of it after Perez refused to touch it. He just boiled a few red berries in the vase and drank the herbal tea, which tasted not bad at all. Then he dragged himself back to his bed.

They lived like this for two days, Luz bringing fruit, lizards and even one time an iguana that was a good eight inches long. She was smart, for when she lit the fire she also put it out every time when the meal was over. Perez was feeling better. His fever had gone and he could stand up.

Luz had learned a few words in Spanish. They could now not only talk about their physical needs but they started to have real conversations. Thus, Perez became the teacher he had been before being a convict. Clearly the joy of introducing this young intellect to a new life had sped up his recovery.

On the second day he ate some iguana and found it delicious. Luz was finding plenty of lizards for them but their water supply was down to the last drops. This shortage forced them to leave.

Perez picked up a long, straight branch and hewed it into a passable walking stick. He put the fishing line and vase into the net, tied it around his shoulders and started off to the west. Having been bedridden with fever he had not been able to explore the thick brush beyond the tree where they had stopped. He saw nothing but more brush and trees. For four or five hundred yards it was the same scenery, desolate and monotonous. Then slowly, gradually, the brush changed. A few different plants appeared, even some wild flowers, which Luz, with her native feminine instinct for style, picked and put in her hair.

They kept walking. Cactus appeared. Perez was happy because this meant that there was water nearby. In fact, around 100 yards away between two rocks they could see something shimmering in the fading sunlight: a source of water. Luz wanted to run over, but Perez saw something else and grabbed her arm to hold her back.

A lion was drinking the water!

XXVI. The Lion

He had completely forgotten about the lion he had heard roaring when they crawled out of the pit. The wild cat had its back to them and obviously had not heard or seen them.

Perez put his finger to his lips, which the child understood, and pulled her out of the danger zone, being careful not to make a sound. Luz looked surprised at him. She had seen the lion too, but she had no fear. The animal reminded her of a big version of the cats in the crypt that did not attack humans.

What was so annoying and even frightening was that the lion did not leave and the two travelers were starting to die of thirst. It didn't matter! First of all they had to find shelter.

Perez did not backtrack. Instead he made a long detour to his right, staying low behind the bushes and vines, hoping to find the stream running into the pond. A vain hope! The pond was apparently fed by a river welling up from underground and the lion seemed to be a jealous guardian who wanted to keep it all for himself.

However, a ten-foot tall tree with a huge, rough trunk fanned out its branches covered with thick, dark green leaves. It could serve as a refuge in case of attack.

A terrible roar thundered through the air. The bushes parted and the travelers turned. The lion was standing there, 50 feet away, its mouth gaping open and its eyes on fire. But the weird thing was that it did not seem to see them. It was as if it had shown up there by chance or chased by some invisible enemy.

This time Luz was scared and she screamed. Suddenly the lion saw them and its rage escalated. It attacked.

Perez did not miss a beat. He grabbed the child and lifted her into the branches of the tree, which she latched onto instinctively, shimmying up to the top. A second later he was straddling a branch next to her. Just in time. The lion was at the foot of the tree, roaring more loudly when it saw its prey out of reach. It stalked around the tree two or three times, beating its flanks like a drum with its strong tail. Then it jumped.

But Perez was keeping a close eye on all its movements. As the feline's monstrous paw clamped onto the lowest branch he leaned over and swung the sword, which cut deeply into the flesh. Howling in pain the lion let go and crashed to the ground.

What makes lions different than other felines is that they do not climb trees. In this respect they have less in common with tigers, panthers and leopards.

This was a lucky fact for the two travelers. But still, if the sword had not injured one of its paws, it could have tried again and maybe climbed up to where Perez and Luz were stuck. Ten feet was not too high for a lion. But this one could not jump anymore. It just sat at the foot of the tree licking the blood seeping out of its wound.

A shout from Luz pulled his attention away from the lion. The child was showing him a thick, gummy, reddish liquid that was seeping out of the tree. She automatically wet her finger and tasted it. Perez did not have time to stop her.

"Malou!" she spit it out.

The fugitive knew that they had taken refuge in a "dragon tree", which grows in the dry regions of Africa and whose bark secretes a red sap that was as appetizing as pure alcohol. As little as Luz had tasted she was already feeling her throat dry up. Despite her suffering she looked at Perez with surprise. Was it possible that he who had overcome all obstacles was going to be beaten by a big cat lying at the foot of the tree?

The fugitive read her thoughts like an open book. He did not need her to urge him on to deal with the feline. But how?

Climbing down to attack it with the sword? He had no illusions that being as weak as he was after the sickness he could not stand up to a lion. In a single bound, with a swipe of its paw and a chomp of its jaws, the furious beast would turn him into a corpse.

As he was searching in vain for some practical way, he noticed that the animal was showing signs of anxiety and worry. After lying at the foot of the dragon tree, keeping an eye on its prey, it suddenly jumped up, sniffed the air and started growling.

Was some enemy approaching? But what enemy could threaten the king of the beasts? Perez could think of only one: man.

Maybe the lion had been hunted, even wounded in the past and knew by experience the deadly effect of firearms. When it saw Perez and Luz its bitterness against the human race was rekindled and since the one was carrying only a sword and other was only a helpless child the wild cat got it into its thick skull that it could have its revenge. It is common enough among men that when they are wounded by someone stronger than them they take it out on someone weaker. Why wouldn't animals do the same thing?

A sudden noise made Perez shudder. It was the sound of a human voice.

The lion also heard it and answered with an angry roar.

The bushes parted and in the place where the lion had shown up three men armed with rifles appeared. Two of them were Arabs, not dressed in flowing burnous, which were impractical for hunting in the bush, but in short jackets and baggy pants like the zouave. The third was a bare-chested negro.

Luz screamed. She had never imagined that black men existed!

Besides their rifles the Arabs had yatagans in their belts—that formidable hand-to-hand weapon. The negro had a short spear slung over his shoulder.

The hunters must have been very courageous, or reckless, to go into the bush just the three of them to chase a lion, an animal that Arabs rarely attacked if they were not on horseback and in a big group, wherein they were wise considering the disadvantage of their long muskets. Obviously the weapons these men were carrying were of a different quality.

The lion had a moment's hesitation. What did these men want by coming here into its domain? It had already escaped them once, which was when it had met Perez and Luz. Once again, sensing that the fight would not be equal, the lion turned tail and bounded away, roaring, into the bushes. But it was too late. The hunters had seen it. A shot rang out and the bullet hit a branch a few feet from the dragon tree.

"Stop!" Perez yelled.

His voice was drowned out by the lion's roar. It was not wounded but it had heard the bullet whistling by and now it was wavering between rage and caution. Two more shots followed. A howl pealed out. A howl not only of anger but also of pain. This time the lion was hit.

Luz trembled during the concert of gunshots and roars. But she had the strength to get a hold of herself and obey Perez who was waving to her to calm down. After his experience with the Riffians and Beni-Coudia the fugitive had no idea if these men would turn out to be any better.

But the lion was coming back. Its huge face, glistening with fury, popped out of the bushes. Clearly, rage had got the better of caution. When the hunters were within 100 feet of the dragon tree the lion took a mighty leap, then another, despite its wounded paw, and with its mouth wide open, its body shaking all over, it dropped to the ground a few feet from them. Just as the negro's spear stabbed its chest and the hunters emptied their rifles at point blank range into its flanks.

The wild cat breathed out a ghastly groan that was cut short by its death throes. It stiffen in a final spasm then turned over on its side, dead.

Luz had just fainted.

XXVII. Nuts

Perez wasted no more time. As cruel as these men might be they were less frightening than isolation, hunger, thirst and the complete lack of resources in this savage land.

"My brothers!" he called out in Arabic.

The hunters, amazed to hear a human voice, looked up and saw Perez climbing out of the dragon tree with Luz in his arms. The child was just opening her eyes and coming round.

"Salam!" the fugitive said, bringing his hand up to his heart, lips and forehead.

During his captivity he had learned a few words in Arabic because all the tribes, including the Riffians and Riata, spoke the same language, although they each had their particular dialect.

The hunters answered his greeting with a quick "salam", mumbled reluctantly. They showed neither open hostility nor hospitality. Obviously they were astonished by the appearance of this man and girl.

"Who are you and where do you come from?" one of the Arabs asked.

It was hard for the fugitive to answer the question. Could he say that he had come from the prison in Ceuta? They might take him for some dangerous bandit and maybe kill him. It would be better to talk about the cave. The Arabs could check out his story by going down there themselves.

Perez pointed to the ground. His silent answer stupefied the hunters even more. They looked at each other and one of them muttered, "Maboul", meaning a nut.

Today this word is used in French not as an insult but with respect. For a Parisian joker "maboule" is a kook; for the Arab believer "maboul" is a fanatic, favored by heaven.

Perez immediately saw that the hunters looked upon him with a kind of devotion. A stroke of genius crossed his mind: since these men considered him a blessed fool, well why not play it out? Under any other circumstances he who had once devoted his life to educating his ignorant compatriots would have been ashamed to take advantage of these gullible men. But he was at their mercy with a child and this double responsibility won out.

"Allah!" he shouted passionately, looking up at the heavens with an ecstatic gaze.

Madness is contagious. Apparently, so is a fake madness.

"Allah!" the hunters echoed, raising their arms and ready to kneel on the ground.

Perez had not learned much Arabic but the little he knew served him well.

"Allahu Kébir! Allahu Kébir! Allahu Kébir!" he repeated, meaning "God is great!", a call to prayer from the muezzin.

The Muslims already had their bellies on the ground, facing east, i.e. toward Mecca, the holy city.

Perez went on, "Ashadu anna Sidina Muhammadun rasul Allah," meaning "I testify that our Lord Mohammed is the prophet of Allah."

It would not be possible to describe the zealous effect of these words. In their religious rapture the three men were ready to kiss the hands and feet of the maboul, inspired by God.

"Poor fanatics," Perez mumbled sadly.

The two sentences he had just declared were almost all he knew in Arabic. From now on he was holy in the eyes of the hunters. Holy also became the child he was protecting. But there was no room for mistakes. If these men suspected that his madness was a fake, they would take cruel revenge for being fooled.

He had delivered the religious creed "God is Great and I testify that Mohammed is His prophet," not only with the mystical grandeur of a religious nut, but even with the correct intonation in perfect Arabic. If he dared to start up a regular conversation the hunters would know right away that he was a foreigner and they would uncover the fraud. It was necessary, therefore, that he not say a word. He had to keep silent except for repeating a few "Allahu Kébir" and "Muhammadun rasul Allah" at the right time.

Then again maybe it would be wise to give them some material proof that he came out of the depths of the earth. He wanted to bring them to the entrance to the pit but first of all he had to quench the thirst that was tormenting him and torturing Luz even worse. The child's throat was so dry and her lips so swollen that she could not speak. Her forced silence, a result of tasting the sap from the dragon tree, was perhaps for the best. Speaking in a language other than Arabic might have put the hunters on their guard.

Perez first put his hands on Luz's head and murmured, "Allah!"

"Allah," the child repeated, looking at her friend.

She did not understand his gesture or the word, so she waited for him to explain it to her. But this was not the time. All that he could do was to put his finger to his lips to tell her to stay quiet.

The hunters had echoed Luz's utterance and did not doubt that she, too, was a chosen creature, this child who pronounced the holy name of Allah and traveled with a maboul... or rather a "santon". There is a slight difference between the two: you can be a santon without being a maboul and a maboul without being a santon. The one is a fanatic nut, the other a religious ascetic, like the dervishes in the Middle East or the fakirs in India, who often fall into ecstasies.

Holding Luz by the hand Perez headed for the water. He walked slowly, taking little steps, pretending to ignore the hunters who were following him. On seeing the water Luz had the urge to run up and drink from it. Perez held her back. It was only after reciting three times the phrase "Allahu Kébir" that he let the child drink. He had to play the role holy man heart and soul.

Still, he felt sad having to pretend in front of the child. He knew how impressionable the brain was at her age and how vividly it remembered words and images. After starting Luz's education in such a rational way, here he was possibly distorting her young mind.

"Patience," he told himself, "I'll spend as little time as possible with these people."

He had turned his back to the water but was not sure whether he should go to the pit or not. Should he take the hunters out of their way to show them the abyss? It was over two miles from here.

The Arabs made up his mind for him. One of them brought a whistle out and blew a long, ear-splitting signal. An identical call answered. Then they heard shouting in the distance and galloping horses.

"Watch out!" Perez said to himself. "A whole tribe's arriving. It's now or never that I'll be a maboul."

Ten men on horseback showed up, shouting back and forth with the hunters. The Spaniard understood a few words: "killed the lion", "met a maboul and child", "gather the Djema". Perez knew that the djema was the tribal council made up of all the adults and gave the caïd or chief merely executive power.

Among the newcomers was a skinny old Arab with a white beard. He spoke a few words to the fugitive who recognized him as the sheik. Without understanding the words, Perez knew what the old man had on his mind. He wanted to know if he was alone with the child, where they had come from and what race they belonged to. Because there was no sure way to tell that they were European: his skin color was like a Kabyle or some other North African people.

To all the questions he answered with his usual, "Allahu Kébir! Muhammadun rasul Allah"

The sheik did not look very convinced. On the other hand, most of the Arabs were and the old chief could not stand alone against the fanaticism of his companions. They belonged to a douar set up a two-hour march away. The lion had attacked their flocks, so the three best hunters armed themselves with the best rifles and set off on foot to track it down while a group of horsemen went ahead as beaters to flush it out.

That was what Perez learned from listening to the Arabs. The few words of Arabic that he understood helped him piece together whole sentences and get the gist of it. But he kept a straight face, totally unemotional, and the people of the douar only heard him muttering under his breath, "Allahu Kébir! Muhammadun rasul Allah".

XXVIII. The Douar

The Arabs went back to their douar, some on horseback, some on foot. One of the horsemen carried the lion skin on his saddle; the carcass stayed on the ground, waiting for the birds of prey or the jackals.

Perez called up all his strength to follow the caravan. He figured that his maboulism would be doubted if he did not have enough energy to endure the march, as painful as it was. Among Arabs religious rapture, bordering on pure madness and mixed with unconscious trickery, produced remarkable effects: trance, catalepsy, hypnosis. Thus, among other things you can see the sect of Aissawa pierce their skin without bleeding, pop an eye out of the socket and withstand other tortures without seeming to feel a thing.

"Let's go! Maboulism made me do it!" Perez told himself, knotting his muscles in a heroic effort.

But he was terribly worried that Luz could not last long on the quick march. For the moment she was running, jogging, next to her friend, gawking at the horses. The route the caravan took brought them near the pit where Perez and Luz had climbed out of the crypt!

"Allahu Kébir," he mumbled, making sure the Arabs could hear him. Then he added a little more loudly, "Bab-el-chaaba," (gate of the abyss), which he knew the meaning.

The sheik was surprised to see that the so-called maboul had finally decided to speak. He tried to talk to him again but Perez had already fallen back into his dramatic silence.

170

The opening of the pit seemed to be known to the Arabs, but they had never thought of going down into it. Their tribe lived a few miles to the south in an oasis that was good for raising sheep. A tribe of 60 people who had come to the area a few years earlier from the west. Being weak and peaceful they retreated before the attacks of stronger, warring peoples. All they wanted was to feed their animals and grow figs. Besides, the mysteries of the subterranean depths did not attract their curiosity. Isolated in their oasis in the middle of the desert, these men had preserved their traditions and their religious fervor.

Luz was deeply awed by the horses. The only four-footed animals she had ever seen in the crypt were the cats. She was thinking that this new world was full of marvels.

One of the horsemen pointed to her and said a few words to Perez who understood what he meant. He was offering to put the child in his saddle. The fugitive nodded. The march was long and Luz was starting to get tired. He, too, was exhausted, but by some miracle of will he overcame his fatigue.

For two more hours they walked on. Perez was staggering like a drunk and the Arabs watched him with growing respect. The swaying of the body is, among the Aissawas like the whirling dervishes, a sign preceding a trance or of religious madness.

The caravan came to the edge of a plateau and Perez understood why he had not seen the oasis when he got out of the pit. It was hidden in a fold of land, a green valley planted with olive and fig trees. As for date palms, there were a few of them but they were paltry and almost fruitless. It was more to the south of Atlas that this fruit bloomed in full.

Here and there, surrounding the gourbis (huts), grew some oleanders and pomegranates and shrubs bearing red berries like little cherries—they were coffee plants. Tall, lush grass mingled its dark green with the golden yellow of corn stalks. And in the middle of this cool oasis was a silver patch of lake linked to a deep cistern by a thin stream.

Around the douar the sheep, heifers and milk cows were grazing. A red bull looked up at the approach of the caravan, then went back to grazing, paying no more attention.

All this cool, calm life, so different from the gloomy limbo where she had lived so far, snapped Luz out of her wonder and awe. But Perez did not notice all these charming details. On his last legs, when the caravan finally stopped he dropped to ground and passed out, face down, arms akimbo. Luz screamed. She wanted to run to her friend but the Arabs held her back, gently. For them he was not a sick man in need of help but a chosen one in ecstasy whom they had to watch over to remind them of the vulgar realities of this world.

And just then the sun was setting. "My brothers, it's time for prayer," the sheik said. He and all the others knelt on the ground, facing east toward Mecca, the holy city.

Out of pure luck, Perez happened to have fallen in this direction as well. If, on the contrary, he were facing west, his maboulism would have looked seriously suspicious.

After finishing their prostrations and prayers to Allah, the Arabs got up. They had not noticed that Luz remained standing, curious about the salaams whose meaning she could not understand. Being hospitable they

172

brought her some milk and honey. She tasted these two unknown foods with a mixture of surprise and delight.

After 20 minutes the fugitive woke up. He was weak and Luz had to help him sit up. Then the Arabs brought their children over, begging him to do something that he figured out: they were asking him to lay his hands on the youngsters' heads and give them his blessing. Perez could not refuse. A line of 20 children was already forming. On each head the fugitive placed his two hands and doing his best to look ecstatic he murmured his eternal, "Allahu Kébir!" It was the extent of his Arabic just like for Figaro "goddam" was all the English he knew.

XXIX. The hospitality of the Beni-Harglou

Once the blessing ceremony was over the women were ordered by the chief to serve the maboul some milk and figs. It was about time! Perez was dying of starvation as much as of exhaustion. This was not all. In honor of the unexpected guest they slaughtered a sheep and prepared couscous.

While eating and listening to the Arabs talk, the fugitive took stock of the situation. He could not stay long in the douar before he was discovered as a fraud. Any minor incident could find him out. It would be better to leave as soon as he and Luz got their strength back.

The *diffa* or feast offered to the envoy of God had been decided by the sheik Ahmed ben Hadded to please the other tribesmen who were happy to have any excuse for a feast. But what would the tribe do afterward? Would it give him an escort if he wanted to go on his way into another part of the desert? There was little hope that the maboul would tell them what he wanted because even though there are jugglers, whirlers and howlers among the Muslim fanatics, this one seemed to belong to the category of silent ones. The problem could only be resolved by the djemma.

While the sheep was roasting and the women prepared the big balls of semolina that would be mixed with the meat and fried in oil to make a couscous, all the adult men gathered under a fig tree.

"My brothers," the sheik presided over the assembly, "let us first praise merciful God for sending this emissary to his elect. There is no God but God and Mohammed is his prophet!"

This introduction was welcomed with an enthusiastic murmur of approval and the eternal formula was repeated by all. Then came the body of the speech, which Perez did not understand very well, followed by the conclusion.

The old sheik was offering to give the maboul some provisions and to let him continue on his way with Luz, meaning to send them away for good. Basically, he was afraid that the intruder, despite his silence, would be a bad influence on his authority.

Others were inclined to keep the fanatic with them with due respect.

Others again wanted to let him go but to keep Luz who was a chosen being through her contact with the maboul and would certainly attract Allah's blessing onto the douar. Not all those expressing this opinion were compelled by religious zeal. There were some who thought that since the number of women and children in the tribe were limited, this girl would make a nice new recruit. The small number of women did in fact force the Beni-Haglou (as the tribe was called) into monogamy. Only Ahmed ben Hadded had three wives—it was the special prerogative of the chief.

The discussion lasted a long time. In the end they decided to leave Sidi Maboul free to do as he wanted. The sheik promised personally to do whatever was right and necessary to get him on his way.

As for Luz, it was decided that they would ask her companion to leave her in the douar. Maybe the fanatic, being so unattached to worldly things, would agree to sell her for a modest price?

The diffa was cheerful and on this day the Beni-Harglou discredited the reputation of sobriety that their race had so righteously acquired. Roasted sheep, couscous, dates and figs, served not at a table but on the ground on big leaves, filled up the bottomless pits of their stomachs.

Perez sat next to the sheik in the Arab manner, i.e. squatting, keeping Luz on his right. He had silently refused to let the child leave his side and his hosts bowed to his will. This was, however, breaking the rules because only adult men dined with the sheik. The younger men sat together farther off and the women made a third group with the children.

The tribe also had several blacks but they were not slaves since they were all Muslims. See, the law of the Koran does not allow the faithful to keep another of the faith as a slave no matter what color skin he may have.

Perez took full advantage of the feast—he knew he had to get his strength back before leaving.

The diffa was followed by a concert, if you could call it that. Two young men picked the guzzla, a fiddle, accompanied by a droning chant but in the evening calm it had its charm.

As the moon rose on the horizon the sheik led Perez and Luz to a little tent that he had set up for them and fitted out with two mats. Both of them fell quickly into a much-needed, deep sleep.

\#

The next day on waking up Perez felt ready to go as if he had never been sick. His friend was also refreshed and rested.

"It's time to get going," he told himself.

Although he had only caught a few words that were said in the djemma, he understood that the sheik, despite his somewhat forced hospitality, wanted him leave and he knew why. The poor man feared the maboul's influence.

He walked out of the tent and the first person he met was none other than Ahmed ben Hadded. The two men greeted each other solemnly and the sheik said a few words. Perez understood "when" and "leave". He desperately tried to call up his knowledge of Arabic.

"This morning," he answered.

"And the child?"

"She goes with me."

He caught a glimpse of satisfaction on the sheik's face followed by a hint of annoyance. The satisfaction came from the fact that Perez was leaving; the annoyance because Luz was going with him.

Ahmed ben Hadded was about to start up a discussion that could not have pleased the fugitive, so, to cut him off, Perez found nothing better than to fake a trance. First he started trembling all over, then his arms and legs went stiff and suddenly he fell face down on the ground repeating the name of Allah three times.

This time the sheik was convinced. He called a young warrior over and gave him orders. The Arab left and five minutes later came back with a woven basket full of figs and dried meat.

Perez, whose eyes were only half-closed, was watching what was happening around him. When he figured it was the right time he got up but looked disoriented as if he were lost in a vision of a far-off world.

Ahmed ben Hadded came up to him holding the basket. "Take some food," he told him, "and go, my brother, wherever the will of the all-merciful God leads you."

Perez fumbled with the basket and mumbled, "May Allah be with you." Then he went back to his tent, waved to Luz to follow him and slowly walked out through the crowd of silent, respectful Beni-Harglou.

He looked completely unaware of everything around him, adrift in a divine vision. But in reality nothing escaped him. He even noticed the disappointment on the faces of his hosts. They could have quickly shaken off their surprise and gullibility and tried to keep the child by force. That was why Perez figured it best to get away from the douar as soon as possible.

After 200 yards, hidden by a stretch of tall bushes, he put Luz on his back and started running, veering off to the south. The child was surprised by the getaway. She could not understand the reason. Why run away from hosts who were so nice to them? But her trust in her friend was boundless. She showed no resistance or regret.

For two hours Perez showed no sign of ever having been sick. He carried Luz on his shoulders and walked briskly. Thus, if the Beni-Harglou changed their minds and decided to chase after them, they would not see the little prints of the girl's bare feet. As for the Spaniard's espadrilles, which were not yet completely worn out, they left little trace.

It was only after putting a good five or six miles between them and the douar that Perez stopped to take a break, get their bearings and figure out what to do.

While listening to the Arabs talk he had caught a few names: Sanfredja, Taza, Fez. Although not very well versed in the geography of Morocco Perez was not at a complete loss. As a prisoner, planning his escape, he had snuck a peek at a big topographical map hanging in the medical office of the penal colony. He knew that Fez was situated around 120 miles SES of Ceuta and closer to the Atlantic shore. Taza was around 60 miles ENE of Fez so that the three cities formed a right-angle triangle whose hypotenuse was Ceuta-Taza. He must have been between Fez and Taza.

As for this Sanfredja, he remembered that it was a mountain range running along the northern route from Fez to Taza. At the foot of these mountains was a river whose name he could not recall.

If he did not go off in the wrong direction, he might be in the Moroccan capital within three days. At first this thought filled him with hope. Then another idea came to mind that dwindled this hope. Before bringing Luz into a city of 70,000 people, so different from the gloomy crypt where she had lived, wouldn't it be better for him to teach her his language so that the two of them could communicate?

He had already started to teach her some Spanish. Meeting the Beni-Harglou, as lucky as it was for them, had cut short the lessons and made Luz learn some Arabic words that were different than what he was teaching her. He could not let this child get mixed up and confused by the two languages.

Above all, she had to fully understand the man who had snatched her out of the life of an animal and also make herself understood by him. It was necessary that this common good—language—prevent any unexpected disaster from separating them.

Now, in Fez Luz would hear Arabic spoken and not Spanish. She would also see things that could warp her uncultivated mind: religious practices of the most extreme fanaticism, racial hostility, the enslavement of women, etc. In the midst of cruelty and ignorance what would become of the conscious, rational being he dreamed of educating?

To earn a living for the two of them he would be forced to leave the child alone most of the time. In whose hands could he put her?

It crossed his mind that it might be better to find some fertile oasis where he and Luz could set up while he provided for their needs by hunting and growing a few things. A life of rustic simplicity and isolation was happy enough for a lot of people. Meanwhile he could shape up Luz's brain and make her understand that not all humans speak the same language or have the same customs. Only when she had understood these basic ideas could he enter an Arab city with her to find transport to some center of European civilization.

Now he just had to find a desert oasis.

"Let's go," he told Luz.

And they got on their way.

XXX. A Little Eden

The two travelers walked for a few more hours without seeing anything but rocky ground and patches of bush that were sometimes very tall. But Perez knew that he was reaching the edge of the arid steppes and approaching the region of cultivated land, which started to the east of Fez. Minor hints confirmed his belief: in the middle of some dusty bushes the green stalk of some unknown plant stuck out; the ground was black-veined, the color of the beautiful, fertile land to the west; and birds were flying overhead.

In the afternoon the change was stronger. Grass was growing and green plains could be seen, separated by clumps of cedar and oak trees. In the distance a flock of sheep was grazing. Sheep obviously meant that there were guardians and owners.

It might have been around three o'clock and the sun was beating down on the landscape, heating it up like an oven. Luz touched her companion's arm and pointed at a bluish line to the south, a little out of their way.

"There's an oasis!" the ex-convict rejoiced.

The darkish area had to be woods and with vegetation there had to be water nearby. Nevertheless, the travelers were too tired to make it there in one go. They took a 30-minute break to eat some of the figs they owed to the generosity of Ahmed ben Hadded. Then, still tired but spurred on by hope, they started off again.

The sun had not set when Perez and Luz, after crossing through clusters of green bushes with red and white flowers, finally arrived at the woods. It was a real oasis: a carpet of thick, green grass surrounded by majestic cedars entwining their leafy branches. The flapping of wings indicated the presence of many birds.

"Little suns!" she shouted.

The naïve comparison made Perez laugh cheerfully when he saw the orange trees. There were half a dozen of them, full of fruit. A few oranges were lying on the ground where they were destined to rot if nobody ate them. Perez picked one up, the most beautiful, completely round, peeled it and split it in two. He tasted one half and found it good, although a little bitter. He gave the other half to Luz. The precious fruit quenched the thirst that was starting to torment them.

"Good! Good! Good!" the child repeated the adjective to emphasize it.

The orange trees were wild, which is why their fruit was a little bitter.

Was anyone living in this Eden? Perez wondered. He and Luz no longer felt tired. The tasty fruit they had scooped up refreshed and reenergized them. The thick green carpet of grass felt wonderful under their feet and the canopy of foliage protected them from the heat of the sun. They were happy.

But their happiness would be greater still.

Walking away from the orange trees and into the thick woods Perez noticed a pile of branches arranged in such a way that it could only have been the work of man.

"Unless I'm mistaken, Eden is inhabited."

He went closer. It was the dilapidated remains of a small, square hut. A wall of cracked mud formed one side. The two other sides were made of branches. There was no fourth side, just a gaping hole around ten feet wide and six feet high. As for the roof, it must have been made of bundles of thin reeds and dried leaves that had collapsed into the shack. Three flat stones blackened by smoke proved the existence of an old hearth.

"They've left," Perez mumbled. "Well, I can fix up this dump and we'll settle in." Then he added to himself, "As long as there are no lions prowling around." This hut would be a sorry protection against a lion like the one that had attacked them the day before.

With the remains of the collapsed roof Perez made a barricade that covered part of the opening on the fourth side. Then he gathered some long, dry branches to finish off, as best he could, the structure. In spite of everything, the roofless hut with mud or wood walls would provide little protection against a serious enemy. Luckily, however, since there were no enemies at the moment, the two travelers could lie on the bare ground and enjoy a fitful sleep until morning.

The bright sun woke them up because nothing was blocking its light from entering from above.

"Up and at 'em!" Perez said cheerfully. "We've got a lot of work to do."

Luz did not understand his words but she smiled at her friend. They did indeed have a lot to do: finish their hut, explore the oasis and its resources, make some tools for hunting and gardening and stock up some supplies.

Perez checked what they had. Their riches consisted of figs, dried meat, a silver vase, a sword, two spent pistols, a fishing line and a net. Plus the two halves of the burnous that they had on and finally a pair of espadrilles that were worn thin.

The first thing to do was to look for water. The second thing was to get more food. The third was to make the hut a real living quarters. All this had to be done, if possible, in 24 hours. The rest was less pressing.

Perez did not have to walk far to see the clear stream running down a low, rocky hill and winding through the twin rows of reeds before emptying into a pond. Blue flowers and water lilies floated on the still surface of the water. Birds similar to black-crowned cranes paced along the edge of the pond. They flew away from Luz when she ran playfully in front of her friend.

Another discovery that was almost as valuable was the beans from a three-foot high plant with purple flowers. "If I remember right, this is the *faba vulgaris*. It came from Asia but is grown all over Europe today. The fava might be *vulgar* but it'll give us plenty to eat." Then another thought came to him. "But the fava bean isn't usually found in the wild. This had to be planted by whoever lived in the hut before. What happened to him?"

Obviously he either died or left. The sorry state of the hut proved that he had been gone a long time.

There were a lot of fava beans, which made it a precious resource. Going hungry was no longer a problem.

After this Perez took care of the hut. It was crucial that their shelter be less crude. The ex-convict had worked on construction sites in the penal colony at Ceuta but unfortunately here he lacked the necessary tools, like an axe, saw, hammer and nails. All he had was the sword, which had already served so many different purposes. How fond he was of this steel blade that had been forged to deal out death but for him had been an instrument of life! He had promised himself to safeguard the weapon whose strength had held up in battle, in accidents on the journey and in anything that was dished out.

This time the sword cut and carved ten long, straight branches that he stuck deep in the ground. Thus, he had a kind of gate at the front of the hut with an opening around one and a half feet wide in the middle. The pickets were stuck ten inches apart and the space was filled in with dirt and grass packed together.

Luz was a clever helper. As a good housekeeper she had already followed her friend's directions and lit a fire and put the vase full of water and fava beans on it. The stream was only 100 feet away from the hut.

While the child was taking care of the frugal meal the fugitive kept working on shoring up the other sides of the hut. The work took him all day to complete. He barely stopped ten minutes to gobble up the half-cooked beans. Despite having no salt they were not bad.

When evening came the hut still had no roof but the night was calm. As for the opening, Perez had barricaded it a little better than the night before with some big rocks from the riverbank that he piled up between the double fence.

The night passed as quietly as the previous one. There were no wild animals living in the oasis.

XXXI. A Slab of Salt

Like everyone, Perez had read the adventures of Robinson Crusoe. He compared his situation with Daniel Defoe's hero. But there were some major differences between them. Robinson was lost in the middle of the ocean but he had the resources of the sea and supplies and equipment from the shipwreck. Perez was only about 40 miles from a big city but in the solitude he had willingly chosen his resources were much more limited than Crusoe's.

"It doesn't matter," he told himself, "in time I'll make what I need to hunt, fish, plant, weave and sew. I'll try to take only a few weeks… or months to do what primitive man took thousands of years to accomplish."

The hut was soon rebuilt. Long sticks crisscrossed over the walls and tied with vines formed the framework of the roof and was covered with a thick layer of leaves. The door was made of three layers of long pieces of bark attached to strong sticks. Although he lacked nails, there were plenty of vines and stringy plant fibers.

In the meantime Luz was in charge of fishing. Perez had taught her to make a net like the one he had and she quickly made two more. The smaller of them was to be stretch across the stream; the other, much bigger one, was tied to a pole and swept through the pond. Without the lake monster of the crypt, she was happy to find these smaller, silver-scaled fish that sparkled red.

They seemed to have enough food with the pond and the trees but Perez decided not to limit himself to these. He made two bows, a big one for him and a smaller for Luz, with 20 very sharp arrows. Then he started to practice his marksmanship on the winged world. He was immediately surprised to see that the little girl had an extraordinarily precise eye. Maybe because of her night-vision. So, the first bird that had reason to curse the travelers' arrival in the oasis fell to Luz's arrow.

However, one thing bothered Perez even though he was not a demanding gourmet: no salt. Now they had enough food but it had no seasoning. Luz thought everything was excellent because she was not used to variety, but the ex-convict was getting tired of bland food.

To multiply his resources he had planted some fava beans. Given the rich soil and the climate they would certainly not take long to sprout.

Not having dishes was also an inconvenience. Perez decided to become a potter. After a long search he ended up finding some mud that could serve his purpose. He made a pot, a jar and a vase, mixing them with sand to be stronger. Then he coated them with the sap that seeped out of the trees that resembled argans and he put them all in the fireplace. The vase did not stand up; it split in two. But the pot and the jar hardened well.

A hammer was necessary. From the stones lying on the riverbed Perez chose one that was cone-shaped and sufficiently big and hard. He tied it firmly to a strong branch that he cut down to about eight inches long to form the handle.

"Primitive men had nothing better!" he gloated.

A needle was another necessity. Fish bones of all sizes did the trick. Thanks to these needles and some thin plant fibers Perez could give some form to Luz's clothes that might not be elegant but certainly more practical. He could also make a pair of crude espadrilles for her and fix the ones he was wearing.

In the midst of this work Perez did not neglect Luz's education. A week had passed since they arrived in the oasis and they were already talking together almost fluently, even though the child was far from speaking good Spanish. She spoke more of a pidgin, but Perez was no less delighted to hear her. On his side he had learned almost all the animalized language but he only used it when absolutely necessary.

Luz's physical development was just as important as her intellectual development. Above all he had taught her about cleanliness, a thing which she knew nothing about. She never dreamt that water was good for anything but drinking. This was not her fault: the animalized in the cave had lost the habit of washing themselves generations ago. After taking her first bath Luz seemed like a different person. Perez felt that ideas were clearer in her mind, she had more energy and, looking at her with paternal love, he thought she was pretty.

Both of them were really happy in this solitary retreat. Work and education kept them busy all day long. Time passed quickly. One day Perez was digging in front of the hut with a stick he had hewn and hardened in the fire so that he could plant some seeds he had picked up that looked a little like peas. It would be one more vegetable they could eat. All of a sudden he heard Luz's voice.

"Father," the child shouted, "me find rock-food!"

He was used to his student's language and right away knew what she wanted to say. She had found something that looked like a rock but was edible. Intrigued, he ran toward her voice but he quickly saw her running toward him and holding out a white rectangle about 16 inches long and 8 inches wide.

"Rock-food like drink water under ground," she panted.

It took Perez a good half a minute to understand her this time but then he was amazed. If he was right Luz wanted to say that this edible stone had the same taste as the water in the crypt, meaning it was salted!

Salt! Could it really be salt?

Perez was anxious to examine the stone. It was crumbly. He scraped the surface with his nail, picked up a few grains of white powder and tasted it. It was salt!

"Oh, Luz, my girl, what a find you've made!" he was very excited. "Now there's nothing that can stop us from spending our life here!"

His excitement was obviously making him exaggerate. What was true was that this discovery was priceless. Salt, which was so far unknown to Luz, is a necessity not only for the civilized European but for the Arab as well. Since time immemorial this product found in the Sahara has been the object of great commerce for caravans.

2,300 years ago Herodotus recorded the existence of rock salt in North Africa. "Beyond the wild beast tract in Libya," he wrote, "there is a vast zone of sand that reaches from Egyptian Thebes to the Pillars of Hercules. Throughout this zone, at the distance of ten days' journey from one another, heaps of salt in large lumps lie upon hills."

The existence of an ancient sea in these regions long since dried up and overrun by the sands can explain the formation of these deposits where the caravans came to stock up.

Perez knew about all these details because economic geography had once been one of his favorite studies.

"Where did you find this stone?" he asked.

"Over there," Luz pointed toward the west. "Over there in big empty rock a lot of things."

"Empty rock: a cave!" Perez thought aloud. "Maybe the place where the former tenant kept his supplies."

He started to carry the block, which must have weighed around five pounds, back to the hut, but he stopped and turned to the girl. "Show me where you found this."

He ran more than walked next to her, burning with hope and desire for another discovery. It was only when he was 50 yards from their home that he realized he had forgotten the sword, the weapon that hardly ever left his side not just for safety but because he used it for almost every kind of work he did.

"Well, it doesn't matter. You don't run into lions every day."

They passed some thick underbrush, crossed a clearing, then stepped into a kind of island of greenery, a tangled mess of bushes and vines wrapped around a stand of tall, straight trees with dark foliage. Between the trees could be seen a little hill made of rocks piled on top of one another by the whimsical hand of nature. They could only see the general outline of the hill, partly covered with greenery, but Perez right away thought that a cave or a big space must have been hollowed out that could serve as a hiding place.

Without worrying about ripping her clothes on the thorns Luz was already pushing through the bushes. The fugitive heard her shouting out, "Father! See the pretty rope!"

He saw her turn around, holding what looked like a thick cable in her hands. A second later her excited shout turned into an unspeakable cry of terror. The cable was

unrolling all by itself and rising into the air. It was a
snake.

XXXII. The Python

At the sound of Luz's scream—a shriek of fear and a cry for help—Perez ran to her. Even without a weapon at hand he leaped forward to help the child in danger. In danger? She was almost a goner...

The snake had already wrapped its coils around her legs and poised its gaping mouth in front of her chest, darting out its tongue like a stinger. It was almost ten inches round and seven feet long. Its body was yellow with black spots.

At first sight Perez knew it was a young python and he shuddered. Although the python was not venomous it was strong and agile enough to be dreaded. Obviously it had been dozing when Luz grabbed it, thinking it was a rope since she had never seen a snake before.

Perez immediately grabbed the reptile around the throat and squeezed as hard as he could. Angered and choking, the snake pounded the ground with its tail but also released its hold.

"Run!" Perez shouted to Luz.

She stood there paralyzed by horror and fear. It was like the snake had changed her into a stone statue.

"Run!" the fugitive yelled again. He was worried that the snake was about to escape and strike back. His scream had broken the spell that had frozen the child. She slipped out of the coils and within seconds disappeared.

"Finally," Perez gasped as he felt his strength draining.

He lifted up the python, planning to smash its head against the rocks but the animal was already slipping out of his hands, threatening with its cavernous mouth and trying to wrap its coils around him. Perez did not take two steps before he felt his leg trapped by the reptile's body.

"I'm a goner," he thought.

This thought was made more agonizing by the thought of Luz, who would be left all alone now. What would become of her?

Struggling with the python that was now winding around him and squeezing its spiral of death, Perez felt a little bitter that the girl whom he had sacrificed so much for had run away and abandoned him. If she had brought him a rock, a big branch, anything he could use as a club, he just might have come out victorious in this new battle. As it was, there was only one possible ending—his death!

A few more minutes went by and under constant, merciless pressure of the coils Perez was being crushed and suffocated. The battle lasted a while longer. The poor man was exhausted by his desperate efforts to get free of the living bonds that grew tighter and stronger, starting to break his bones. Twice he grabbed the snake's head. Twice it escaped hissing in anger. Finally, with his feet tied up Perez wobbled and fell over. He was losing his breath, just about to pass out.

At this moment the bushes parted. The fugitive saw a hazy figure jump through and something flashed in the sunlight before vanishing in the reptile' open mouth. Luz was there, sword in hand. She had stuck it with all her might between the animal's gaping jaws.

When she had got some feeling back in her legs she had also cleared her mind. Knowing that they needed the weapon to defeat the reptile she had run full speed back to the hut and grabbed the sword. When she got back, out of breath, she plunged the blade down the python's throat just when it thought it had crushed its enemy and was getting ready to eat him.

We know that a snake has to crush, knead and put lots of saliva on a prey that is bigger than it. Preparing their meal, transforming a living creature into long, doughy substance to swallow, takes a certain amount of time. This delay allowed Luz to get back to her friend before he become edible.

The python was struck in the most vulnerable part of its body. It shook and trembled furiously. Its head was thrown back and a flood of black blood poured out of its throat. At the same time it loosened its hold a little.

Almost unconscious Perez shook his head and came to. But he was crushed, unable to pull his legs out of the mortal coils. And then the reptile was about to attack again, with a choice of two victims.

Luz was still holding the sword whose blade was dripping with blood. She swung at the body but the scales shielded it from her feeble blows.

"Give me," Perez wanted to say but he could not utter a word because the snake was still squeezing him. Instead he motioned with his hand so that Luz understood. She handed him the sword and just holding the steel blade seemed to give him strength.

Still lying on the ground but leaning on his left elbow, he stabbed hard into the front of the snake where its vital organs should be. He thrust the steel a few inches through the thick, living tube. Right away the coils stiffened. The wounded snake was convulsing. A second later it whipped its tail violently at Luz and almost knocked her over while its head dropped onto Perez, its eyes still burning with anger.

They started fighting again, furiously, but the outcome was uncertain. Luz had disappeared again but was back in no time holding a big rock that she had taken from the hill. Perez could see victory. Putting the sword between his teeth he put all his strength in clutching the snake just under the jaws and pinning it to the ground. Luz immediately dropped the heavy rock on the python's head.

Now it was the animal's turn to be trapped. If it was not crushed at least it was knocked senseless. Perez only had to keep his left hand on the throat while his right hand sliced with the sword and beheaded it. Meanwhile Luz was unwinding the coils from her friend's body.

With its throat severed down to the vertebrae the snake was helpless. It died in agony. One last quiver shook its body and its tail beat the ground a final time. That was all.

For a few minutes Perez lay exhausted next to the corpse of his victim. He was lucky not to have run into a medium-sized python because these giants of the reptile world can grow up to 25 feet long. In that case it would not have been a happy ending.

One thing surprised him: he thought that these animals were only seen in the south. He started to worry about the dangerous neighbors in this oasis because even if this snake was dead, its parents could still be slithering around. From now on he had to be on his guard.

While thinking this Perez massaged his legs; Luz rubbed his back. His blood was starting to circulate normally again and soon he could stand up and walk as steadily as if he had not just survived a mortal combat.

XXXIII. Paradise without the serpent

The fight with the python had made Perez forget about the aim of their excursion. It was Luz who reminded him of their purpose.

"We look for something."

"Let's go."

This time he walked in front of his little friend, watching the underbrush carefully before taking a step. What if the unknown treasure had other guardians! But they arrived safe and sound before the hill.

"There," Luz pointed to the hollowed out opening formed by three blocks of rock. The cavern was around five feet deep and two feet wide. Perez hesitated a moment before sticking his arm into the dark hole where some dangerous host might be crouching.

But Luz already had the top of her body inside. "Wait!" the fugitive screamed, pulling her out. The girl came out holding a long roll of brown, woolen tissue.

Perez shouted with joy. Clothes were something they needed badly despite the clever adjustments he had made to their two halves of the burnous. Now he and Luz would have plenty to wear because the rolled up material must have been 15 feet long and three feet wide.

This was not all. Perez took his turn to explore the cavern and brought out a piece of leather. They could make real shoes! Then a goatskin bag, three rusty irons that looked like spearheads and a bunch of different seeds.

All of this was a priceless find. Thanks to it he could make clothes, shoes, tools and plant a garden. His situation was becoming as good as Robinson Crusoe's and he had the advantage of being close to a big city.

These "hiding places" are built all over, especially in the mountains. The Arabs in Morocco and Algeria are in constant danger of being robbed by prowlers.

Once again Perez wondered what had happened to his predecessor in the oasis. Was he dead? If so they would have found his remains near the hut unless some wild animal had devoured him whole. Or had he left? Perhaps.

In any case, since the puzzle seemed unsolvable, Perez let it drop.

But one thing did worry him: the possibility of running into other pythons. He knew that the famous sect of Aissawas mixed their juggling tricks with frenetic fanaticism and used a lot of snakes in their practices. But the animals were usually hunted in the south and mainly in the province of Souss. Moreover, Perez wondered how a python could live here seeing that they are not exactly vegetarians. Its presence in the oasis meant that there were other animals that it could eat.

Perez decided to continue exploring the forest. However, he postponed it until the next day. For the moment he wanted to skin the python. He would keep the skin and the meat, salted and smoked, would make a few nice meals. The rest of the day was spent on this work as well as bringing all the supplies back to the hut. Perez and Luz tasted the roasted snake meat and thought it was delicious.

"Me never eat thing so good," Luz smiled.

The slices of meat were strung up and put over the smoke. The snake skin was stuffed with grass and dried leaves then sewed up.

The next morning Perez and Luz started off carrying the sword that had saved their lives in so many battles along with their bows and few supplies in a basket—the exploration might last long.

They walked with a spring in their step and joy in their heart, admiring the luscious beauty of the plants. The sun was shining in the clear blue sky, its rays filtered by the trees drawing circles and triangles on the ground.

"Pretty!" Luz observed.

The fugitive was happy to see that this child who spent her gloomy life in the darkness of the crypt was open to the sense of beauty. The majesty of a tree crowned by its thick foliage, the contrast of purple fruits and green leaves, the shifting skies changing from the gray of dawn to light blue to indigo and orange then purple only to fade away again into the sepulchral dark of night—all this awoke in the child feelings of deep admiration.

"Look!" the girl suddenly shouted.

They had just passed the rocks where they had battled desperately with the python the day before. The ground before them was weird: sometimes sandy, in other places black and circled with thick vegetation. Luz was pointing to the ground where a few faint prints appeared in the sand.

"Looks like hoof prints... maybe a small herbivore," Perez muttered.

He wanted to follow the tracks but no sooner did they show up than they disappeared, only to surface again. After half an hour the travelers had made no progress.

"So," the fugitive thought aloud, "what animal could have made these prints. Looking at their distance the animal must be around a foot and half long from front to back feet and half as wide. So, it's something like a goat or an antelope."

Just then Luz shook his arm. "Baahs!" she said, pointing at something in front of them in a dark thicket.

Perez had to squint. He saw nothing. With her night vision and ears accustomed to the faint, indefinable noises of the crypt, Luz's sight and hearing were more acute. When they were with the Beni-Harglou she had seen the horses, cattle, sheep and goats and since she did not know what they were called she had named them by their sounds. The horses were "Neighs", the cows were "Moos" and the sheep and goats were "Baahs".

"Yesterday we got salt and today we're going to get us some milk," Perez dreamed. "It's too good to be true."

He had to step cautiously so as not to scare off the goats and sheep. The hardest thing was to capture them because the ex-convict did not think for a moment of killing one. Isn't needless killing, even of animals, a crime? Since violence between certain species is an inflexible law of nature, why should we make it worse by killing peaceful creatures? Perez had more than one loud argument with his fellow Spaniards when he slandered bullfighting as a school of savagery.

"They're the only schools you have," he had said. "That's why you're the tail end of European civilization."

They walked for a few minutes, hiding as best as they could behind the bushes and trying not to crack the dry branches on the ground. All of a sudden they stopped. 50 feet in front of them a white goat was feeding two young kids. A half dozen other goats were grazing around her under the protection of a bearded billy goat.

"Baah!" Luz yelled excitedly.

Perez could not hold her back before she ran as fast as she could to the herd. At the sight of the child the billy goat whistled and they all disappeared except for the mother and her kids. As for the male, he was obviously not ready to surrender the territory without a fight. He stiffened up on his rear legs and jumped at Luz since she was already less than 15 feet away.

The reckless girl was hit head-on in the chest by the curved horns and fell to the ground. The billy goat had vented his anger, so he scampered off and disappeared. Perez ran over and helped the girl to her feet. She was dazed from the fall but not hurt. Then he went to the goat.

Like a good mother she had not abandoned her kids. Trembling a little she stared at the newcomers with gentle eyes. To comfort and reassure her Perez offered her some grass, petted her and petted the kids.

"Now I understand," he said, "what the python was eating. I'm glad I killed it. It would've ended up eating every last one of them."

The fugitive had brought a rope wound around his waist. He tied one end to the mother's horns and held onto the other. Then he put one kid under each arm and gave Luz the basket of food.

"Let's go home!" he was beaming.

He wanted to bring the goat and her kids back to the hut to feed them. These animals were destined to be both a resource and amusement for the exiles in the oasis. The goat was more than willing. Not only did she see to her motherly duty by following her kids but she seemed tame already: she nuzzled her neck against Perez's leg.

"We're starting to live in a real paradise now that the serpent is gone," the ex-con mused. "As long as it lasts!"

XXXIV. The Moqqadem Ali ben Kadour

The goat became a house pet. They did not need to keep her tied up. She never left her kids alone and always came up to be petted by her masters. They, in turn, used her milk, but not too much—they did not want to deprive the kids of their necessary ration. Perez was also hoping that the goat would lure the rest of the herd to the hut so he did not want to have to chase it around.

Two weeks had gone by since they had come to the oasis and they were so happy that at times it was painful for Perez to think that they would have to leave for the sake of Luz's education. As enchanting as this Eden was, they could not spend the rest of their lives here.

One morning Perez saw the goat, who always slept in the hut with her kids, looking apprehensive. She lifted her head and sniffed hard.

"Is there some wild animal prowling around?" the fugitive wondered.

Luz saw what he was thinking in his eyes and bravely grabbed her bow. Perez was about to snatch up his own when the sound of a whistle made him shiver. He was sure that the whistle came from human lips. Friend or enemy, a human creature was approaching.

He ran outside the hut holding his sword but he had not taken two steps before he lowered the weapon. In front of him stood an old Arab whose beard was as white as his burnous. A few silver hairs peaked out under the camelhair turban that was wrapped around his head. He looked venerable because of his age and the long, flowing garb, but in his thin hermit's face two sparkling, hypnotic eyes were, at the moment, burning with rage.

"Dog!" he shouted when he saw Perez. "Who said you could fix up my house and live in it?"

The fugitive understood the angry words. Bracing himself with patience before the old man who, all things considered, figured his ownership rights had been breached, Perez tried to explain himself. But on hearing him talk in bad Arabic mixed with Spanish the old man became even angrier.

"Dog! Son of a dog!" he repeated. "You're just a roumi and you dare enter the house of Ali ben Kadour el Hadji[10]! You dare defile with your impure presence the roof that protects the moqqadem[11] of the Beni-Choussas!"

Just then, at the sound of the shouting, Luz appeared in the doorway holding her bow.

Ali ben Kadour started laughing wildly. "It gets better! You've brought this demon child into the house of the moqqadem? Watch what I'll do."

And the weird old man walked up to Luz and stared deep into her eyes with a steel-hard gaze. The child went stiff, tried to utter something but could not. Her eyelids drooped; she was in a trance.

Perez rushed over and took her in his arms. He had put up with the moqqadem's insults patiently but now that he had attacked this child he was fed up. He stood in front of the old man with his sword raised. The Arab stared at him with a dreadful look, concentrating all his will power in his eyes, but Perez just shrugged his shoulders.

---

[10] Hadji is a name taken by those who are consecrated by completing the pilgrimage to Mecca.
[11] The moqqadem is the chief of a fanatic group that travels around giving performances of juggling and magnetism.

"Phony!" he yelled. "You can hypnotize children and gullible fools but what happens when you try it on me?"

The moqqadem whistled a strange tune and the folds of his burnous parted: the heads of snakes peeked out, their squirming coils twisted around his chest and waist. Then they started uncoiling and threatening Perez. He stepped back not out of fear but out of disgust while Ali ben Kadour grabbed one of the reptiles, a venomous asp, and tossed it at the Spaniard.

If Perez had not had his blade up already he would have been a goner. But by reflex, he parried the attack and the steel blade sliced the asp into two hideous, bloody pieces that writhed and wriggled on the ground.

The moqqadem howled in rage. He grabbed two other snakes and threw them one after another at Perez. But he had jumped to the side so the squirming missiles missed him. The Arab kept the others in case his enemy tried to jump him, but the fugitive did not want to risk Luz's life by taking a chance on a fight like this. He held the child in his left arm and to shield her turned his right side to the snake charmer, holding out the tip of his sword.

Ali ben Kadour saw that he was dealing with a formidable adversary. Whistling again he called back that asps that had fallen to the ground. The snakes crept up and wrapped around his waist with the others like a protective belt. Perez was wondering what he should do next, but this brief moment of hesitation was enough to allow the moqqadem to disappear into the bushes.

If alone the ex-convict would no doubt have chased him down to finish off the dangerous enemy and his snakes, but he just could not risk Luz's life in another fight or leave her behind. The most important thing was to wake her up if he could.

The Arab enchanters, like the Indian fakirs, were masters of magnetism and sleight of hand, to which they owed their influence among their superstitious fellows. Perez had witnessed hypnotism several times. He knew that the cataleptic state in which the powerful eyes of the moqqadem had cast Luz was nothing miraculous. But how long would the artificial sleep last? That was what he did not know.

Now, he could end up waiting forever for the girl to wake up. The situation was too serious for her stay like this for long without being hurt. He carried Luz back into the hut and tried to bring her around by blowing on her eyes and rubbing her temples with water. To his great relief he saw that she was starting to open her eyes.

"Me sleep," she mumbled out of her cloudy mind.

"Come," Perez said and he led her to the stream.

A good bath brought her completely back to her senses as if she had never fallen under the magnetic influence of the eyes of Ali ben Kadour. But Perez had to think. He was disappointed to admit that their stay in Eden where they had been so happy had come to an end. The fanatic enchanter with his bitterness and spite would be sneaking around, hiding, watching the roumis, holding a grudge and never forgiving them for taking his place.

Of course Perez felt no guilt. Had nature given the moqqadem property rights over this corner of the earth that he had not created or even kept up? All he did was enjoy the natural fruits of nature's labor. And the fugitive who had nothing? Had he wronged anybody by staying here and fixing up an abandoned shelter? Obviously not.

But the moqqadem, urged on by his religious hatred, would have none of it. Day and night—especially at night—they would have to be awake, watching the bushes and rocks, the corners of the hut for some slithering snake bite, the unseen instrument of the moqqadem's vengeance. Such a life was unthinkable. It would be better to leave.

Even more so since Perez saw how impossible it would be, in the very unlikely case that an opportunity might arise, to make his enemy listen to reason. And he felt absolutely sickened by the thought of washing his hands in the blood of an old man. In the heat of battle he would end up killing the guy with no regrets. Because he had the right to defend himself. But when he thought clearly he knew that if murder could be avoided it was his duty to do so.

Now, there was only one way to do this: leave. And this was also what wisdom counseled.

Certainly he felt bitter, more for Luz than for himself, at the thought of leaving this spot just when their life here was becoming sweet. Was it, then, his destiny condemning him to wander the earth restlessly, escaping one ordeal just to fall into another?

What does it matter! They would leave before nightfall, which was ripe for ambushes.

XXXV. An Encounter

The preparations for leaving were finished quickly. Although Perez was giving up the oasis to the snake charmer who considered it his legal property, he was not naïve enough to leave him their essentials.

He and Luz were now wearing clothes, shoes and hats—well, they had hoods. They both carried a big basket of provisions on a string: the preserved python meat; the silver vase, a souvenir from the crypt; pieces of salt; boiled fava beans; oranges; resin torches; ropes; and finally their different tools like needles, nets and fishing lines, etc.

The wineskin found in the hiding place and full of goat milk slapped against the side of Perez. This drink would give them strength during the long and no doubt arduous journey they were in for. Regretfully they had left behind the goat and her kids. It was almost like abandoning friends, but these friends would make a hard trip even harder despite their four legs.

Perez got his bearings: Fez ought to be to the right, so it was this direction they headed, but cutting into the country so they would not have to cross the whole length of the oasis. They had to avoid the dark woods and thick bushes where Ali ben Kadour and snakes might be lying in wait, invisible. Out in the country the trip would be tougher but safer.

After saying a regretful farewell to his Eden the fugitive breathed cheerfully on stepping onto open land where no ambushes were waiting for him. The moqqadem would probably wait until the evening to surprise the roumis in their hut and had no inkling that they had left.

For a good two hours they walked without stopping. It was better to tire themselves out while putting as much as distance as possible between them and the snake charmer. Then all of a sudden Perez called a halt. He had just seen a figure moving on the horizon. It could not be the moqqadem who must have been in the oasis, i.e. behind them.

"A man on a horse," Luz said, speaking much more correctly now.

Perez knew how well his little friend could see and hear. Therefore, he had no doubt that the individual was a horseman. Should they hide? Why? And how? If the person had seen them and had evil intentions, it would be easy for him to catch up to them by spurring on his horse.

"Come on," Perez said.

Since the horseman was heading in their direction it was not long before they were close enough for the two on foot to see the man. It was an old man, or almost, draped in long, black clothing and riding not on a horse but on a donkey...

When there were less than 20 yards separating them, the man dismounted but held the bridle in one hand. He stood next to his donkey, bowing his head, waiting for Perez and Luz to pass by. At first the fugitive was amazed at this sign of humility. A moment later he understood: the black clothes, the donkey, the show of respect, all indicated that this man was a Jew.

Jews made up a good part of the Moroccan population. More than 40,000 out of perhaps 8 million Arabs. Still, they were barely tolerated and the Muslims made life hard for them. They had to live in ghettos called *mellah* and wear black, a color despised by the Moors; they were forbidden to ride horses, so a donkey or mule, much less noble animals, were all they could mount; when passing by mosques or the houses of a marabout (a holy man) or a noble they had to take off their shoes; and finally if they were riding and met a Muslim on foot it was common courtesy and wise policy to get their own feet on the ground and wait for the true believer to pass by before getting back on their donkeys.

All this respect did not always protect them from fanaticism. The Moors, being less brave and more cruel than the Arabs, were especially hard on them. Maybe because the Moors were a Semitic race descended from the Carthaginians and saw the merchant Jews as fierce competition. As for the fanatic sects such as the Aissawas, they also considered Jews lower than dogs. Unfortunate the Youddi whom the furious fanatics met during their religious practices!

Perez knew these details of custom. He was glad to have met a Jew rather than a Muslim. Maybe this man who belonged to an oppressed race would take pity on the wanderer and the child. Moreover, he knew that almost all the Jews in Morocco spoke and understood Spanish. Most of them were descendants of those peninsular Israelites who had been chased into Africa by the tyranny of Catholic kings and the Inquisition.

Be that as it may, the man had dismounted and was bowing. When Perez was only a few feet away he cried out, "Salam! I salute you, Lord. May the heavens pour blessings on you!"

Perez answered in Spanish, "Brother, I salute you. May you be prosperous and happy!" Not believing these greetings were truly genuine or effective, he usually did not bother to say them, but he made an exception in this

209

situation, believing that politeness should be responded in kind.

On hearing these unexpected words the old man stood speechless a moment, thinking. Then he answered, this time in good Castilian speech, "Would I be correct in believing that you are Spanish?"

"I am indeed."

"Tell me, brother, can I be of any help to you?"

This kind-hearted question came out naturally at the sight of the sword hanging at his side and the bow resting on his shoulder. The old Jew was wondering if this tough, armed traveler might be hostile and it would be better to stay on his good side.

"Thank you. I won't take advantage of your kindness but I would like to ask you for a little information."

His kindly answer brought a smile of satisfaction to the old man's face. Curious to know who this man was, coming from the east with a child, he chattered, "I'm Samuel Azar, a Jew as you can see. My ancestors came from Spain when the Christians chased them out. I live in Fez. And now it's your turn."

By offering his name and race the clever man had obviously meant for Perez to do the same. But his curiosity was not satisfied.

"I'm Antonio Mires," the fugitive said. "My story is too long to tell. I'll only say that I'm an honest man and down on my luck, with no money and I'm only asking for some work. Can you help me with that?"

Samuel looked hard at Perez and answered his question with another, "Where do you come from? Before hiring anyone you have to know them."

The ex-convict quickly made up a story on the spot: he was a passenger on a sailing ship that crashed against the rocks on the Riff coast. The others drowned while he fell into the hands of the Riffians. From this point on he only had to tell the truth, which he did. He was sold as a slave to the Riata, escaped, found the cave and stayed there until he brought Luz out of it.

Hearing this marvelous tale Samuel declared, "Who has ever heard such a thing? And yet it must be true. Morocco has pits everywhere because the abysmal fires once shred it up and the sea moved in. Sometimes, if you believe the Arab tales, you can find marvelous things: stone men, the skeletons of giant animals and blocks of crystal containing gold. But an ancient human race living for centuries at the bottom of an abyss, that's really fabulous!"

"If you doubt me," Perez said solemnly, "ask the girl. She knows enough Spanish now to answer you."

"No, I believe you. But go on."

The fugitive continued the now truthful story of his adventures. He told of meeting the lion and the Beni-Harglou, staying in the oasis and the arrival of the snake charmer who forced them out.

At the name of the moqqadem the Jew turned pale. "Ali ben Kadour, you say. The moqqadem of the Beni-Choussas. Oh, if he's mixed up in this you'll never get far enough away."

"Why? Who's this ben Kadour and the Beni-Choussas?" Perez asked anxiously.

He had hoped that his leaving would have snuffed out the hatred of the old Arab. Samuel proved him wrong.

"The Beni-Choussas," the Jew explained, "are a religious sect affiliated with the Aissawas. Like them they're jugglers, hypnotizers, scorpion eaters and snake charmers. Like them they pierce their bodies without pain and can pop their eyes out of their sockets. Unfortunate the Jew or the roumi who gets in their way. Every year they travel across Morocco from Rabat to Oujda performing their customary religious practices. They split up around Fez but can gather together at a signal from their moqqadem. Their moqqadem is Ali ben Kadour, a cruel and dangerous man whose power and influence is boundless."

"Caramba! Sounds like a real piece of work," Perez always felt disgusted by charlatans of all stripes.

"During the off season," the Jew went on, "Ali ben Kadour lives in the oasis where fate led you. No one would be reckless enough to enter it. His presence alone has made it a holy place, forbidden even to faithful Muslims."

"I see," Perez said. "Maybe the python I killed was one of his pets. But the hut looked like it was abandoned for a long time."

Samuel thought for a minute, then answered, "It's possible that the moqqadem was gone for longer than normal this time. It would've taken just a gust of wind to blow down his hut. But Ali ben Kadour probably has another one somewhere in the oasis. Anyway, you can be sure that he won't forgive you for violating his home. Watch out! He can send the Beni-Choussas after you."

Perez was worried. He completely understood the gravity of his situation. He had made a serious mistake letting the enchanter escape. He remembered the French proverb: better to kill the devil than be killed by him.

"Some advice," Samuel added, "Don't go to Fez."

"Why?" the fugitive was frustrated now. "We can hide in a big city and I can work."

The Jew shook his head, "You can't hide and work at the same time. Who will take you in? Besides, the Beni-Choussas are getting ready to tour the city. You won't be able to be there without running into them."

He explained the topography of the country, drawing lines in the sand with a stick.

"You guessed it: you're between Taza and Fez, closer to the latter. But you're still a two-day trek away because you haven't been walking in a straight line. Fez is to the southwest with two rivers between you. The smaller one is the Oued Inaouen that empties into the big one, the Oued Sebou, running to the northwest toward the ocean. I advise you to go along the Inaouen until you get to the Sebou, then follow that so you avoid Fez and the Beni-Choussas."

Perez was unsure. This itinerary fouled up his plans and his hopes.

Samuel saw his trouble. "Don't be discouraged," he said. "It's safer. To the north of the Inaouen you might run into the Philistines. They won't help you but they won't hurt you either. Then you'll cross a fertile zone followed by marshes all the way to the sea. You'll find some Europeans there who can help you. Courage and farewell!"

With these words the Jew climbed up on his donkey and trotted off.

XXXVI. Chase and Battle

Perez stood undecided and thoughtful. Should he take the Jew's advice, cross through the region of unfriendly Philistines, put some distance between him and the big cities and walk to the coast out of fear of the Beni-Choussas?

He hated to have to do this but prudence told him it was the better decision.

Finally he made up his mind. Samuel had continued his way to the northeast. Perez veered off to the northwest.

Luz walked bravely, without complaining about being tired. The open air, the exercise, cleanliness and healthy food had made the puny child of the crypt a pretty little girl who was graceful and strong—the plant that once withered in barren soil was blooming now, full of vitality.

The transformation of her mind was no less marvelous. Her knowledge of the outside world she had never suspected of existing three weeks ago was like a five-year old European child's. Her intelligence, on the other hand, was far beyond her age.

In her friend's eyes, without him saying a word, she read his thoughts: Let's keep walking to escape the snake charmer. "Yes," she answered as if he had spoken aloud.

The delay caused by meeting Samuel had lasted almost 20 minutes. The sun was showing noon on the celestial clock. The warm air was turning hot, carpeting the earth with its vapors. How nice it would be at this time of the day to be resting in the cool shade of the oasis!

For another hour they walked through the desert where the grass was burning hot. Scattered around, however, were a few meager clumps of trees, some cactus and dusty palms. Here and there were also dried up riverbeds and on the horizon the blue fringe of mountains.

All of a sudden a white patch sparkled in the sunlight before them. "The Inaouen!" Perez shouted with joy. "Now our direction is mapped out. All we have to do is follow it."

But he and Luz were both getting tired, more from the heat of the day than from the distance they had traveled or the weight of their supplies. They lay down on the ground to rest and drink a little milk.

"Nice like this," Luz said.

It was highly unlikely that Ali ben Kadour's anger would reach out to them in this place. Besides, there was nothing around them but empty space. So, they took a longer break to eat some python meat and fava beans.

Perez wondered about the Philistines that the Jew talked about. Completely preoccupied with the Beni-Choussas who had forced him to change his plans, he had forgotten to ask about them. The name was weird. The real Philistines were people in Palestine, not Morocco.

As strange as it was, Samuel Azar had told the truth. The name of Philistines is still used today in Morocco by Hebrew tribes that came into the region before Christianity and who were tolerated by the Berbers. These Philistines were considered heretics by other Jews because they accepted only the Old Testament mixed with some Chaldean practices. Their early arrival in Morocco showed, in any case, that the Semites had no need of Christian persecutions to make them into a wandering race.

Perez and the girl had been resting for more than an hour when Luz, who was lying face down, suddenly looked up.

"What is it?" Perez asked her, looking around and listening carefully.

"Horses running."

Her answer made him very worried. Was it possible that the moqqadem had gathered his men and started hunting for the fugitives?

He put his ear to the ground but heard nothing. Nevertheless, he did not doubt Luz, knowing how sharp her hearing was.

Where could they hide? The land was absolutely barren. Maybe the Inaouen would fence them off from the hunters. But the river was almost two miles away. Could they hope to reach it before the horses caught up to them?

"Let's go!" he pulled Luz to her feet.

They started off again in a hurry. One thing stumped Perez: how had the moqqadem been able to know what direction the two fugitives had taken?

He had his answer very soon: on the wind, just a breeze really but quite clearly he heard dogs barking. Ali ben Kadour had sent the bloodhounds after them. And now the horses appeared like moving dots.

Perez was already weighed down. He had even thrown away his bundle without caring about the obvious traces he would leave. But he still picked up Luz, whose little legs could not keep up with him, and ran as fast as he could to the river.

Fortunately the horsemen had not yet seen them and at times they stopped their horses to examine the ground and wait for their dogs. They were delayed two or three times before resuming the chase. This was because some

Arab shepherds had led a flock of sheep across the area earlier in the morning and the prints of men and animals were mixed up with the fugitives'. But it was only a few minutes break before the dogs and horses were back on their track.

A howl suddenly broke out. The fugitives had been spotted and the hunters were not far away: just over half a mile. And the Inaouen was still some 700 yards farther on. If Perez had any doubts that these were Ali ben Kadour's men, the determination and zeal of the hunters was enough to dispel them.

What to do? There was no chance of being saved. So, wouldn't it be better to stop this useless, exhausting chase and face the enemy, die fighting? But what would become of Luz if her protector died? Was she destined to be eaten by dogs or poisoned by snakes? Or would she become the slave of the Beni-Choussas?

All of a sudden Perez flinched: the wind had changed and the warm gust caressing his face gave him both an idea and hope.

The grass they were trampling was not very high but it was everywhere and very dry. The slightest spark would set it aflame. Perez still had his flint and the pistols. In the blink of an eye he pile up some grass and started striking his lighter. A flame sprang up.

"Come on," he said to Luz, whom he had put down.

The two of them ran toward the Inaouen while a sea of fire rose up and surged through the grass between them and their pursuers. The latter stopped for a moment. They were not bothered as much by the flames as by the thick, stinging smoke.

"To the right!" yelled a voice that Perez recognized as the moqqadem.

It was indeed Ali ben Kadour on his black horse who was leading the chase. Maybe old Samuel had guessed rightly and the hermit had another shelter in the oasis where he kept horses, dogs and his servants. Or maybe he did like others of his kind and used carrier pigeons to communicate with his devotees.

What was certain was that within three hours after Perez and Luz had left, a group of four men on horseback, led by the moqqadem, set out after them with three *sloughis*, those skinny Arab greyhounds that run as fast as the wind. The dogs had quickly sniffed them out but at one point they hesitated. It was where the fugitives had met Samuel Azar. After following the Jew for a short while they went back to the spot, barked wildly and got back on the right track. The sheep and shepherd prints made them hesitate again, which the fugitives took advantage of. Nevertheless, they were on the verge of being caught when Perez got the idea to set the grass on fire.

Since the wind had changed direction it blew the flames and smoke toward the hunters, burning the hooves and paws. They had no other choice but to follow the moqqadem's order: go to the right where the barren ground had less fodder for the fire and they could ride.

Perez and Luz got to the river. It was around 50 yards wide and the current was pretty strong. For a moment some holes appeared in the veil of smoke and they could see the horsemen. And they, too, spotted their prey. There was a volley of gunfire but they missed their targets.

"Climb on, grab my neck and have no fear," Perez said. He jumped into the river and started swimming across, not trying to fight the current that was carrying him downstream.

The sloughis dove in behind the swimmer, but their stamina was not as strong as Perez. This was only natural seeing that dogs were considered vile creatures by Arabs and generally undernourished.

The current dragged away one of the dogs. The two others were only in the middle of the river when Perez and Luz climbed ashore. The child was not afraid. She had been careful not to squeeze too tightly when Perez was struggling with the water.

"Here," Perez grabbed Luz and hid behind a big rock surrounded by bushes that was on the riverbank. They lay flat on the ground behind the shield.

It was just in time. The Arabs had reloaded their rifles and fired another round, as harmless as the first.

"Idiots!" Perez thought. "They're wasting their ammunition instead of waiting to get closer. Now it's our turn."

They had thrown away their supplies but not their weapons. He grabbed his bow and an arrow whose tri-dent-shaped head was made of three strong fish bones. He aimed at the nearest hound. The arrow whistled off and a howl of pain echoed through the air. The three-pronged point was buried in the eye of the dog. Luz already had her bow ready. The arrow she fired was no less accurate. Another howl and the second dog had its snout torn apart. The two wounded animals stopped swimming. The current carried them away just as it had the other sloughi.

The hunters, however, a little surprised at this resistance that they hardly expected, stopped in their tracks. First of all they reloaded, then the moqqadem shouted orders and they split up. One of them rode up the Inaouen to cross it farther upstream; two others went the opposite direction looking for a crossing downstream. The moqqadem stayed behind with the last one. But right away they urged their horses straight ahead into the waters of the Oued. Ali ben Kadour risked getting shot by an arrow, of course, but he was brave and his men believed he was invulnerable. His prestige would be badly wounded if he backed off from this wretched roumi.

"It can't be helped," Perez mumbled. "We've got to get rid of this crazy old man."

He had nine arrows left. He took one, notched it in the string of his bow and aimed straight into the face of the moqqadem.

"You hit the other horse," he told Luz. Even in this desperate fight for their lives, Perez still had feelings. He could not bring himself to let this little girl take the life of another human being so he told her to shoot the horse. This, of course, was being generous but profoundly unjust because it was the human being who was attacking them and not the horse.

The two arrows shot off at the same time and they heard a cry. The moqqadem was hit in the eye. He fell out of the saddle and into the river whose current was already dragging him away. His companion was not hurt but his horse was struck in the nose and had reared up. Being bucked off and seeing his chief shooting off downstream the Arab jumped into the water and started swimming. But his flowing burnous weighed him down.

Meanwhile the two horses went back to the other side of the river. Which is when a crazy but ingenious idea came to Perez. The Arabs who were supposed to cross the river upstream and downstream were 100 yards away on either side. Perez grabbed Luz and slipped back into the river.

"Hold on tight and hold your breath," he told her.

He dove down and came up 15 yards into the river, took a breath and dove back down without being seen by the Arabs.

As for the moqqadem being swept away by the current and his companion swimming to help the wounded old man, they had no inkling of the fugitive's bold move. Dripping with water he climbed onto the other shore with his breathing bundle and stood in front of the two horses. He immediately grabbed the wounded animal's bridle, tied it to the black steed and jumped on the latter with Luz still clinging to his back.

It was at this moment that the Arabs reached the other side of the river. Perez kicked the sides of the horse, which leapt forward and shot off at a mad gallop.

XXXVII. The Flight

The flight went on for a long time. Sometimes the fugitive looked back to see if they were being chased but he saw nothing on the horizon.

The moqqadem's horse was a noble animal, completely black and as fast as the wind. Its partner, although less elegant, was able to keep up. Luz's arrow had torn up its nose and it was bleeding, but it was not a serious injury.

The moqqadem's wound was certainly worse. Ali ben Kadour could no longer magnetize people with his eyes. He must be eaten up with rage!

Perez had turned right to head north, changing his plan again. He instinctively thought that if the Arabs got back on his trail it would be to the northwest. The ground was still warm from the fire so their prints and scent should not hold long.

All their supplies had been left behind, as well as their tools except for the sword, bows and arrows and the two pistols that the fugitive still kept in his belt even though they were utterly useless without ammunition.

"Father, look at this!" Luz said.

She was pointing to a small bag hanging from the horn of the saddle. Perez opened it and shouted for joy: the bag was divided into two compartments, one containing powder, the other bullets. Small, round bullets that could just fit into the barrels of the pistols!

"We're saved," he smiled.

He might have been exaggerating but with the ammunition they could defend their lives, more or less, against both animals and men, the latter often being more dangerous than the worst wild beasts.

"And this," Luz held out another bag of about the same size.

This one had dates in it. No doubt the moqqadem thought the chase could last a day or two and he had taken the necessary precautions. Dates are not very bulky food and they can feed an Arab for a pretty long time in his tent.

Then Perez saw that two similar bags were hanging from the saddle of the other horse. Without stopping his horse he reached out and grabbed them. He had to keep in mind that they might be forced to leave the other horse behind. But thanks to the food and ammunition their situation was a lot better now.

After the barren landscape they came into a halfah prairie. The horses bounded through the clumps of grass that grew over three feet high. Today this has become an important crop that is used to make rope, wickerwork and paper. Perez figured that the halfah prairie must mean that men were in the vicinity. What kind of men? Peaceful workers or fanatics infused with hatred for roumis?

The prairie went on as far the eye could see and no hunters showed up behind them. Perez stopped for five minutes to give the horses a breather and switch their ride. He did not want to tire out one horse more than the other. As for Luz, straddling in front of him, she was holding up like a veteran.

While the horses chomped the grass Perez checked their saddles. "If we sold one of the horses we might just have enough to get us to the coast."

Now that they were back among men, money, which they had been able to do without so far, was going to be indispensable.

They got back on their way. The sun was setting in the west and in the east the moon was rising to light the prairie stretched out before. Nothing was more striking than the difference in color across this silent landscape. To the east the pale night star drifted through a dark blue sky; to the west the last purple traces of the vanishing globe of fire were fading away.

The fugitives stopped one more time for half an hour to stretch their legs and give their horses a little rest. They ate a few dates and were sorry they had nothing to drink since they had to throw away the milk at the Inaouen. But regrets were useless.

They changed horses again, got back in the saddle and galloped off. The monotonous landscape of the halfah prairie finally gave way to a more varied vegetation of laurels, roses, orange trees and coffee bushes. A wide stream wound through the tufts of heather and lemongrass, glistening like silver in the moonlight. By instinct the two horses rushed over and stretched out their necks. They lapped up the water with obvious delight. Perez and Luz jumped down and after tying the horses to a bush they also drank at the stream.

All of a sudden a voice rang out, "Who are you?" It was spoken in Arabic.

Perez looked up and saw the ghostly form of man wrapped in a burnous standing in front of him. All he could see clearly was the face: a man around 45 years old whose skin was more yellow than brown and whose eyes sparkled.

"I'm a traveler and this is my daughter," Perez answered in bad Arabic mixed with Spanish. "We were attacked by robbers but got away."

The stranger examined the saddles very carefully. "And these animals," he asked, "where did you get them?"

Perez hesitated before answering. For a second he even wondered whether it might not be better to jump into saddle with Luz and ride off. But he thought that other Arabs were probably in the area and their fresh horses would easily caught up to them.

"Well?" the Arab asked.

"The robbers slaughtered everyone and killed my horse. Since some of them had jumped to the ground during the fight I grabbed these two here and escaped."

The answer was given almost entirely in Spanish on purpose. Perez figured that his hesitation could be blamed on his poor knowledge of Arabic. Moreover, he would have an excuse for not answering other awkward questions by pretending not to understand them.

But the Arab had grabbed the horses' bridles. "If what you say is true, in the name of all-merciful Allah you will be the guest of Ben Said, even if you are roumi. But if you are lying, your head will be cut off and your daughter will remain our slave."

His grave words were followed by a loud, hoarse cry and almost instantly more white forms came out of the dark blue night. Perez found himself surrounded by Arabs.

XXXVIII. Guests or Prisoners?

At this point on their wild ride the two travelers came into a douar whose tents were scattered on the other side of the halfah prairie. 100 Arabs of both sexes were living here and using the plant that nature had put at their doorstep to make mats, baskets, ropes and *alpartagas* or espadrilles that they sold in nearby markets. In the middle of all these tents, surrounded by laurels, roses and orange trees, stood two whitewashed buildings, one with many narrow arrowslits and topped by a crenelated parapet—this was the *Kasbah*—the other with a rounded doorway and a tower—obviously a crude, basic mosque.

Ben Said led the horses by the reins. Perez and Luz walked next to him, surrounded by the Arabs who made any hope of escape impossible.

"Are we guests? Are we prisoners?" the fugitive was asking himself anxiously.

And yet these people did not seem vicious. Even though they protected themselves from desert-roamers, at least they looked nothing like the cruel fanatics of the moqqadem.

Perez and Luz were brought into an empty tent that was used for storing feed. Bundles of dried grass were piled up. Ben Said came in with two mats and a couple of old blankets.

"Sleep with your child," he told his impromptu guest. "Tomorrow the djema will see whether you told the truth. If so, we'll help you because the prophet Mohammed says we should help those in need, even infidels."

And we went out, leaving the two travelers alone. But Perez guessed that the Arabs around the douar were keeping an eye out and he could not think of escaping. In spite of the problems looming over their heads while waiting for the djema's decision, the ex-convict was not as worried as one might imagine. Maybe it was just that he was dead tired. Luz was already asleep. Her friend lay down beside her on the second mat and quickly fell into a deep sleep.

Dawn found them rested and ready, all the exhaustion and trials of the day before almost forgotten. Then a melodic voice rose in the distance, chanting this call:

"Allahu Kébir! Allahu Kébir! Allahu Kébir! Ashahdu innala ilaha ila Allah!" And ended with the holy words, "Ashadu anna Sidina Muhammadun rasul Allah."

It was the muezzin in the minaret of the little mosque calling the faithful Muslims to prayer.

"The djema's going to meet," a voice said. "Come with the child."

It was Ben Said who had come to fetch his guests. Perez followed him, accompanied by Luz. He was starting to worry again, but he did not let it show. Making sure he could not be heard by the Arab he used the bad Latin from the crypt to tell Luz, "If they ask you anything, just say that we were attacked very far from here, over in that direction." And he pointed to the east. It was important not to lead the Arabs to the moqqadem and his gang.

The djema was gathered, about 30 of them, all the adult males of the tribe. They sat in the grass forming a circle around a majestic old man who presided not so much as chief but because he was the oldest. Perez and

Luz were brought inside the circle and the old Arab started speaking thus:

"This man is a roumi. This is no reason to treat him as an enemy because the prophet told us to be merciful to all humans. We deal with roumis when they buy our halfah and they sell us powder."

"It is so," a few in the audience approved.

"However, we have to examine very carefully the story of this man who is not one of ours neither in faith nor in blood. I ask, therefore, to question him in front of you all and for you to judge his answers."

"Amine!" the Arabs shouted, which is an exact equivalent to *amen* in Latin languages. No doubt the Muslims had borrowed it from the Christians in North Africa.

Perez was questioned by the old man who could throw enough Spanish into his Arabic to be understood. This time he had to answer and in detail. The fugitive pretended to be a colonist from the Tell, traveling with his daughter westward across Morocco to El Araich.

"We were part of a caravan with 12 other people," he said. "We had horses and mehara, camels. Three days walk from this douar in that direction," he pointed to the east, "we were ambushed by bandits. All the others were massacred."

"How is it that only you and your daughter managed to escape?" a suspicious Arab asked.

"It was God's will!" Perez pronounced solemnly.

This short and simple answer had more effect on the gullible minds than any speech he could have made. The gathering was suddenly sympathetic to this roumi who invoked the holy name of Allah. They did not even question the girl.

"My brothers," the old man said, "we have to show respect to the guests that heaven has sent us. Don't you agree?"

"Amine!" the Arabs shouted.

"You can go on your way or spend two days with us," the elder told Perez.

He wanted to leave right away, but he realized that being in too much of a hurry could rouse suspicion and possibly darken their good mood.

"Thank you, my brothers. I accept your hospitality for the rest of the morning but then, if it please Allah, I will get back on the road."

Then the djema dealt with some other affairs. The session was not quite over when a young Arab arrived and sat down. They welcomed him and urged him to speak because he had spent several days around Taxa and was bringing news.

"My brothers," he said, "I'll tell you what my eyes have seen and what my ears have heard."

"As long as you didn't hear or see the moqqadem Ali ben Kadour," Perez wanted to say.

"I found the tribe of Beni-Harglou very disturbed," the young man went on. "A gang of pirates—May Allah curse them!—had attacked them during the night, killing three warriors, kidnapping two women and slaughtering some of their cattle."

"They're probably the same wretches who attacked the roumi our guest," the old man said.

A murmur of approval showed that the djema shared his opinion. Perez understood just enough of the messenger's news. He marveled at the coincidence that backed up his tall tale. At the same time he felt sincerely sorry for the Beni-Harglou whom he had found to be kind and generous.

"Still," the young Arab continued, "they believed they were protected by Allah because they had taken in a santon who performed miracles and was accompanied by an angel."

The ex-convict had to hide his astonishment on learning that Luz had been promoted to the ranks of supernatural creatures by the Beni-Harglou. Less than three weeks had passed since they had left them and their short stay was already becoming the stuff of legend!

XXXIX. The Philistine

After a frugal lunch of couscous balls and figs, washed down with fine, clear water, Perez said farewell to his hosts. He was carrying a bag of boiled fava beans and, what was no less valuable, precise geographical directions.

"If you travel without stopping in that direction," the old man had told him, pointing to the northwest, "you will reach Ouazzane, the holy city, tomorrow. The region is watered by the Sebou that is navigable all the way to the sea. If you keep walking one-day's travel from Ouazzane you will find El Ksar and one more day El Araich."

El Araich, called Larache by Europeans, is the northernmost Moroccan port of any size on the Atlantic shore. There are many Jews and Spaniards there.

Therefore, barely four days separated the fugitive from a European city. After crossing the high northern plains of Morocco from north to south Perez was about to go back up from south to north toward the ocean. His journey, detoured by so many adventures, will have lasted around two months! In two months he had been held prisoner by the Riffians, then by the Riata, explored the unknown cave, made off with Luz, met the Beni-Harglou, lived in the oasis and escaped the vengeance of the moqqadem. He certainly made good use of his time!

Ali ben Kadour's horse did not seem very sensitive to the change of masters. Maybe because the old moqqadem did not ride it very often and then only at an easy trot. As for the other horse, it was no less friendly.

The wound from Luz's arrow had been bandaged by Ben Said and did not seem to bother it.

As the sun was sinking on the horizon, a white line appeared a little to the north of the route taken by the travelers. "Could that be Ouazzane already?" Perez wondered. "No, it's not possible."

All of a sudden he remembered that his hosts had spoken of a rather big market that was held in the area. The idea popped into his head that they might make one little detour to sell a horse—one horse was plenty for them.

He veered off in that direction, spurring on the horse with his voice and feet. They needed to get there before nightfall.

The market was already taking shape: an irregular square formed by tents with chaotic, moving masses here and there, probably animals brought to sell. Heading towards it Perez noticed two men on donkeys advancing slowly before them.

"Look father," Luz said. "That old man…"

The fugitive narrowed his eyes at the one Luz pointed out. He almost fell out of the saddle when he recognized Samuel Azar. What should he do? The old Jew knew something of his real situation and could guess right away that the two horses belonged to the moqqadem's gang. But it was too late to turn back, even if he wanted to. Samuel and his companion were only a short distance away. Above all, during their last encounter the Jew seemed pretty nice. There was no reason for him to change his attitude.

Samuel had just recognized the travelers. "Hello Antonio Mires," he cried out. "I'm glad to see that fortune is smiling on you. The last time we met you were on foot and here you are with two horses."

The ex-convict, whom the Jew called by his borrowed name, could feel the irony in the compliment. Maybe the old man suspected him of stealing the animals. After a brief hesitation he answered.

"I was attacked by robbers. I managed to escape by taking these horses you see. The next night I was given a warm welcome by the douar that's set up back there." And he pointed to the horizon behind them.

The two groups of riders were now together and while Samuel listened, his companion watched on. He turned his donkey around to examine them. This companion had a fat, dark face framed by frizzy hair that squirted out from under a dark blue skullcap. His bright eyes were crowned by two gray, bushy eyebrows; his nose was hooked; his thick lips covered the teeth of a real cannibal. Whereas Samuel was the typical refined Semite, this one's crude face oozed all kinds of brutal, greedy sentiments.

"A fellow Jew," Perez asked.

The two men shook their heads at the same time.

"Hannon Kanaan is a Philistine," the Jew shot back while the other repeated quickly, "Filistino."

Perez saw that a difference in rituals or biblical interpretation must have separated the Jew and the Philistine into two distinct religious sects as hostile as Catholics and Protestants among the Christians. And yet this religious rivalry did not stop them from doing business together.

Hannon spoke a dialect of Hebrew mixed with Arabic. He knew barely half a dozen words in Spanish. Anyway, he was not trying to start up a conversation and was paying much less attention to Perez or Luz than to the horses.

"Ask him if he wants to buy that one with its saddle," he told Samuel, indicating the riderless horse.

The Jew relayed the question to the Philistine who immediately turned cold and barked a few scornful words.

"What did he say?" Perez furrowed his brow.

"He said," Samuel translated, "that it's not his habit to buy merchandise from just anybody when he doesn't know where it came from."

"I told you where it came from. I took these horses from robbers who tried to kill me."

"That's the law among Arabs," Samuel agreed somberly and he gave the response to his companion.

"Also tell him," Perez added, "that if I don't make a deal with him I'll find somebody else."

Hannon just shrugged his shoulders when he heard this. Looking like he did not care he raised three fingers in the air and spit out, "Three metikals."

Perez jumped in the saddle. He knew that three metikals equaled 7f 89, about two dollars. To give away a living horse and its saddle for such a price was too much

"He's crazy!" Perez stared at Samuel. "I'll find another buyer. Goodbye."

The Jew stared back at him. "He told you his price. Tell him yours."

"So be it. 100 metikals."

The difference did not seem to surprise the Philistine who had offered such a ridiculously low price only to prevent the seller from offering a high one.

Suddenly he raised his price, "10 metikals."

"You add seven, so I'll minus the same. 93 metikals. Take it or leave it."

Perez gave this like an ultimatum. But in truth he wanted to sell as badly as Hannon wanted to buy.

The Philistine said, "I will give you 15 metikals and not a cent more."

The fugitive hemmed and hawed. Samuel made a discreet sign to him to accept.

"So be it!" Perez exclaimed.

The money was immediately counted out and he wrapped it in a piece of the burnous that he tied to his belt. Buyer and seller had both won: the first because he got a beautiful animal for a low price and the second because the horse had cost him nothing. Of course 15 metikals was very cheap. Nevertheless, Perez felt more confident, more secure with some money in his pocket. Samuel could see this in the ex-convict's eyes. Despite the mystery surrounding his life, the Jew had taken a liking to the Spaniard.

"Listen," he told him. "Now that you have some money, don't dawdle in this region. The vengeance of the moqqadem can still catch up to you. Keep heading west and whatever you do, don't go into Ouazzane. It's a city full of fanatics. You might not be welcome. If you get to El Araich you can see a friend of mine, Izrail Mouny, the orange seller. Anyone in the mellah, the Jewish quarter, can point him out to you. Maybe he'll give you some work."

"Thanks."

Samuel was already kicking his donkey and waving goodbye. The Philistine was ahead of him, leading the Arab horse that he had just bought.

"He's a pretty good man," Perez reflected as he watched them trotting off. "He could have turned me in but he didn't. Let's go! I believe that, as he said, the best thing for us is to keep moving."

XL. The Headless Corpse

Twilight came. The purplish blue sky after the setting of the sun turned to light gray sparkling dimly with stars and covering the earth like a veil. No sound could be heard. Perez and Luz felt like they were alone in the world.

Leaving the market on their right the fugitive had gotten back on the road to the west. His horse trotted steadily over the flat ground where only a few clumps of high grass grew. In spite of the semi-darkness, it was easy going, so Perez proposed to take a break when they were far enough away from the market and could find a safe place.

Luz was amazed by all the mysteries, from one escape to another, one fight to another. Such things had never crossed her mind. Even if the humans in the crypt were sad and miserable, at least they never waged war.

Her friend understood the thoughts hatching in her young brain but he did not break the awkward silence. On bringing her to the surface he wanted this child, who was born in a dark underworld, to see only the splendors and joys, the intelligence, kindness and fraternity of men, but far from it she was seeing the fanaticism, lies and hatred.

"Father," she suddenly spurted out, "what are those shiny stones the man gave you when he took the horse away?"

She could find no better name for the metikals than "shiny stones". Even though Luz was speaking Spanish pretty well, Perez had a tough time explaining the role of money as a representative value of exchange.

"So," she said, "with lots and lots of these stones you could have everything you want?"

"You could buy a lot of things," he answered, "but there are some things you can't buy."

"Like what?"

"Intelligence, kindness, affection."

Luz paid careful attention to this serious conversation that was maybe not beyond her age but certainly beyond her upbringing. She struggled to understand.

In the meantime Perez was thinking: "What would this poor child say if she knew that for these shiny stones, as she calls them, human beings hate each other, tear each other to pieces and kill."

The horse, left to himself, had slowed down. The moon had just risen and was lighting the lush prairie and the narrow stream wandering through it. Crickets were chirping in the grass. A few orange trees exhaled a perfumed scent from their flowers. In the middle of the scene a big cedar tree spread its leafy branches. It was a pleasant place.

After letting the horse drink from the stream Perez tied it to the trunk of the cedar and lay down next to Luz on the dry moss to get some sleep. The beautiful, serene night really did emanate a sweet poetry that enveloped the soul. Perez was cradled by a reverie that carried him far into the infinite—he was not sleeping or awake. And Luz could not sleep. From time to time she would look up and contemplate the countless stars in the heavens.

All of a sudden she raised her head and touched her friend's arm.

"What is it?" he asked, although his mind was still somewhere else.

At the moment he was in his home country, Spain. Not in contemporary Spain where smokestacks belched and train tracks slithered, but in Spain during the Middle Ages where scholars and poets rubbed shoulders with knights in shining armor. In Cordova, the Arab civilization was casting its brightest rays while Christian warriors, ignorant and stoic, were gathering in the grottos of Asturias (in northwest Spain) to plan the reconquest.

The silent call form Luz snapped him out of his dream.

"What is it?" Perez repeated.

"Animal that scratches."

He listened hard and thought he could, in fact, hear a faint noise. He got up and made sure his pistols were loaded and his sword still sharp. The blade that had been used for so many different purposes without being kept in a sheath must have been forged with exceptional skill not to have lost its edge.

"Not big animal," Luz explained.

Her words were reassuring. At first Perez thought a lion might be in the area, but the king of beasts rarely used its claws to dig in the ground.

"Over there," the child pointed to a dark spot, obviously a row of bushes.

She stood up, ready to go with her friend, but he hesitated. Should he expose the child to a possible danger? But then again should he leave her alone? He made up his mind: "Let's go!"

They held their breath and stepped forward. 50 yards in front of them a thicket grew. Suddenly, from behind the leafy wall, laughter broke out. But really sinister laughter, like a lunatic, which sent shivers up Perez's spine and made Luz jump back.

The fugitive stood frozen, unsure what to do. At once, the laughing creature appeared. It was not a human being.

"A hyena!" he breathed a sigh of relief.

It was, indeed, a small hyena that got frightened by the intruders, ready to run away and come back later when they had left.

"Is there a carcass around here?" the idea popped into Perez's mind. He knew how these animals acted. They were not bold enough to attack living creatures so they fed on dead bodies that they often dug up.

The hyena slunk away a short distance but kept up its gloomy giggling. Perez, with Luz right behind him, went to where the animal had just come out. He stopped and shuddered. A human arm was sticking out of the ground!

The carnivorous beast had started digging up a corpse. The fugitive controlled his nerves and with the tip of the sword scraped away the dirt. He stood petrified with horror. It was a woman's body, expensively dressed and without a head!

What tragedy of barbarous life had taken place in this corner of earth? Greed had certainly not been the motive for the crime because the murderer had not touched the victim's clothes: a silk blouse and a skirt of the same material, both decorated with gold sequins; silver jewelry wound around her wrists and ankles; her stiff fingers wore heavy big rings.

Perez thought of the horrible anger of Arab husbands whose bitter jealousy made them judge and executioner of their wives, cutting off their heads on a mere suspicion and burying their remains in some hole like an animal. The poor woman before his eyes had probably had the misfortune of displeasing her lord and master!

What confirmed his conjecture was the fact that the corpse was of a young woman with a shapely body. Her murderer must have had lots of money and not cared about it since he left her with all the expensive jewelry. In his rage he had also not bothered to remove the clothes she was wearing.

Perez stood there thinking for a minute.

Philosophically he respected life and held no superstitions about death, which he saw as a simple transformation of universal matter. He was outraged at how much money was so often wasted on hypocritical garishness to decorate tombs when so many living beings lacked the basics of life.

Certainly, in ordinary circumstances it would never have occurred to him to steal from a grave, especially since he put no value on stupid wealth. But this was no ordinary circumstance. After sacrificing his own fortune to enlighten his fellow man, he had been thrown into the hell of the penal colony, an innocent man. And now he was a fugitive, wandering in the middle of a savage country, with no friends or family, with no support, meaning with no money (less than 40 francs!) and with a child to save and educate.

Wouldn't it be foolish to leave these unexpected riches to the wild animals or to the pirates of the desert?

Perez made up his mind: he took off the rings, bracelets, gold sequins, all the expensive jewelry that was ridiculous on a dead woman and he put them in the piece of burnous with the metikals. "Poor woman," he sighed. "Her death is going to keep us alive."

And he thought of that great law of mysterious nature that in the infinite cycle of transformations crushes one life to assure the lives of others.

But he was soon shaken out of these melancholy thoughts and came back to present reality. They had to give the remains of this poor woman a more decent burial. With the help of his sword and of Luz he dug a narrow grave about four feet deep in which he placed the decapitated corpse. Then he covered it with dirt and packed it down. It took him two hours.

"Now, let's go," he said.

But they had not gone 50 feet when the infernal laughter broke out again. The grave-robbing hyena was back. Perez let out a frustrated sigh and went back. He took one of his pistols and stepped in front of the carnivore. The animal stopped short. Unafraid of the man and unsure of his intentions because he had not chased him earlier, the hyena let him come close. A shot rang out and the hyena fell, hit in the chest, bleeding a river of blood and letting out one last, eerie laugh that turned into a death rattle.

Perez and Luz went back to where they had tied up their horse. They lay down nearby to finish their sleep but the macabre scene they had just lived through kept them awake. Perez lay there thinking while he heard Luz mumble with her eyes half-closed, "Here men are mean."

XLI. Lost!

At the first light of dawn Perez got up. He was eager to get away from the tragic site where the calm beauty of nature had been sullied and bloodied by ferocious humanity. If he had not wanted to let the child rest and also the horse that was carrying them, he would have set off again right away. But it was Luz who forced his hand.

Her first words on waking up were, "Father, let's go far, far away."

They got back on the road without touching their dates or boiled fava beans. The vision of the headless corpse was haunting them. They could not eat. Perez even made a detour so they would not see the sad site.

Some small woods stood just over half a mile to their right so it was this direction they took. It would be better to ride under cover. Not only to enjoy the fresh morning but also because despite the hospitality they received twice, the inhabitants of this region full of fierce moqqadems and homicidal husbands did not inspire them with trust or security. It would be better to avoid them as much as possible until the coast where the European influence could be felt and it would be easier to get along with people.

It was absolutely necessary to avoid the dangerous zone of Ouazzane, the holy city that might be teeming with Ali ben Kadours.

"Father, look," Luz cried out.

They were at the edge of the woods and the child was pointing to something like a huge fruit hanging from the end of a branch.

"Ach," Perez recoiled in disgust.

The fruit was a human head!

Overcoming the mixture of disgust and anger that was washing over him, he went up to the tree and looked at the head that was hanging ten feet off the ground by its long, black hair. It was a young woman, obviously the one whose body they had found the night before. Even though its eyes were closed and its mouth open and twisted into a sinister grin, he could see that the victim was young and had been beautiful. Gold earrings hung from her ears.

Perez was petrified with horror for a moment. Then he was suddenly seized with rage. "This hideous trophy won't stay here," he shouted.

He raised himself up in the saddle and with a swipe if his sword he cut the hair. The head dropped straight down to the ground. At the same time Perez jumped off the horse and picked it up. Looking at it more closely he recoiled in horror again: the head had been salted!

This was one of the barbarous customs in Morocco. It was not rare that in the markets and inland cities, hanging from posts or the tops of walls you could see the heads of criminals or vanquished enemies, most often rebels, that is Arabs who refused to pay the tribute to the sultan. They were preserved by putting on a thick layer of salt and exposed to the public to make an example of them.

Perez dug a hole deep enough to bury the grisly remains. He had not yet finished filling it in when a shriek made him turn pale and almost fall over.

The horse was no longer being held by his strong hand and took the opportunity to bolt. It was running off with Luz still on its back.

"Father! Father!" the child cried, clutching desperately to the saddle with one hand and to the horse's mane with the other. They were already far away and the girl's cries were getting lost in the distance.

Perez stood there dumbfounded. His daze lasted only two seconds before he started running full speed to catch them. But as fast as he could run, he was no match for the horse. Soon it had disappeared in the trees because it had headed deep into the woods, figuring perhaps—who knows how animals think?—that in the thick of the woods it could lose the man, its master and tyrant.

Perez could not think straight. As long as the horse was in sight, he ran, jumped, flew with supernatural strength. When the animal disappeared, with Luz on top, he caved in. Where should he go? Every step now could be taking him farther away from the horse. Maybe it had kept going in a straight line. Or maybe it turned one way or another to throw him off its course.

The poor man was beaten. The vanished child, whom he had snatched from the abyss, protected, started to educate, had become his whole life. Now that she was gone he felt devastated.

How could he have lost sight of her for even a second, left her on a loose horse? He alone was responsible for everything that happened.

What now would become of this eight-year old girl, alone, without resources of any kind, lost in the desert, unable to communicate even if she happened to meet some Arabs?

Like a madman Perez bounded through the bushes, swerved around the trees, ran in circles calling out her name and firing his pistols in the air.

Nothing answered him. After three hours of random searching, worn out and bleeding from the thorns, his mind a blank, his heart racing, he tripped over some roots, fell to the ground and passed out.

.

XLII. The Horse and the Panther

Perez's fainting spell apparently lasted for a long time because when he came to the sun was just starting to set. Birds were singing in the forest; purple-flowered trees stood tall with leafy crowns; a few palms spread their emerald fans a few feet away from cedars and pines; tall bushes grew in these luscious jumbles of greenery; and above the dome of leaves stretched the infinite dome of the sky.

Nature in its tranquil beauty seemed to be insulting the fugitive's grief.

What to do? What decision should he make? All the obstacles, all the dangers, as grave as they were—he would face anything to find Luz. But where was she hiding?

One second of neglect was all it took to separate them… probably forever.

He could see her in his mind's eye, exhausted, falling off the horse, cracking her head open on the ground, or wandering around, dying of hunger, thirst and fear, calling out to him for help. He saw her torn apart by wild beasts, hyenas, panthers or lions. Maybe she was captured like an animal by men and being kept as a slave!

From now on his life had no purpose. Death was meaningless to him. What was the point of fighting?

The glorious energy that had filled him when he was confronting visible dangers had vanished now. Tears ran down his cheeks.

He stood up, however, and without a clue where he was going he started walking again, searching, calling out, but not expecting to find her. Then all of a sudden a wild scream startled him. It sounded like the cry of an angry cat ending in the roar of a lion.

"A wild animal! Damn, what if she's about to be eaten!"

This terrible thought crossed his mind but at the same time boosted his spirits. With a pistol in one hand and the sword in the other, he ran toward the frightening scream. He also screamed out to draw the attention of the wild beast.

50 feet away he saw it and his blood froze. It was a panther. A huge panther that he was leaping after its prey. Suddenly in a clearing he saw the horse running away. He cried out, Luz!" but it was already out of ear-shot. After so desperately wanting to see her again the fugitive had only one desire now: that she get as far away as possible from the wild cat.

The panther was still chasing the horse but despite its mighty leaps and bounds it was losing ground. Unless some accident occurred it looked like the prey was going to escape. But in the mad race for freedom, wouldn't Luz fall off? How long could the frail child hang onto the horse? Who knows, maybe she had already fallen off. In this case she was doomed!

The three creatures chased after one another for a long time. The horse was out of sight and the panther was just a dot jumping around in the distance. Soon it, too, disappeared. Perez kept running. He did not feel tired or out of breathe. A supernatural force possessed him. He was ready to fight all the panthers and lions in the world.

Then a desperate whinnying followed by an angry roar echoed through his ears. "Too late!" he yelled, going crazy with grief and frustration. "But at least I'll have my revenge!"

200 yards in front of him he saw the awful scene. In its flight the horse had caught its bridle on a tree branch and all its desperate efforts could not shake it free. The panther had already stopped but now it pounced and a horrible fight ensued between the two animals. It would have ended quickly in the victory of the wild cat if it had not been so eager and jumped just in time to get kicked in the face by a hoof that sent it rolling ten feet away. The panther lay there, stunned, for a few minutes. But the skull of big cats are thick and this one got back on its legs.

After being knocked down by the powerful kick the panther kept a respectable distance between it and the horse, growling furiously like ten angry cats.

Perez was still too far away to hit his target but he shot his pistol anyway, hoping to draw the panther's attention and anger away from the horse. But either its brain was still ringing from the kick and it did not hear or its anger was too focused on the horse—it paid no attention to the newcomer. Slowly, carefully, it crawled toward the enemy who felt another attack coming on and tried furiously to shake its bridle free. All of a sudden the panther leapt and landed on the horse's hind legs, which immediately turned purple.

The attacker had roared in triumph but it turned into a cry of pain. Only 15 feet away Perez had unloaded his second pistol into the animal's flank. The panther fell to the ground. If it had not already been bucked hard by the horse it would probably have mounted a desperate defense. But Perez did not give it time. Sword in hand he ran up and stabbed it in the heart.

He had won. But where was Luz?

She was not anywhere near the horse whose leg was bleeding badly. Perez went wild, calling out her name with a shaky voice but got no answer. He searched the nearby forest but found nothing. There was no trace of the child.

Was it possible that the panther had already eaten her before attacking the horse? No, the cat was obviously hungry when it went off on its wild chase. If it had found Luz and eaten her, it would have given up on the horse.

Anyway, it was easy enough to check. Perez split open the still warm cadaver and the guts spilled out. With a trembling hand he sliced the stomach, expecting to see the formless pulp of the remains of the poor child. And in the midst of his despair, he felt unspeakable relief when he saw that the stomach was completely empty. Obviously the panther had been fasting for days.

All of a sudden another thought made him jump: Luz was very intelligent. If she was still alive she was searching for him. He had to make a signal that she could see from afar: fire!

In no time he had two piles of branches and leaves. Dead branches for the flames and dried leaves for smoke. One or the other would guide the child. Then with his flint and sword he lit the fire. Twin columns of flame rose up, reddening the air with blazing light, mixed with thick smoke that swirled blackly into the heavens.

At the same time Perez loaded and shot his pistols again and again. But wouldn't Luz think there was some dangerous battle going on and run off instead coming closer? No, she was smart and brave. She knew what her friend would do to signal to her. Plus, she could sneak up before deciding to either show herself or run away.

He knew her well. He especially knew the deep, daughterly affection she had for him. He knew that at this moment if she was not dead she was crying and had only one thought: to find him.

Hours passed. After a short-lived hope Perez was feeling anxious and heartbroken again. Then all of a sudden he heard a shout.

"Father, here I am!"

And Luz came through the trees, out of breathe, her clothes torn, running straight into his arms.

XLIII. The Oued Ouargha

It would be impossible to describe the emotion, the happiness of both Perez and Luz when they were back together after thinking they were separated forever. The fugitive could not stop hugging the child. He had feared that she had suffered a horrible death and here she was, saved again.

"Are you hurt?" he asked, examining the cuts and scratches from the thorny plants.

"No, nothing," Luz answered.

"Poor child. Or poor me for having lost you. So, you fell off the horse?"

The little girl was so shaken up with emotion that she found it hard to talk. Perez knew, however, on seeing that the horse kept running instead of slowing down, that she had bravely slipped off it. Then he understood that she had tried to go back but quickly got lost in the woods. She sat down and cried, calling out his name. When she finally saw the smoke and flames she ran toward them, spurred on by the absolute certainty of finding her protector.

Happy now Perez smiled at her confidence. In the midst of the worst dangers she believed in him with absolute faith.

"Horse very mean," Luz said.

Her comment reminded the ex-convict of the poor animal whose mischief was the cause of this all. The panther's claws had cruelly atoned for its fault, if it really is a fault for a four-legged or two-legged animal to try to regain its lost freedom!

The horse was lying in a pool of blood, whining mournfully now and again. Perez examined the wounds. They looked more painful than serious.

"You deserve to be left to your fate," Perez told it, "but we still need you."

With some leaves he chewed up he made a kind of plaster that he put on the wounds. Then he cut up the panther's corpse and picked up the best pieces. The meat of big carnivores is nothing like a herbivore's but it is still edible. This was the important thing.

It was dangerous to camp in a place haunted by panthers but they could not leave the horse behind and it was not ready for them to ride them. Perez decided to get the animal on its legs, which it obeyed readily, and lead it by the bridle. They had not gone far, barely 50 feet, when they came in sight of water.

The sight perked up the horse. It neighed happily. Perez let it trot over and it dove in up to its chest. After this he tied it to a tree on the bank.

It was crucial to get their bearings because the race through the woods had thrown them off course. The sun, of course, could serve as a reference point but it was dying in the west. The wide band of silvery water that glimmered in the fires of the setting sun, was it a lake or a river? If the latter it might be the Sebou and they only had to follow it.

There was almost an hour left before nightfall. He could use the time for a quick reconnaissance. With his little friend whom he did not want to lose sight of again, Perez walked along the water's edge. At times, as they progressed, some big bird, mostly ducks would soar up out of the reeds and plants. Leafy bushes ran along the other bank, around 100 yards across the river, but very few trees. In fact, the woods ended here.

"Man sings," Luz stopped suddenly.

Perez stopped too, listening. The breeze carried faint echoes to him: a vague, droning chant. A song in this solitude, under tall trees or on the calm surface of the water, implied a nature inclined to pleasure or poetry rather than violence and ferocity.

"Come on," Perez walked toward the voice. He was hoping that the singer, a woodcutter or fisherman, could give him directions.

The song continued, becoming clearer. All of a sudden, behind a clump of plants the travelers saw a half-naked man, very tan, with his head shaved bald. He was sitting in a still boat, chanting his sweet, droning song, watching his nets.

"Salam!" Perez cried out.

The man sat up, surprised to see travelers. "Salam," he responded, adding a few words that the fugitive did not understand.

It was weird to talk at a distance. On a sign from Perez the fisherman took his long pole and pushed his boat to the travelers. He was very surprised to see that they were roumis, but he figured out pretty easily what Perez wanted to know and he gave them information: the river he was fishing in was a branch of the Ouargha, which was a tributary of the Sebou.

Perez got an idea: what if the fisherman could take them? The trip would be a lot easier. He had on him, not counting the jewels, enough money to pay for him and Luz. Sure, but what would they do with the horse? There was not enough space for it on the long, narrow boat that was as flat as a raft and would capsize with too much weight.

On the off chance the traveler asked the Arab.

"It's easy," he answered. "You and the *muchacha* get on my boat. The river is wide but not too deep and the current is weak. We'll tie the horse to the boat and I'll take you to the Sebou."

"Perfect," Perez was excited.

The deal was made, costing three metikals, but the boatman refused to go any farther than the Sebou.

"It's not my country," he declared.

The departure was set for the middle of the night. The moon was full and bright over the river and Abu Zeb (as the Arab was called) knew all the nooks and crannies.

Perez and Luz went back, lit a fire and roasted some panther meat because food was not included in the deal. Meanwhile the fisherman gathered up his nets that had captured a few loaches and eels. He was a happy, self-sufficient fisherman, this Abu Zeb. The Ouargha and its tributaries were "his country" because he spent his whole life, so to speak, on these waters, but the Sebou was a foreign country to him, which he had no interest in exploring.

It was almost midnight when Perez and Luz climbed on the boat after tying the horse to the bow. As soon as they stepped on the Arab pushed off hard and they were on their way. Far from putting up a fight the horse followed along, sunk up to its withers, its neck sticking out of the water. It lost footing and had to swim. Luz slept, her head against her friend's chest, silently, dreaming of the past and the future while the boatman stood in front, always chanting.

An artist would have loved to paint this scene lit by the soft light of the night star.

Just then a furious stampede and threatening shouts came echoing through the woods like the pandemonium of death.

"No mercy for the roumi, the filthy dog, the body snatcher and thief."

It was the murderous husband. When he did not see the severed head of his wife, he announced the "offense" to the anger of his fellow believers. Since rumors were already spreading about the arrival of a roumi accompanied by a little girl, it was obvious that he was the offender. As for the girl, maybe she was a demon! An angel for the Beni-Harglou, Luz was now turning into a creature of darkness. Superstition fits all sizes!

Fortunately Perez had met the boatman and every thrust of the pole pushed the boat farther away from the furious mob.

XLIV. A Good Renegade

The journey continued more peacefully for the rest of the day with a few stops to give a little rest to the horse. Luckily it did not complain about the long bath. Its wounds were healing. Two or three times Perez untied it and let it run along the riverbank while Abu Zeb threw his nets in the water.

This life of fresh air and adventures was doing wonders for both the body and mind of Luz. She was no longer the frail child of the crypt, descendant of a race grown sluggish from its underground seclusion.

The travelers were sailing now on the main branch of the Ouargha. The river flowed between twin rows of palm trees behind which they caught sight of shacks. Sometimes big wading birds with pink wings, flamingoes or ibises, disturbed by the boat, soared off into the heavenly blue.

Later in the evening Abu Zeb tied his skiff to a tree on the bank near a ramshackle hut abandoned by its owner. Perez and Luz spent the night here after lighting a fire to scare away wild animals.

At dawn they were back on the river. As the Oargha got wider they could hear the sound of other waters.

"The Sebou," the boatman declared.

They had come to the end of their voyage and he got his three metikals. But he did not want to leave his passengers with nothing, so he gave them some advice, "Ride along the Oued for half a day. You'll see a big market. There you can get rid of your horse and rent a boat that will take you to Mehdia."

Mehdia is at the mouth of the Sebou. Just being on the ocean made it an important city. Perez wanted to go directly to El Araich.

"Too many marshes," the boatman told him. "First go to Mehdia. From there you can go back up in that direction." He pointed north.

The two travelers were already in the saddle. Perez waved goodbye and let the horse lead the way since it was so happy to be back in its native element.

"May merciful Allah protect you!" Abu Zeb cried out. He pushed off with his pole and floated over the calm surface of the Ouargha.

The countryside around the Oued Sebou was charming and green. Date palms were hanging their clusters of yellow fruit; at times, through the depths of foliage, appeared vast fields of wheat; the air carried the voices of cows and sheep. They were in a land civilized by farming and ranching.

Shacks or shepherd huts showed up now and again, then there was a town, a real town of settled farmers. No more tents but houses built of clay, whitewashed and with thick walls cut with narrow openings like arrowslits in a castle.

A group of veiled women filed down to the river to fill the big jars they carried on their heads. On seeing Perez galloping by, they scattered like a flock of frightened birds.

A little farther on they came to the market. A huge crowd of white roofs over piles of various objects: oranges, pomegranates, watermelons, dates, vegetables, leather, colorful swathes of cotton and silk, blocks of salt, packs of cane sugar, bundles of incense. Animals were kept in nearby enclosures: horses, donkeys, lambs and sheep joined their concert of neighing, braying and bleating to the deafening cries of the merchants while flocks of geese, ducks and chickens screeched and shrieked at full volume. And filling out the chaotic mess was a mob of buyers in white burnous or dark robes.

Luz was stunned, literally speechless. This was the first time that she had seen life buzzing so actively. Perez was deeply moved: he had been a pariah or alone for such a long time. On leaving the penal colony he had only one fervent desire: to be alone and free. And now his old blood was flowing. He realized that man is made to live in society.

A little old man wearing a yellow coat and a gold skullcap, selling trinkets and cloth, caught his attention. Perez went to him and spoke his bad Arabic mixed with Spanish. But he had barely uttered two words before the man interrupted him and pronounced in pure Castilian, "Who are you, mister? Spanish, I see... merchant or explorer?"

Perez spontaneously shot out his hand. He was unbelievably excited to meet someone he could talk to in his native tongue.

"Spanish, yes. I've traveled far with this child and we're trying to reach the coast. Mehdia or El Araich. Could you sell my horse and rent us a boat to go down the Sebou?"

"You got papers?" the merchant asked.

These words rained down on Perez like a cold shower. "No," he answered, "I didn't know that the inland areas were so demanding."

The old man started to laugh, "You're roumis and therefore suspicious. Who knows if the horse you're riding and want to sell wasn't stolen from a believer? Excuse me for this speculation, which shouldn't offend you. I'm Spanish myself."

"You! I should've guessed by your accent that you were from Madrid."

"I was, indeed, born on Calle de Hortaleza. But since my interests have drawn me to this country, to Rabat where I come from to sell in the inland markets, I became Muslim. You see that I'm a true believer. Still, I'll try to help you out."

This lucky encounter pulled Perez out of a sticky situation. A few minutes later the old man introduced him to the moklasseb or chief of the market and the honest man bought his horse for 15 metikals.

Bou Naher, as the old merchant was called in Arabic, had some influence. Thanks to him Perez found a boatman who was willing to take them to Medhia for 8 metikals. Two more metikals were spent on food and a big bag to hold it.

The merchant went with Perez all the way to the Sebou and when the traveler was about to step on the boat he handed him a little package wrapped in paper.

"Take this," he told Perez. "You remind me of my homeland. I pray you see it again. Goodbye."

They went their separate ways, Bou Naher back to the market while the boat cast off with its passengers.

XLV. The "Heraldo of Madrid"

For a long time Perez watched the shore he was sailing away from. Little by little the white stars of the market faded away, replaced by tall bushes between cultivated fields. Soon there was nothing but marshes.

The boatman had set up a mast and unfurled a sail that billowed in the breeze. Luz admired the strong wind that could carry a boat and three passengers over the water.

The fugitive decided to examine the gift from Bou Naher. He unfolded the paper and found two objects that made him gasp with joy: a knife and a small mirror. Both were of little monetary value but extremely useful.

But something even more important made him forget about these objects. The objects were wrapped in paper and this paper was not blank. It was covered with printed words. Perez instinctively glanced over it and was hypnotized. He had just read the following:

"Desde Ceuta se informa que el presidario Perez y Rosal…" *From Ceuta we are informed that the convict Perez y Rosal…*

The fugitive was shocked. So violently shocked that he dropped the paper. And just then a gust of wind carried it away over the river. Perez shouted. He thought that he was dead to the world, that he did not care about a society that had so cruelly convicted him. And now he needed to know what the newspaper said about him. Because he was sure that it was a piece of a newspaper that he had seen. His eyes and fingers both recognized the Heraldo de Madrid.

All the way to Mehdia, which they reached two days later, Perez was pensive. Was it his escape that the authorities of Ceuta were reporting? Were they or did they think they were on his trail?

Mehdia is not a very big town. However, there are a few Jewish and Spanish merchants living there, lost among the Moors and Arabs. Perez went to an inn that did not look too shabby. It was located at the entrance to the European quarter. The sign Fonda del Universo, the Universe Inn, revealed that the owner was Spanish. The fugitive's first priority was to get the name of a Jewish merchant where he could cash in some gold sequins for hard currency. The money-changer gave him an honest rate of 75%.

With this indispensable aid Perez bought European clothes for himself and Luz and a suitcase to keep the jewels in. Then he reserved two seats on a coaster leaving the next day for El Araich.

Now he was not scared of meeting anyone. Who would recognize the ex-convict in these proper clothes? His black beard and the silver hair around his temples had grown for two months and completely transformed him. A barber's shears trimmed this hairy tangle, making the ex-convict look like any other European traveling on business.

As for Luz, her European clothes bothered her a little, but she got used to them. However, she sensed that it was not over yet. Her intuition told her that her friend, who did not talk much with the other men, was hiding some secret thought. She, in turn, became more serious and said almost nothing.

Besides, there was one sight that consumed her. A monotonous sight but incomparably majestic: the sight of the sea. Faced with this blue vastness, which she had never dreamed could exist, which mingled with the blue vastness of the sky, the child of the crypt got lost in thought.

The next day Perez and Luz embarked on the coaster *Abdallah* that would sail all day long in sight of land. The Moroccan coast rolled by with its marshes through which the Sebou flowed. After the paludal plants came a drier land of olive groves. In the distance, reaching the blue mountainsides stretched yellow fields of wheat.

Luz marveled at the countryside but Perez remained thoughtful and quiet. The memory of the piece of newspaper swept away by the fickle wind was haunting him. What were they saying about him? Should he be scared or excited?

In a hole like Mehdia there was no hope of finding a newspaper but he swore that once in El Araich he would scour the European quarter and buy everything he could to catch up on two months of news.

Before that, however, he had to deal with customs. Perez had little respect for the Spanish administration and he learned that the Moroccan administration is even worse concerning both its intelligence and honesty. The hands of the chief customs officer reached out irresistibly for the jewels sparking in the suitcase. But Perez knew how to defend his treasure against greedy authorities and after threatening to go straight to the Spanish Consul, he settled on paying a series of exorbitant duties.

Once free to get off the ship and protect his suitcase from the hands of porters, almost as greedy as the customs officers, Perez got taken by a guide to the edge of the *mellah*. A very mixed crowd was roaming up and down a long, narrow street. The guide pointed out a house whose ground floor was a big shop. Behind its windows mountains of oranges glowed red.

"Is that the house of Izrael Mouny?" the Spaniard asked.

The Arab nodded with the scornful sneer of all true believers when it comes to Jews.

"In that case, thank you. That's where I have business."

Perez paid his guide and followed by Luz he walked up to the merchant's house. He was a little old man in a long black robe, advancing toward the strangers with eager politeness.

"What can I do for you, sir?" he asked in good Spanish.

The fugitive right away brought up the name Samuel Azar, not to ask for work since his luck had changed and he came into possession of the headless corpse's jewels, but rather to offer to sell the jewels.

The name of his fellow Jew from Fez brought a smile to the face of the orange merchant. The details that Perez recounted of the two meetings with Samuel convinced him that this stranger was not an impostor. Nevertheless, it was mostly the prospect of a lucrative deal that made him friendly.

Perez had opened the suitcase and was pulling out a stream of gold: sequins, bracelets and rings.

The merchant stood stone-faced for a minute and finally said, "Listen, I don't have the means to buy all these beauties for what they're worth. But they'll be hard for you sell anyway. They'll ask you where they came from and maybe the police will give you a hard time. Personally I don't care about your adventures or your life... I'll offer 1,500 duros."

"2,000," Perez replied firmly.

"So be it!"

Izrael got a great deal. He counted out 2,000 duros on the spot and took the jewels.

"I made a sacrifice for the sake of my friend Samuel," he sighed. "If I can do anything for you…" The sale was over, the merchant was gone and the friendly man was back.

"Listen," the fugitive said, "I need two months of the Heraldo de Madrid."

"Here in El Araich?" Izrael looked astonished.

"I'll pay for them if I have to."

The merchant giggled. "That's a bold statement you should never make. But I won't take you on your word. Come back in three days and you'll get what you want."

Perez shook the Jew's hand excitedly and went to get a room at a cosmopolitan hotel that looked decent enough, run by a German and called The Star of Morocco.

Under the name of Antonio Mires he rented a comfortable room for him and Luz.

He hardly lived during the next three days. Once so calm he now felt agitated, wavering between fear and hope.

On the third day he ran to Izrael. "Well?" he asked.

"Here they are," the merchant answered, showing him a stack of newspapers arranged by date.

Perez rushed over to the mountain of papers but had no patience to wait for them to be brought back to his room—he started going through them right away, feverishly, paying no attention to the merchant. All of a sudden he yelled. He had just read the following:

"From Ceuta we are informed that the convict Perez y Rosal has died in the water while trying to escape. His body has not yet been found. The death is all the more tragic because the innocence of this man, formerly convicted during the troubles in Alcala del Valle, has just been fully acknowledged. His Excellency the Minister of Justice was about to issue the pardon when the sad news arrived."

Perez stood there in a daze, unable to say a word. So, now he was both innocent and dead!

The merchant worked up the courage to ask him why he was troubled. The ex-convict, who had nothing more to fear, told him the whole story. He felt this need that the strongest of men feel sometimes to have someone understand them, someone to pour out their thoughts to.

"It's fantastic!" the Jew exclaimed, congratulating him and shaking hands. "But do you want my advice? Well, leave it alone. Don't go bragging about your adventures and especially don't start making demands. They gave you justice because they thought you were dead, that's normal. But watch out if you show your face. Who knows what hatred and resentment might rear up again…"

It was sage advice. Old Izrael knew about men and other things.

\#

Perez set himself up in Morocco. The political events, the French landing at Casablanca, the fight between the two rival sultans Abdulaziz and Abdelhafid came and went without bothering him.

With the money he got from Izrael he settled in an area near the coast that was inhabited only by a few peaceful shepherds. He lived and split his time between farm work and raising Luz.

Luz became a pretty, cultivated girl who kept nothing of the little savage from the crypt except her generous nature. She loved her adopted father who would bring her to Europe someday to complete her education.

In the meantime, there is another journey the ex-convict is thinking of. The story of his adventures were received skeptically by most of the official scholars, but he had managed to earn the respect and trust of a few intelligent men who knew that "the truth may sometimes seem improbable." And it was with their support that he planned a well organized expedition into the deserts of the central plains to find the entrance to the mysterious crypt and bring back up to the surface the strange beings still living down there.

MEMOIRS OF A GORILLA

CHAPTER ONE

I am a gorilla, born in the heart of the great forests of central Africa, of parents who will leave no trace in history. I should say, however, that I'm not at all ashamed of this humble birth because I've always been a democrat and know that an individual is judged solely on his own grounds. So I can say—if a primate whom men look upon as an inferior race is allowed to brag—that although I'm the offspring of my parents, I'm also the offspring of my actions.

Who knows who the ancestors were, millions of years ago, of these gentlemen who are so proud of themselves? I've heard and I've read—because when I was staying with humans I learned to read and write pretty well (at least I never put more than two "U"s in stomach)—that the kings and lords of old used to gloat over their ignorance and there was even a time, so long ago that scholars have only found traces of it, when men wandered through the forests without clothes or weapons or tools of any kind and were not much different from us. It seems they call this period prehistoric. I'm glad to teach you about it, girls and boys. Maybe in exchange you'll give me the respect I think I deserve.

Well, it's really too bad that I couldn't learn to speak the language of humans like I learned to read and write! Oh, to have a world of ideas in your head and not be able to express them! I think I could've put up a good fight against those orators I heard and who owe their reputation to nothing but their booming voices and dramatic gestures.

But I'm digressing into matters that have nothing to do with my subject—my life story that I want to tell you like all the other true or false great men who wrote their own.

As I told you at the start, I was born in Africa, in a dense, green forest through which ran the big, fast-flowing Congo River. Several gorilla families lived in this region where coconut, banana and date trees provide lots of food. We lived as vegetarians and were none the worse for wear. Even though there were a few more sophisticated types who chewed the big tobacco leaves. This indulgence was always shocking, I remember, to my delicate youth, but now I've seen men do the same thing.

As a child I went with my parents on their walks, their visits to friends and their outings in search of food when we ran out. Apparently I was exceptionally bright and imaginative for my age and the old females, my mother's friends, couldn't stop talking about it. See, it's a big mistake to think that we don't have a language—it's only that humans aren't able to understand it yet.

The Bateke natives, long before I was born, had once tried to hunt us for no reason at all. But the gorilla race is the bravest in the world and who knows if its courage isn't destined for great things someday[12]. Not only did our ancestors fend off the unjust attacks of the Batekes, but their chief was clubbed to death and his three widows carried away by the victors. Later, on reading through histories, I saw that the Roman people had done the same thing when they took the women and girls of their neighbors, the Sabines, except that with all due respect we didn't trick them by inviting them to a feast like the Romans did only to steal what was most precious to them. Ah, humans!

I was barely a few months old when one day while I was sleeping next to my mother I was woken up by a sound like thunder. A howl of pain answered this noise and I saw my father fall out of the tree where we had lived for a long time. He had a bloody hole in his chest. His last words to my mother were, "Save yourself and the child!"

Many years have passed since this awful moment but my eyes still fill with tears when I think of my poor father dying and my mother frantically clutching me to her chest.

At the foot of our tree was a group of men, men like I'd never seen before: white skin, covered in weird fabrics, with straw baskets on their heads, which I later learned to call hats, and holding what I first thought were strangely carved sticks but I now know were rifles. The stick of the man walking in front was still smoking: this was the weapon that had killed my father.

My mother was unsure whether she should avenge her mate who lay lifeless on the ground at the attackers' feet or run for safety. But she didn't hesitate long.

---

[12] It must be said that the gorilla race is not the only one to have such flattering opinions of itself.

They'd seen her and a barrage of gunfire brought her down, as dead as my father.

Falling with her to the ground because she didn't let go of me, I was captured by the merciless victors. By some miracle I wasn't hit by a single bullet. What were they going to do with me?

I closed my eyes, scared, waiting for death because one of the murderers had just said, "Got to kill this one too. These apes are so vicious!"

How true it is to say that before you see the mote in someone's eye, you should take the beam out of your own. Over the course of many, busy years, I can boast a little that I've met all kinds of supposedly fierce animals, both in books and in real life: lions, tigers, hyenas, vipers, mosquitos, fleas, but I've never found any of them to be as cruel as man, who kills for no reason, for the simple pleasure of destruction. But this didn't keep my parents' murderers from cursing and slandering us.

Unable to defend myself, I almost stretched my neck out for the knife that one of the hunters was holding, when the one who seemed to be the chief, an older man, brown-haired and stocky, stopped his partner's hand.

"This animal," he was talking about me, "is very young. We might be able to domesticate him. My daughter's always wanted a monkey. This one could do the trick."

So, they just tied up my arms and legs and one of the men carried me in his arms. Such was the tragic incident that snatched me from a life of freedom in the great forests and brought me into the society of men.

CHAPTER TWO

Mr. Heindrick Piffenfluth, as my master was called, was a Dutch colonist, an old hardliner, one of the honorable industrialists like so many others in the new countries—and in the old, too—who say that nothing is more honorable than having money and so you should get it any way you can.

Set up on a beautiful grant of land that the great African river washes with its seasonal waters, he became in turn farmer, merchant, hotel owner, slave trader and moneylender. All around his estate, half farm and half hotel, were fertile fields growing strong, busy with the constant coming and going of white and black workers. But even though Heindrick Piffenfluth dealt in corn, sugar cane and tobacco, he dealt much more in trafficking slaves.

This might surprise you if you've heard that slavery had been abolished thanks to the work of civilized countries. Unfortunately there are still vast territories in Africa that are little known outside their borders where Europeans venture to sell cheap alcohol at exorbitant prices along with rusty old guns. In these territories they still trade human flesh with no repercussions.

When Heindrick Piffenfluth landed on the West African coast with nothing but a case of rum, he started by doubling his quantity of this liquor by adding a little water and pepper. This clever combination brought an untimely end to the Bateke chief Boula Gifla, dead in a fit alcoholic fury that is scientifically called delirium tremens. But it did profit the clever merchant who had nothing stopping him from pursuing his lucrative operations.

The first days after my arrival at the Piffenfluth house passed by in a kind of lazy trance mixed with blurry surprises. The image of my murdered parents kept haunting my mind and I felt alone, truly alone, among the enemies of my race, the murderers of my family. Little by little, however, the sight of all the new things helped to shake me out of my sorrowful lethargy and I ended up paying close attention to everything around me.

The daughter of the colonist, Miss Irma Piffenfluth was a tall, brown-haired girl, 10 to 12 years old, precocious and stubborn, who was probably no meaner than any other child but who had one big fault in my eyes: she was the child of the man I hated.

If she had the insight to understand my situation and the sensitivity to try to comfort me, maybe in the long run my hostility toward her would have faded away. But Irma thought she was so much better than me that she couldn't see me as anything but a living toy and right away, without being intentionally cruel, she let me know it.

"Let's go, monkey! Come here! Lie down, monkey! Oh, the wicked beast tore my dress! Come on, sit up and beg!"

That's what the little girl said to me. Without the least bit of imagination she named me "monkey".

Materially I lived a good life. I had a nice bed of straw and leaves to sleep on, laid out in a small alcove near Irma's bedroom and changed twice a week by a negro servant. During the day I was left pretty much free to do as I pleased in the big salon with all the windows closed and some of the servants checking in on me.

That's where Irma came to play with me. Sometimes she even put me on a leash and brought me to the other parts of the house. They figured that I was too young to try to regain a freedom that I had barely known.

As for food, even though I didn't have the best, I had plenty of it. There were always old bananas and cabbage stalks around my masters and they threw a lot of them to me. The coconuts, which I had a hard time breaking open with a rock, had tasty pulp and wonderful sour water. Finally, given my young age and the huge amount of milk at the Piffenfluth's, every once in while they brought me a fresh bowl of this frothy drink, which, unfortunately, I had to share with their spaniel, Jewel.

I should tell you a few things about this creature I took an instant dislike to. Was it because he was four-footed whereas I was four-handed? Or was it for a certain look in his eyes, half-defiant, half-snobby, that he gave me when we faced each other over the milk bowl for the first time? I don't know, but it was easy for me to see in the eyes of this pretentious little animal as much hostility for me as I felt for him.

And since Bijou took the liberty of growling at me when I approached the bowl, I gave him a couple of good slaps that threw him into a funny rage. He tried to pounce on me and bite me. I straddled his back and started pulling on his ears and tail. The spaniel whimpered loudly, "Waa, waa," which didn't make a big impression on me because it was the first time I'd ever heard such a thing. A negro servant girl ran over, separated us, gave Bijou a piece of sugar and me a few whacks on the head. I tried to protest. On hearing all the noise Mr. Piffenfluth came in and decided that I lacked due respect for justice. To teach me about it he tied me to a tree and whipped me with his belt.

This was not only a painful punishment—since the wretch didn't pull any punches—but it was also a mortal outrage to my gorilla dignity. On that day I resolved to get away as soon as possible from this house where they had no consideration for youth, especially when the blood ran a little hot sometimes.

However, I had to hide my feelings because no escape would have been possible otherwise. So, the next time I saw Bijou with his bruised ear and dragging tail in front of the milk bowl I pretended to make up with him. He did the same. But deep down we were both seething.

Something unexpected, however, almost made me give up on escaping. One day a negro brought in a cute little female gorilla with a hurt shoulder who had been captured on a hunt. The captive was trembling all over, scared and confused. Oh, how the sight of her troubled me, especially when she looked at me with her eyes full of painful bewilderment. She had an incomprehensible look on her face, as if she were asking me for help. I was about to rush over to her and shout, "All apes are brothers! My dear, you can count on me. I, too, am a victim of humans." But I was lifted up by the scruff of my neck and taken to a small room next door where they locked me in while I heard Irma yelling, "You have to keep them apart! That one (meaning me) is so vicious that he'll kill her."

Slander is always accompanied by the excessive use of force! The next time I saw Ramona, as they called the prisoner, was a few days later and having learned through experience I took great pains to control myself. All I told her, in our simian language that is the most eloquent of all languages, was how much I sympathized with her grief. I urged her to look forward to better days. Who knows, maybe the two of us could soon find our lost freedom and live happily someplace far from our tyrants!

Still trembling, she listened to me but only responded with a few timid words to say how nice it was at this tragic time to meet a fellow gorilla who had a sensitive soul to understand her.

We lived like this, side by side, for more than a week, not counting the days and coming up with hundreds of projects for the future. But captivity had had a profound impact on Ramona and on top of everything the wound in her shoulder, which had just started to close up, suddenly split open again after a fall and this time it was much worse.

What can I say? Everything I tried to do was useless. Ramona died. While she gave me one last look, her final words were, "Friend, living in slavery is no life. Try to get free and be happy."

Her death made my life unbearable and my hatred for my masters grew stronger every day. I did everything I could to show it: broken dishes, plundered pantries, torn curtains, bitten servants, I piled up the damage in spite of the whippings that rained down on my shoulders. In the end it got to a point that they put me on a chain and starting talking about killing me as if it was the most natural thing in the world. They would either throw me into the river with a rock tied around my neck or line me up before a firing squad. Not for a second did those men discussing the best way to send me into a better world ever have the decency or sensitivity to ask me for my opinion.

Drowned or shot, the result was the same for me and I wouldn't have been able to write these memoirs if my lucky star had not brought to the house one day, at the head of a group of French sailors, a lieutenant on a ship that was leaving on an exploration.

Monsieur Fernand Amaral, as this officer was called, was around 32 years old. He looked strong and honest. His face was lit up by big, blue eyes and framed by thick, blonde sideburns, making him look both gentle and firm at the same time. As I learned later when my understanding was more polished, he had just arrived from Libreville, the main port of Gabon, on board the frigate *Joyeuse* in order to explore the territory between it and the right bank of the Congo on foot.

Along with 12 sailors and 20 negroes who carried the baggage and supplies in this country full of cannibals and crocodiles but not a single hotel, Amaral had crossed the land of the Fangs, fearsome cannibals who were not satisfied with just eating human flesh but sold it as well. That was why two negroes of the group disappeared one night. The next day the others found their heads and limbs neatly severed and hanging outside a hut whose owner was chopping up a buffalo. A fight broke out in which two more Gabonese died and around ten Fangs. After this Amaral got back on the road and crossed the Ogooué River fending off 200 or 300 natives who were hiding in the bushes and attacking them with rocks, arrows and spears. There again the explorer lost a few men including a Frenchman. Despite the attack and the desertion of some porters who took the bags with them, the officer continued his travel and ended up finding the Piffenfluth house.

My master wasn't an especially hospitable man, but he knew how to count and Monsieur Amaral paid well for all his expenses. So, the explorer got an eager welcome and plenty of attention, not so much to his person as to his purse.

He happened to see me just when an old negro had stepped in to settle the issue of drowning or shooting me: it was decided that they'd hang me by the neck from the strongest branch of a banyan tree.

"That's a nice-looking ape and looks smart too," he said to Heindrick Piffenfluth.

These were the first kind words out of a human mouth that I'd ever heard spoken about me. Despite the dark state of mind I was in, they made me feel good.

I saw in the colonist's face that he was about to answer that I was a wretched creature unable to do anything, but he thought twice about it and with a deal in mind Piffenfluth declared that I was the pearl of primates. In truth the officer wasn't listening. He was examining me instead and seemed very thoughtful.

"Would you sell him and if so, how much?" he finally asked.

It was a godsend for my master since my death would have brought him nothing. However, he didn't want to look like he wanted to get rid of me.

"If you'd like," he answered his guest, "I'll sell him to you. Even though I'm very attached to him because you don't find such smart, gentle apes every day, you know. Of course, I'll be sorry to see him go but whatever I can do to make you happy…"

The sales pitch was not lost on the Lieutenant who obviously knew what self-serving courtesy was all about.

"How much?" he asked again.

"500 francs," Heindrick Piffenfluth said flatly.

Monsieur Amaral was startled. But he was rich and even though he didn't lavish expenses on the expedition, he wasn't stingy with his own pocketbook. He held out a blue slip of paper to the colonist who swiftly pocketed it with satisfaction, mumbling the usual, insincere cliché, "You got a bargain."

Up to this point I had watched them without moving or uttering a sound, following all the phases of the negotiation in which my destiny was at stake. When the murderer of my parents put the price of my freedom in his pocket I understood that a fateful hour had just tolled in my life.

I had changed masters! My ideal would've been to have none at all, but like some grand philosopher once said, "Apes desire but events decide."

CHAPTER THREE

I had nurtured such a strong hatred for my first master that I started to love the second before I even got to know him. Every creature, especially the young, feels the need to love. Only the type of love varies: some love their own kind, others cherish an idea, others again devote themselves to pieces of gold and silver. Heindrick Piffenfluth was one of the latter.

Fernand Amaral was nothing like him. A good man, wise and generous, who knew lots of things, he was certainly the man, more than any other in the world, who could make me forget the loss of that most beautiful of things—freedom.

First of all he was very perceptive: the sight of my chains, some bruises on my body and the total lack of concern in giving me a name, all this showed him very quickly that I was not the pampered animal he was led to believe.

"Poor thing," he whispered, petting my aching back, "you look like you've gotten more lashes than caresses, but it'll all be different with me."

Moved to tears at the sound of these kind words, my goodness, I threw my arms around his neck and hugged him affectionately. Monsieur Amaral was all the more surprised by this unexpected gesture. He stared at me, patted my head and I heard him mutter, "Am I dreaming? He's got a look in his eyes that's completely human."

Then he touched my skull, felt around my forehead and uttered a few words that I only understood much later. Still, I saw that my new master had a high regard for my mind and that he wanted to make me forget my ordeals. For my part I promised myself to pay back his kindness in turn. Moreover, I decided to get the most out of living with humans by learning a bunch of things that the gorilla people don't know about and haven't even dreamt of.

After a few days we left the Piffenfluth house where everything had changed for me because the servants now respected me. What can I say? They went so far as to flatter me and the colonist himself said some hypocritical drivel that I answered with a cold sneer. I was glad when we left the cursed place that gave me no good memories except of poor Ramona. Should I admit this? I wanted to steal the glowing pipe from one of the servants and toss it on the straw roof of one the buildings. Only the fear of serious retribution held me back from this revenge because I was just starting to feel that life was worth living.

We started off in the evening, with a beautiful full moon lighting everything around us with lovely blue light so that we could see like it was daytime. We followed a well beaten path along the long river that was like a motionless snake defending mysterious central Africa. We could hear the fast current of the water on our right. To the left grew thorny bushes full of red berries bursting with poisonous juice and behind them leafy groves of banana and date trees alternating with clearings.

We walked single file, the guides in front, then my master with half the sailors. After them came the porters while the other half of the European detachment brought up the rear. I was riding on the shoulders of Monsieur Amaral. During those final days spent at Piffenfluth's they had taken off my chain. During the trip, however, my master was scared of losing me so he put a collar around my neck and tied it to a long leash, so thin that I barely felt its weight. I didn't even think of putting up a fight to get it off.

Whenever we passed by a banana tree I was tempted. I reached out to pick one or if it was too far I jumped into the tree and grabbed the cherished fruit. If I stayed too long a little tug on the rope reminded me where I was and I hopped back onto my master's shoulders.

Making the trip under these conditions was very pleasant. During the nights when the moon was not shining so brightly and during the scorching hot afternoons, they called a halt. The porters unrolled the light, waterproof tents that Amaral ordered pitched on whatever open land he could find to defend against any surprises. They lit big fires to keep the wild animals at bay. And they set up guards while everyone slept or at least tried to sleep.

We were heading northeast and for a long time went up the right bank of the great African river. Then we veered off to the north crossing a bunch of big, native villages whose names I can't remember except for Okanga.

What I saw in this place left an indelible mark on my memory. On our arrival there was a lot of loud shouting and the tom-tom started beating low and fast. My master, figuring that we were about to be attacked, had us form a tight column and told everyone to be on guard. At the first attack the men were supposed to fire away, but we were able to keep going without being stopped. But then, after passing by the first huts and getting to the center of the village, we saw something that struck us all with horror.

A corpse lay on a pyre, covered with purple rags and wearing a tall hat whose form indicated that he was the dead chief. In front of the pyre was a gruesome, skeletal negro wearing a loincloth while his chest and waist were wrapped in living snakes and he was making weird, creepy movements. In his right hand he held a long knife dripping with blood and in his left hand a lit torch whose sparks were flying in the wind. At his feet lay a half dozen negro men and women with their throats slashed. In front of him 15 others, still alive but tied to poles by their necks, arms and legs, were waiting for their turn.

It was the powerful sorcerer of the Okangas who, as I learned later, faithfully observed their customs and was sacrificing slaves at the funeral of King Malokoko. The domesticated snakes coiled harmlessly around his body added to his prestige.

All around him, squatting respectfully in the open space, the Okangas were saluting the slaughter of every poor devil with shouting and drumming. Once all of them had been put to death in order to serve their master in the afterlife, the sorcerer would set fire to the pyre, as custom dictated.

But our sudden appearance upset their little celebration. Just when we arrived the sorcerer had gone up to one of the prisoners and after cutting him free was preparing to slash his throat with the knife. The slave didn't put up any resistance. Personally I was offended more by the victim's apathy than by the executioner's cruelty. Obviously degraded and debased by slavery the poor guy about to die truly believed he was a lesser soul than his masters and considered it a crime to try to escape his fate. Maybe also the sight of all the onlookers supporting the killer made him believe it was useless to resist.

"We have to save those poor men," Monsieur Amaral said. He took out his revolver, aimed at the sorcerer and fired.

My master was a first-rate shot and he had an excellent gun. I should add that he was no more than 60 yards away because we had come out so suddenly from the bushes. For all these reasons the sorcerer fell, not killed but shot in the leg, and he dropped to his knees before his victim.

The first reaction—the good one, if we must believe the philosophers—of the Okangas was to hightail it out of there. The second was to grab stones, arrows and spears to welcome us. I was already cursing the generosity of my master who was maybe about to spill more blood than the native sacrificer had done.

"Since these people accept their fate," I was telling myself with selfish wisdom, "why massacre them to stop them?"

But there was a third reaction, totally unexpected. An Okanga, as agile as one of my kind (if I'm not doing too much honor to the human race by comparing them to the race of apes in this) jumped on the wounded witch doctor, grabbed his knife and plunged it deep into his chest. At the same time, he shouted something to the others that I didn't understand but that they answered with a unanimous cry of approval. And as we came out of the wide passage between the huts into the central space, shocked but defiant and ready to shoot, the Okangas threw their stones not at us but at their feet and lowered their spears. Then they came to meet us with exaggerated signs of friendship.

We learned then that the one who threw the lifeless sorcerer next to his victims was a failed rival who had once tried in vain to get the important job of witch doctor. Now he had a good opportunity to take it and he wasted no time: he was truly of the human race, this one!

While sticking six inches of iron into his rival, who was too bashful to answer back, he blasted him for bringing down the "heaven's fire" (my master's bullet!) for his careless and clumsy sacrifices to the fetishes and sacred rites and he threatened the Okangas with the greatest woes if they kept being led by this kind of individual who, between parentheses, after the death of King Malokoko the night before had added civil powers to his religious duties.

The official sorcerer didn't respond and therefore his old rival was immediately and right before our eyes saluted by the crowd as witch doctor and king under the name of Oumatife, which means "Justice of the land" in Okanga language.

Monsieur Amaral, who held liberal ideas, would have preferred to set up a republic, but he figured that with the servile customs of the Okangas a republic would have been only in word. So, he let these people organize as they wanted. The only thing that he demanded was the immediate release of the poor devils who were tied to the poles, watching everything with gloomy coldness, waiting for their turn to be sacrificed.

Oumatife, who owed his promotion to Amaral's gunfire and who had a clearer idea than his fellow tribesmen about what firearms could do, gave in to this demand. He even showered us with gifts that were paid in kind with European objects because my master never accepted something for nothing. Except that when we got back on the road and far enough away—as we learned later—Oumatife, now the magnanimous sovereign, celebrated his coming to the throne by massacring not 20 but 300 of his subjects.

CHAPTER FOUR

I will spare you readers all the everyday incidents of a trip that went on for around a month and during which, being devoured by a thirst for learning, I took every opportunity to educate myself. I already understood most of the words of the human language, all the while noticing that they themselves didn't understand everything since they spoke a bunch of different idioms. Also, I was very astonished to see that side by side with individuals who did surprising things like my master, there were others who were lower than the lowest of my kind.

I was amazed to see some make fire, milk cows, make butter, sew clothes, build houses, communicate their thoughts by writing; but I was sickened at seeing others get drunk, fight, lie and make others tremble. I constantly wavered between admiration to contempt.

My master, who had given me the very African and nice enough sounding name of Popo, had noticed my inclination to study and first on a whim, then out of natural kindness, he tried to cultivate it.

One day I heard him saying, "Let's see how far this ape can go. He will certainly never speak an articulate language but he just might learn everything else."

We were in Libreville, [Gabon], and since the *Joyeuse* was anchored for a few months, my master had set up house on shore in a big, comfortable bungalow surrounded by palm trees and looking out on the beach. Every morning he went on board to take part in the inspections and sometimes to have breakfast with the captain. But since they had given him special work he spent most of his time on shore.

I was interested in everything I saw and even though they left me completely free I hardly ever thought about going back into the forest. I have to say that I even started walking like men; and I had the unquestionable superiority of being able to use four hands instead of two.

One day a friend of my master, sitting at his desk, decided on a whim to draw my portrait: I went along with it willingly, quite surprised to see my likeness appearing on paper. Then I got the idea to do the same. You know that the spirit of imitation is in our nature. I grabbed a big sheet of paper, a piece of charcoal and looking back and forth at the man and the paper I sketched the visitor's face. This first drawing was no masterpiece, I admit, but such as it was it literally stunned my master and his friend. From this moment on Monsieur Amaral gave me drawing lessons every day and soon I became an ace.

Seeing the dexterity in my fingers and the sureness of my hand, my professor reflected and then managed to develop them a lot more by bending in, little by little, with a strip of cloth, the palm of my right hand so that I could oppose the thumb to the other fingers. The non-opposable thumb is, like not being able to articulate sounds, one of the unfortunate differences for our race that keeps it separated from humanity. Thanks to my master's patience and my willingness, this first difference disappeared. As for the second, despite my constant efforts I never overcame it: for centuries our throat was made so that while it could emit distinct sounds, even richly varied sounds, it could not manage to produce the particular sounds that form human language.

My skill at drawing aroused a surprising idea in my master, an achievement that would otherwise have been unthinkable: to teach me to write because writing is drawing. In truth, it was just a matter of copying not visible images but sounds that represent things, beings or thoughts. For this he had to teach me not only to trace letters and know them by name, which was pretty easy, but also to understand the meaning of their combinations, basically to read.

In spite of our mutual willingness, both of us, teacher and student, almost gave up the lessons countless times. The reason for the differences between printed writing and handwriting completely escaped me. It took me almost two years to put together reading and writing. As for math, I had to give it up almost completely.

During these two years we traveled. More than once while staying in Libreville I went with my master on board the *Joyeuse*. To tell you about all the surprises and awe I felt on seeing the ship would be impossible for me.

The first time that I stood next to Monsieur Amaral in the dinghy, chopping through the blue surface of the sea that looked like a mirror from a distance, I was scared, really scared, I admit. The movement of the foaming waves on which our boat was dancing, paddled by six strong rowers, made me deeply worried.

Far from land, my element, I felt like a weak toy at the mercy of unknown forces. I was breathing more freely when our boat reached the port side of the *Joyeuse*. I climbed up the ladder and stepped onto the deck. Then I became the prized object of curiosity: the captain, officers and all the crew looked at me with astonishment, which flattered my ego and made me even more curious.

The masts, yardarms, sails, rope ladders, everything I saw was new to me. The sailors' actions were really interesting to me, but even without fear of falling into the gaping abyss I would have jumped up to the top of the masts quite differently.

When my master and I left Libreville on board the frigate to go to Saint-Louis, a big city in Senegal, it was something else. The steam engine started to shake the ship while it shot billows of black smoke out of its chimney. The sails swelled halfway with the faint breeze: sails and steam combined drove us at 10 knots an hour, a good speed.

The double movement of the ship rolling from starboard, meaning the right side, to port, that is the left—see if I don't understand maritime things—as well as the dancing back and forth, was quite a bother to me. I had just started in on a big meal of boiled potatoes when I suddenly felt nauseous and had to stop. I felt so sick for a few minutes that I even thought I was about to die. I got over it, however, by offering my breakfast to the sea. Two hours later the nausea went away and since then I've taken other trips on water without ever feeling like that again.

Three weeks later, or thereabouts because math, I repeat, was never my strongpoint, we cast anchor in Dakar. I wasn't broken up about it: despite all the care and attention the crew showed me, I was starting to get tired of the sea.

In Libreville I had barely caught a glimpse of the city being built because I didn't leave my master's bungalow, except to go to the *Joyeuse*. At Saint-Louis I was awed by a real city: docks, houses that were several stories tall, elevators, lampposts, factories, shops glowing with electric lights at night. All of this dazzled me and would have given me a very high opinion of man if at the same time I hadn't seen a prison where some policemen were dragging a man who had stolen a leg of lamb from a butcher's stand. This messed up all my thoughts: among us apes, despite our imperfections, we never needed to build prisons.

I'll skip over the minor incidents of a life that rolled by pretty unclouded for two and a half years. I had made incredible progress in everything, understanding almost all the words of the French language and a little English—even though I never learned how to write it because of the pronunciation—and I figured out some African dialects that I thought were, for the most part, derived from ape language.

Monsieur Amaral had a whole family in his quaint house on the upper bank of the river. It was there that I spent those happy days, even when he had to leave because of his work. His family, which was nothing but kind to me, consisted of an uncle, Monsieur Aymeric Amaral, retired captain, widower and easy-going; his sister Prudence, an old maid who looked a little stiff but was good at heart and was great at making guava jam; and Mademoiselle Angele, the captain's daughter, 15 years old, with beautiful pink skin and two blue eyes that in this country where all are black seemed to me to be the most beautiful in the world. Mademoiselle Amaral, however, didn't have blond but rather light brown hair that fell freely over her shoulders and was almost as long as she was tall, which if I'm not mistaken was about 5'2".

A whole troop of black servants filled up The Palms, as the house was called in honor of a novel by Georges de la Landelle that takes place, for the most part, in Senegal[13]. The Amaral girls (the aunt and niece) had romantic tendencies. Moreover, they loved this country that, if you forget about the malaria, the sunstroke, the eye infections, mosquitoes, poisonous animals—I won't even mention the insects that vanish in a flash—the poisonous plants and the native looters, is really quite nice and charming. Also, when they were sitting on the riverbank knitting in the shade of a palm, I often heard them repeating this song that had been improvised by some dark-skinned poet:

"Salam! Salam! Senegal is a black snake slithering through the green trees, biting the golden sand!"

It was this excellent family that took charge of continuing my education when my master was away. It was not often, though, because his extensive knowledge of West Africa had got him appointed by the Navy Ministry to stay on the coast and carry out a bunch of work on the water system.

Every time an expedition was not too long or too dangerous, my master went along. That's how I got a chance to visit Fouta Djallon, the Ivory Coast and even part of Dahomey, a country whose king, Behanzin, had been dethroned and exiled by the French two years before [1894].

One day I landed in Porto-Novo with my master. It would be an exaggeration to call this place a city but it is still the biggest port on the coast. Here I happened to see a negro who was standing in the middle of crowd of curious onlookers, colonists, soldiers, sailors and natives, doing some magic tricks and acrobatics. Nevertheless, there weren't many coins falling into his straw hat that was lying on the ground instead of a beggar's bowl.

---

[13] Les Géants de la mer (The Giants of the Sea).

Even though I think all negroes look pretty much the same, this one's face looked familiar to me. And then when he saw me and my master he stopped jumping around.

"Now where have I seen this crazy fellow?" Monsieur Amaral mumbled, surprised and racking his memory.

The fellow helped us out by telling us his name and status. "Oumatife, king of the Okangas," he said, stepping proudly forward as majestically as he could.

He was indeed the usurper of King Malokoko whose accession to the throne my master had unwittingly boosted by firing his revolver at the rival and who apparently became the victim of some revolution, being reduced to swallowing knives or reeds and walking on his hands for a living.

Monsieur Amaral gave His Fallen Majesty a 40-sous coin. Dazzled by such generosity he put a sudden end to his performance and started telling us his sad story.

Oumatife said that the Okanga people had never been happier than under his paternal government. In the six months of his absolute power he had made war on three tribes, burned five villages, enslaved 1,200 neighbors and sacrificed 800 people of both sexes and every age in the religious ceremonies that had never been as glorious as under his reign. The taxes had hardly even doubled to support the cost of this glory and all the unmarried Okangas from 20 to 40 years old had been enlisted in the royal guard. Unfortunately, so many benefits had not touched the heart of the people, who are eternally ungrateful, nor had they weakened the audacity of vying parties. An obscure and terribly vicious man, Kalibamba, sentenced to have his right hand and left foot cut off for not kissing the ground when the sovereign passed by, had the gall to escape the just punishment awaiting him by running away and then whipping up the vile people and leading them to Oumatife's hut where the royal guard didn't even put up a fight. The sovereign was dethroned and considering the customs of the land he was waiting to be cut up into little pieces. But Kalibamba was a practical man: a slave-trader—because you know, dear readers, that this business still flourishes in central Africa—was in the area. Kalibamba got in touch with him and for the price of some faded calico and rusty rifles he sold Oumatife and the other big shots of his reign.

From absolute ruler to slave, what a comedown!

But we should give credit to Oumatife: he had the soul of philosopher. Hardly were his neck and hands clamped in chains and the trader's whip caressing his shoulders to speed up his march to German positions where he would be sold secretly along with his partners in misfortune, when he realized that men were made to be free. Deep down inside he condemned, as they deserved, the barbaric traffickers in human flesh and swore to do all he could to escape.

He succeeded, not easily, thanks to the help of another prisoner who was able to file through their chains so they could run away together. The two of them, guided by the sun, stole what they needed to live, found hiding places to sleep, and after a month and a half of walking, exhausted, hungry and bleeding, they got to Cameroon, the main German base on the Gulf of Biafra.

There Oumatife left his companion who got hired for one thaler a month plus rice and water by a Dutch merchant to wash bottles and brush horses. Oumatife was left alone and went back to his life of adventures: he was, in turn, a clerk, handyman, kitchen helper on board a merchant ship and winded up in Porto-Novo where he started putting his acrobatic skills to work so as not to die of hunger.

Deep down he nourished the hope that the French government would help him reconquer the Okanga throne, which he had so sadly lost. Therefore, he poured flattery on all the simple soldiers by calling them "captain" whenever they happened to offer him a bowl of soup.

But I doubt that Oumatife would ever get back the club that he used as a scepter and with which he caressed the shoulders of his subjects so benevolently.

CHAPTER FIVE

No happiness is untainted. After two and a half years of a life that was very sweet to me, my master, or rather my friend because he'd never made me feel like a slave, up and died of a fever.

Ah! West Africa! What beautiful country but oh how it swallows the lives of Europeans!

The death of my poor Ramona had certainly been deeply painful for me. But how much deeper was the pain I felt standing in front of the corpse of the man who had been my teacher and made a good impression on me on behalf of the human race. He was in The Palms when he gave up the ghost, in the arms of the Captain, Miss Prudence and Angele, all three full of tears while outside on the banks of the river the voice of an old negro woman chanted mournfully:

"Salam! Salam! Senegal is a black river flowing through the green trees, biting the golden sand!"

I was sitting in a corner and grieving in silence.

Everything that Monsieur Amaral possessed went to his family. I was part of the inheritance and became the property of the Captain. I had nothing to complain about even though a big change had just happened in my life. So far I had been a traveling ape. With my master I had visited a lot of different places: Fouta Djallon, Dahomey, Gabon and all over Senegal all the way to Bafoulabé. From now on I would be a sedentary ape.

Study and work are the best ways to avoid melancholy. Since I couldn't talk I wrote a few words on a piece of paper to ask my new master to lend me some books. I was sure the Captain wouldn't deny me this but he went one step farther: he kept up the lessons that his nephew had given me and for my part I worked as hard as I could. It was at this time that the idea of writing my memoirs came to me.

The news spread far and wide that Aymeric Amaral, retired captain, Chevalier of the Legion of Honor and member of geological society of Carcassonne, had an ape endowed with extraordinary abilities. A commission of scholars showed up one day at The Palms to examine me.

This commission was made up of five men, all old, bald and wearing glasses, which didn't make them better looking, only very serious looking.

What can I say? As sensational as I felt, their first impression intimidated me, even more so when I heard them muttering a bunch of big words in Greek and Latin that I had no idea what they meant.

The president of the commission first of all stated that I belonged to the branch of vertebrates, to the class of mammalia and to the order of primates, which made me very proud. Then he declared that I had warm blood, a body covered with hair, the appearance of being strong and agile, a sharp eye and excellent teeth.

These physical characteristics, which any average clerk could see, being established, after a preliminary discussion full of ominous words, the president took off his glasses, cleaned them, put them back on and started interrogating me, speaking very slowly to give me time to understand.

"Listen," he said to me, "my good Popo, I see that you are intelligent... oh, yes... isn't that right? I'm going to talk to you like a man. If you understand me, nod your head... like this... (and the scholar nodded his venerable scalp)... If you don't understand me, shake your head like this... (another lesson in body language)... Do you understand?"

I answered immediately as he just asked me to.

"Marvelous!" the president shouted, letting his glasses fall in his outburst of emotion.

All the others repeated after him, "Marvelous!"

One of his colleagues added, "What a pity that he can't answer us except with a yes or no."

I stared at him and shrugged my shoulders, a gesture that far from irritating him seemed to delight him to no end. Then I signed to him to give me his notebook. Literally dumbstruck, he obeyed automatically. This time it was the ape giving orders to man. I won't hide from you how delighted I was at the thought of this.

I pulled out the pencil and on a blank page wrote, "I will write."

The surprise ran through all of them. I was basking in glory deep down inside.

"Gentlemen," the president called out when he got over his stupor, "nature is glorious. It is a man and what's better an intelligent man whom we see here in the skin of a ape." He was so excited that I thought he was going to hug me.

My examination continued: to all the questions asked of me I answered without getting a single one wrong, either with signs or in writing. The members of the commission, completely fascinated, left after shaking my hand.

A few weeks later my master received a very pressing invitation to send me to Paris to be presented to the Academy of Sciences. This invitation was written in the most flattering terms, both for "the intelligent animal who could be raised to the human level" and for "the patient professor whose lessons performed this miracle".

The captain didn't like Paris much or rather having lived a calm and peaceful life at The Palms for so many years he was a little nervous about being in the noisy rush of the big city. So, he answered politely but firmly that it was up to the Academy to come to him and the matter was left there.

For me who had once so badly wanted to see Paris, which I'd heard so much talk about like a magic city, I was almost as indifferent as my master or rather it put me in a weird mood.

It's not good for man to be alone, they say—the same goes for an ape. Of course my isolation was only relative since I had around me some people who loved me a lot, but these people, as good as they were, were still my masters and not my equals. We understood each other, of course, but we couldn't really talk together since I didn't speak the human language and they didn't speak gorilla, which should stand right beside English and German in the school curriculum.

Also, despite the care and attention I was surrounded by, despite the freedom I enjoyed, my sweet, peaceful life was sometimes darkened by sudden sadness. Maybe also it was the voice of my ancestors waking up and calling me back to the forest where groups of happy apes leap through the grass in the shade of the trees.

Oh, if only I could have with me another of my race who understood me, who shared my thoughts and feelings, with whom I could talk using something other than signs and writing!

I had thought I could raise myself up to human society and live there, but some unknown power that was lying dormant for a long time started reminding me of the apes. My brain was stuffed with extraordinary knowledge but at times I got pretty depressed: I wanted to forget all about reading and writing down to the last word of the human language. A suppressed urge was bursting my muscles while I was seeing visions of gorillas living happily far from cities as part of primitive nature.

Well, of course, the mind can develop, grow under the influence of an environment, but the habits transmitted in the blood bring us inevitably back to the past, to the far past that we never even knew, to the past of our ancestors. It is not only thoughts that separate different creatures but more than anything the habits.

Sometimes when one of the Amaral girls was sitting in front of the piano making the ivory keys resound, an odd melancholy took hold of me. Music is a language that we learn without understanding the words. It cradles us gently or transports us on dizzying wings to unknown worlds. Oh, that piano that sometimes brought tears to my eyes! But they are tears that I don't regret!

What can I say? At the same time that I felt a moral barrier separating me from those I loved, who were so good to me, I also felt a kind of contempt for the black servants living there. Was it because they were black? I don't think so because even though my skin was a little less dark than theirs, as I got older it was covered with thicker and thicker hair.

No, my distance from them must have come from their inferior ideals. These men and women, who served another man and other women, which was a shocking enough situation for a freeborn ape, couldn't read or write or calculate time. Their conversations were stupid, all their fun was crude and, another strange thing: as they looked on me like all servants do a favorite pet, I suspected that they thought they were better than me.

I loved the Amaral family a lot and many times I pushed away or tried to push away these feelings that called me to another life. But soon these feelings became obsessive. What to do? Stay where I was and die of mental suffocation in the midst of material comfort? Or commit an act of ingratitude and leave?

One event put an end to my hesitation. I learned that a young tax collector from Saint-Louis, Laurentin Mouginot, who sometimes came on Sundays to The Palms to accompany Miss Angele on the piano or to play tric-trac with the Captain, had just asked him for the hand of his niece and he was not rejected.

This made me very sad. I saw the face of the serious public servant coming to change the life of The Palms by taking away the girl who had turned into a woman.

I made up my mind to leave.

CHAPTER SIX

My decision was made. I didn't want to tell the Amaral family with signs because I was afraid of some tragic scene that would hold me back. But I didn't want to just disappear either, without giving some explanation and saying goodbye to the good people who loved and raised me. I used the knowledge and skills they taught me: I wrote.

I took a pencil and wrote the following on a sheet of paper:

Friends,

I still love you but I feel the great forest calling me. The ape is made to live free. This is not my fault, I'm not a man and it was useless for me to try to submit to a life in which you tried your best to make me happy but in which I was suffocating. Forgive me and believe that I will never forget you.

Your friend,

Popo

I folded the letter and put it in an envelope on which I wrote in huge letters, "To Monsieur Amaral". Then I left.

Being an honest ape I didn't bring anything with me. Like a philosopher in the old times that I heard talk about, I possessed all my treasures inside of me.

\#

It is early in the morning, 4 am. I go away without a noise, but I look back once in a while on those four walls within which I spent so many calm and happy days.

I walk leisurely, in no hurry, like a biped. My heart is beating fast, however, and as I near the forest after half an hour, my natural instinct carries me away: I fall onto my four hands and leap into the thick under-growth, letting loose a shout of joy that has nothing human about it.

For a long, long time I get drunk on freedom. The sun seems brighter, the sky bluer and the air more pure. I breathe in the strong scent of trees and the fragrance of the plants goes straight to my head. Sitting on the branch of an oak I forget everything in the endless contemplation of nature.

Around me birds are flying and chattering; insects are swarming; sometimes I hear the cry of an animal disappearing into a thicket.

But time flies and my grumbling stomach brings me back to reality. As it happens a coconut tree is nearby, fanning out its leaves over the other trees. It offers me everything I need to calm both my hunger and thirst.

I stand up, leap… and fall to the ground 20 feet below. During my life away from the forest my limbs have forgotten their former agility. I am certainly not a man, but I am no longer an ape.

#

The sun was starting to set on the horizon when I woke up from the blackout that could have cost me my life if some snake or wild animal was around. When I fell my head had hit the tree trunk. Any skull less solid than mine would have cracked open. Luckily my joints felt all right—I hadn't broken anything.

My adventure was a little humiliating because it showed me that I would need some time to get used to life in the forest again.

With a little more caution I went to the coconut tree, climbed up without another accident and picked some fruit that gave me a comfortable meal. Once my hunger was satisfied I got back on my way. Where was I going? I had no idea. Straight ahead, why not, until I found what I was looking for: my kind.

Gradually I felt the instinct of the forest come back to me after all those long years. I could see through the thickest bushes and hear the almost inaudible sound that the snake makes while slithering through the grass. Off in the distance, without seeing I recognized the plants by their subtle scents.

Night came. I was moved—and I have to admit a little afraid—by the great silence of the trees and other things. It was the hour when the wild beasts stole silently out of their lairs and my heart beat faster because I was alone, exposed to attack, in an unknown country.

Just in case, I snapped off a strong, straight branch and using a vine I tied a big rock to the end. Thus armed with an improvised club I went and spent the night in a rock crevice after barring the entrance. Just like the ancestors of men did centuries and centuries ago.

For several days I wandered through the forest without finding its end. Luckily there were plenty of bananas and coconuts and wild fruits. Caves or thick bushes were comfortable enough to sleep in. In short, every day I found what I needed: food and shelter, while my body got back its agility and strength in the wide-open life in the fresh air.

But of my own kind, which my gorilla soul was aching for, I didn't meet one.

In my journey to the unknown I saw strange-looking animals. Antelopes, wild camels and leopards had come and gone, quick as shadows, before my astonished eyes. I even watched, for the first time in my life, a family of hippopotamus taking their graceful morning bath in the clear water of a river whose name I don't know but that must be one of the tributaries of the Senegal River. I wasn't afraid but the sight of the open mouths of these animals made me jump back and I stepped on the tail of a snake lying in the grass, probably sleeping after a heavy meal. The serpent reared up and hissed at me. I lost no time and disappeared.

It wasn't hippos or snakes I was looking for but apes.

After around a week I finally found some monkeys! And what monkeys! A whole tribe of capuchins, most of them young, small, skinny, stuck up and sneering, speaking a conceited language that was absolutely unintelligible, and holding their tails high while jumping around on their four hands and doing all kinds of acrobats. In short the "dandies" of our species. I was ashamed of these degenerate cousins who for their part reacted to me with a feeling of fear mixed with scorn. I ended up turning my back on them.

More than once, with my hopes disappointed, I felt the urge to go back to human society. I thought about my friends at The Palms and scolded myself for being ungrateful. But an inner strength pushed me on, always walking forward.

The forest stopped sometimes to make room for a clearing or a river, which didn't slow me down much because I just grabbed some branches, tied them together with vines and made a raft, guiding it from one bank to the other with a long pole made from the stalk of a strong bush.

Around 15 had days passed since I'd run away and I was wondering if I might not be condemned to live alone when I heard, with unspeakable joy, the following words:

"Don't eat bananas that are too green. You'll get sick."

These words were spoken in gorilla!

Oh, dear language that fondled my ears when I was born and that I was scared of losing before I die because I wouldn't speak with another of my race. Oh, how its sounds made my heart skip a beat!

The one who had given the sage advice not to eat bananas before they were ripe was a venerable old gorilla (I could tell by the gray hair) who still stood straight and firm. He resisted leaning on the stick that he held in his hand and instead used it to tap the shoulders of his listeners, of which there were two, one of each sex, both young.

I was full of emotion when I went up to them saying, "Greetings, friends."

They looked at me with surprise. The young didn't feel safe, probably not knowing that there were other gorillas in the world outside their tribe. The old one looked thoughtful, scratched his nose, then held out his hand to me saying, "Greetings to you, son. Though I don't know where you were born, I'll consider you a friend because all gorillas are blood brothers. You see my family here. If you'd like to come with us I'll introduce you to our tribe."

He spoke like a reasonable and honorable gorilla who had seen a lot. I was soon to learn that the others called him Rou-o-ro, meaning the wise orator.

Rou-o-ro told me that he was a widower and the two little companions were his grandchildren whose mother had been choked and swallowed by a boa in her sleep and their father had died after eating too many green bananas. Hence the warning that the old gorilla was giving his descendants. The little boy, Pifi, was younger and more scatter-brained than his sister, Oumé, who seemed gentle and serious, a little timid and full of modesty that was befitting a well-raised gorilla. I took a liking to her right away.

Although the gorilla often lives alone, his natural tendency keeping him far from noise and commotion so he can spend his peaceful days in philosophical meditation, Rou-o-ro lived with a tribe made up of ten members.

After a long walk we got to where the other gorillas were living. I was pleasantly surprised to see their shelters made of branches, some set up in the bushes, others in rock crevices, others again in the tall trees. Here were the beginnings of a human village.

Human? Why not? Is the distance that separates us from man so insurmountable? I myself was proof that it was not.

That evening, sitting in a circle around a simple but copious meal, while we were chatting away, I was sure that in their brains there were seeds of higher intelligence than what we're given credit for.

They asked me to tell them my adventures and I did. In truth, I caught them a few times smirking with skepticism. Some of my listeners even went so far as to voice their doubt. But all of them were enchanted by the tale and if they took me for an impostor, they admitted that at least I was interesting. It was not every day that they got such an earful. As for Oumé, she spilled more than one tear and I saw in her eyes a little of my dear Ramona.

I had held back from showing them proof of my high intellectual education. Now I took two dry branches and while talking I rubbed them together over a small pile of dry grass. They watched me, intrigued. After a few minutes some sparks flew off and fell onto the grass, setting it on fire.

I'll let you imagine how amazed they were at the sight of this sudden and wondrous fire. I knew from my reading that this was how savage people who had not yet seen a matchstick got fire. I had practiced it several times in secret at The Palms and trying it again in front of my new friends I knew I could do it.

In their enthusiasm the gorillas wanted to offer me their government with full support, but I always preferred friendship to leadership. Moreover I told them that since they'd got along fine without masters so far, they could continue to do so without any problems and there was no issue of rank that would keep me from sharing with them the treasure of knowledge that I had amassed during my stay among humans.

Rou-o-ro supported me warmly. Maybe, deep down, even though he held sway naturally due to his age and experience, he had been humbled on being brought down a notch by a young stranger. There is always a little egoism in the noblest of sentiments.

Therefore, I didn't become a monarch but my popularity only grew stronger for it and I took advantage of this to introduce all the improvements that their habits could adapt to. Every day brought more progress. After showing them how to make fire and cook their food I taught them to make rafts, weave baskets and mats with coconut leaves and I even initiated them in the art of fishing with poles, which was the greatest victory that ape or man had ever won.

In their frenzy, my friends lifted me on their shoulders and carried me around for a full hour, singing a song in my honor that one of them, Fouyo, a poet full of emotion, had composed on the spot.

I had found the way that I had been looking for, confusedly: I would devote myself to educating my brothers, to improving their tools and their morality. I would become the equal of those founders of ancient civilizations, those philosophers whose names I heard my master pronounce with such respect.

I lived like this for a few months with the gorillas. Everyone loved me and Oumé sometimes looked at me and sighed, lowering her eyes. She was a lot younger than me, but we apes are ready a lot sooner for the joys of mating. Plus, my lessons had done wonders for her mind and I had great respect for her moral qualities. I couldn't find a better companion anywhere: affectionate, intelligent and pretty. As for the dowry, I didn't think of it for a second. My mind was made up. I was going to ask, very respectfully, her grandfather for her hand in marriage.

He hugged me so hard I almost choked. With tears in his eyes he said, "Popo! This is the happiest day of my life."

As for Oumé, she almost fainted with joy. I can say, with no false modesty, that she considered me a little like a superior creature.

Gorillas don't dawdle. That very day the wedding took place, simple and cheerful. Pifi, always friendly, played all kinds of jokes; Rou-o-ro allowed himself a little palm wine, which put him in a very good mood; there were no musicians but plenty of singers since everyone chimed in on the song improvised by Fouyo, which modesty alone keeps me from recording here.

CHAPTER SEVEN

After six months of being Oumé's husband no cloud had come to darken our happiness. However, many times I thought of how abruptly I'd left The Palms. I must certainly have seemed ungrateful or at least very rude to the family. Slowly I became obsessed with this thought and my companion noticed my worry.

"What's wrong, Popo?" she asked, thoughtful and affectionate as always. "Are the palm hearts we ate yesterday giving your stomach a hard time or were the bananas this morning not ripe enough?"

I let her know what was starting to form a dark spot in our rosy sky and she snapped back, "Well, we just have to go pay a visit to those fine people. You made it here all alone so it'll be a lot easier with the two of us going back."

Her words filled me with joy and I kissed her. Oumé, in order to make me happy, was willing to face unknown dangers on a trip through a country that she didn't know.

Rou-o-ro and Pifi were absolutely set on coming with us, at least half the way. Thanks to their company and especially to my charming Oumé, the time would pass quickly and their knowledge of the forest was invaluable in planning the route.

Finally we left. It was not advisable to enter The Palms with too many of us. On seeing all of us at a distance without recognizing me the servants of the Amaral family might have taken us for native looters or for just any tribe of gorillas and started shooting.

Oumé and I, therefore, said goodbye to Rou-o-ro and Pifi, deciding that they would wait for us in the area and expect our return in one week. At the time we were three days away from The Palms and there was only one way to get there.

\#

I'll leave you to imagine what surprise and joy the inhabitants of the tranquil abode felt on that morning when the Captain had left his window open and I climbed in, followed by Oumé, and threw myself into the arms of the good man.

At first he couldn't believe his eyes. Thinking I was some enemy he had grabbed his revolver, but I snatched it away as respectfully as possible—you must never play with firearms—and sitting at his desk I wrote a few simple words on a sheet of paper in place of a calling card:

"Popo and his wife Oumé."

Monsieur Amaral was stupefied. When he got hold of himself he hugged me tenderly, kissed the forehead of my companion, who was a little intimidated, and spoke to me:

"Oh, Popo you rascal, what grief you caused us! But since you're back, everything's forgotten... Besides, maybe you had good reason. An ape can't live without being free. It's to his credit anyway. Well, I can't keep you from going back to the forest, but you can come and see us from time to time with your family."

Moved to tears I could only make a few exaggerated signs of agreement. It seemed to me that Oumé already understood human language because her eyes were also moist.

The Captain called his sister and niece. You can imagine how surprised they were to see me, just like the servants who came running at the voice of their master.

Angele was still not married, in fact. Her wedding would take place in three months. She and her aunt not only gave me a very kindly welcome but were also very gracious to Madame Popo, which was very touching to me.

At breakfast the Amaral family sat us at the table with them. They did the same at dinner. I behaved—it goes without saying—like a well-raised gorilla and it was the same for Oumé, despite her limited experience in using a fork.

We spent two whole days at The Palms, pampered and spoiled. Then I wrote to the Captain that it was time to go back to meet Rou-o-ro and Pifi who were waiting for us in the forest and must have been terribly worried that we hadn't come back yet.

Monsieur Amaral was kind enough to ask me to introduce my family to him, but since it was unwise for a group of gorillas to get near human habitation without taking precautions he gave me four blue, wool shirts on which Madame Amaral embroidered in big red letters the names Popo, Oumé, Rou-o-ro and Pifi, followed by the phrase "Tame Gorillas belonging to Amaral—The Palms." This simple clothing, which was no bother to us, was our safe passage: it would keep any hunters or colonists from firing on us or trying to capture us.

We went back, therefore, to my father- and brother-in-law who were waiting anxiously. They were very relieved to see us come back. It was not easy to get Rou-o-ro to follow us because like a lot of philosophers he tended to be misanthropic. Still, to make us happy, he finally gave in. As for the young and curious Pifi, he couldn't hold back his joy.

The welcome that all four of the Amarals gave us was as friendly as the first one. In spite of Pifi's pranks—he was dead set on wearing the Captain's cap and drinking from his inkwell—our hosts looked as satisfied with us as we were with them. And Monsieur Amaral was really beaming when Rou-o-ro, who spoke little but thought much, gave me this sage advice:

"Why don't you teach this good man the gorilla language? That would be a lot better than communicating in writing."

It was indeed an excellent idea and the Captain agreed immediately while I felt very proud of taking a turn at being the teacher of the man whose student I was. And not only Monsieur Amaral but also his sister and niece wanted to take lessons.

We all started to teach but Oumé, Rou-o-ro and Pifi had no method and couldn't use writing to help them. The Amaral ladies stopped when they saw that the fun they were looking for was becoming tiresome and I remained alone with my former master.

But he made clear progress—we talked a little more every day. The love of useful knowledge along with our friendship gave him extraordinary patience. In one week he knew enough of the language to get along just fine with my family when I wasn't around. This result made me proud and happy and for a moment I wanted to get some calling cards printed that said, "Popo, Professor of Gorilla Language, Taught in Seven Days."

All good things must come to an end. The four of us staying there might have become a burden on our hosts. Moreover, Oumé, feisty Pifi and grave Rou-o-ro were starting to miss the forest. So, we left. But loaded with presents that each of us carried in a small suitcase attached with a strap that we slung proudly over our shoulders. The presents were priceless to us. They consisted of:

For Oumé a mirror, needles and thread, scissors, a little cloth, a thimble and colored ribbons.

For Rou-o-ro a fishing line and net.

For Pifi some rope, a rubber ball and a kite.

For me a French grammar and dictionary, a hammer, nails, paper, pencils, pen and ink, two erasers, blotting paper and a small chest.

Such things to make a comfortable life to satisfy both material needs and intellectual pursuits. Such things to amaze all our gorilla friends!

Our life is happy now. No one dreams of harming us, but I can tell you that if need be we will be apes who can defend ourselves.

Once in a while we go visit The Palms. I'm the father of two children now. Both show great promise and they come with us to see our friends, also wearing a blue shirt custom-made for them—our safe passage to visit the society of men.

Mademoiselle Angele Amaral became Madame Mouginot but she is as kind and charming as ever. Her husband is quite likeable... for a civil servant. Both of them come often to The Palms when we are there.

And Prudence became a real expert at making banana jam. She gets all excited when we come with rare-scented plants that we pick in the forest.

The Captain is passionately devoted to science but he's still an excellent man.

After such a full life. Which is not yet halfway through its natural course—but who knows what tomorrow will bring?—I thought that there might be here, at the same time as an inner satisfaction for me, some benefit for readers with an open mind and a generous heart to read these memoirs of a gorilla who sometimes believed he was a man.

I hope I have held your interest without tiring you out!

THE RAT AND THE OCTOPUS

A Kanak Tale from New Caledonia
(1885)

A rat, a gull and a purple moorhen lived together as friends and searched for food together. Now, at one time it happened that food ran short, so the two birds and the rodent had a powwow.

"Let's go fishing", said the gull. "Let's go to the reef. The sea will be low soon and we can get lots of fish."

"Good idea", said the purple moorhen.

"Ah!" sighed the rat, "that's easy enough for you with your wings, but me, a puny little quadruped, how can I follow you?"

"We'll build a raft", said the purple moorhen, "and you can come with us."

"Great!" cried out the other two.

They got to work. The rat gnawed, cut and hollowed out the sugar cane. The birds formed the pieces into a pirogue; hull, mast, sail, rudder, everything was made of sugar cane. The work was soon finished. The purple moorhen and the gull put the boat to sea and the rat jumped happily on and sailed off, escorted by his two partners.

They came to the great reef, which was dry at the time, and the gull and the purple moorhen said to the rat, "Stay here. We'll go fishing and come back with our catch." Then they flapped away and disappeared over the horizon.

Time passed and the two birds didn't return. Driven by hunger, the rat started to devour the sail, then the mast, then, tired of waiting for nothing, the rudder and, finally, the rest of the boat. He had hardly finished the last morsel when the two birds appeared, holding in their beaks the fish they'd caught.

"Okay!' cried the purple moorhen, "we've had good fishing, but where's your pirogue?"

"Argh!" answered the rat. "I waited a longtime for you. You didn't come back. I was hungry. I ate it."

"How's that?" screamed the gull. "We work hard to build a boat for you and you eat it. That's how you repay us! Fine. Since you're here, stay here." And with that the two birds left, leaving the rat sad and crying.

Already the tide was beginning to rise. "I'm a goner," said the rat. Spying a little rock that was still dry he jumped onto it just as the tide was about to wash over him.

"Argh," he murmured, "soon the water will reach me here and I'll have to die."

Just as he was about to start weeping, an octopus passed by and noticed him. "What are you doing here, little one?" he asked.

"I'm waiting to die," answered the rat sadly. "The gull and the purple moorhen abandoned me." And he told him his story.

"Ah! Ah!" said the octopus, who was a good creature, "you're really in a mess, but I'll help you out. Jump on my back. I'm not too fast, but I can still take you to land."

Cheered up, the rat jumped onto the head of the obliging animal. It's true he didn't swim very fast, but little by little they neared the land until they were only a short distance away.

The rat felt pretty relaxed now that he had escaped death. He laughed and danced like crazy and, with no respect for his savior, he peed on the head of the octopus.

"Hey, what are you doing, little one?" said the sea creature who felt the other one prancing about on his back.

"It's nothing," answered the rat. "It's the sight of land that's making me excited." Then, when they were only a few feet from shore, the rat, full of joy, took a dump on the head of his benefactor and leapt suddenly onto the land. "Now look at you," he yelled at the octopus and he keeled over laughing.

The octopus knew then how the ingrate had repaid him for his service. Furious, he wanted to rush forth and chase the rodent, but the rocks tore up his long arms. All bruised from the effort, he had to return to the depths of the sea.

Bibliography

Entre deux amours, 1880

La Maube et le Quartier, 1880

Avant l'heure, 1887

Philosophie de l'anarchie, 1889, reissued as *Philosophie de l'anarchie: 1888-1897*, 1897

Prison fin de siècle, souvenirs de Pélagie, with Ernest Gégout, 1891

Révolution chretienne et Révolution Sociale, 1891

De la Commune à l'anarchie, 1894

Le Bagne sous la Troisième République, 1895

La Reine des mers, 1895

Les Joyeusetés de l'exil, 1897

Contes néo-calédoniens (written as Talamo), 1897

L'homme nouveau, 1898

Barbapoux, drame satirique en deux actes, 1901

Les Mémoires d'un gorille (Talamo), 1901

Un jeune marin (Talamo), 1901

Les Enfants de la liberté (Talamo), 1903

Luisa Michel: la vita, le opere e l'azione rivoluzionaria, 1904

La Vie de Louise Michel, 1905

La Grande grève, 1905

Les Classes sociales au point de vue de l'évolution zoologique, 1907

L'Assassinat de Ferrer, 1911

Perdu au Maroc, ca 1915

Pierre Vaux, ou les malheurs d'un instituteur, 1915

Le Nouveau Faust, drame philosophico-fantaisiste, en quatre actes, 1919
Los deportados: Novela de aventuras, 1923
Les Forains, 1925
Mémoirs d'un Libertaire, 1937-38
César, pièce satirique en deux actes, no date

SF & FANTASY

Adolphe Alhaiza. *Cybele*

Alphonse Allais. *The Adventures of Captain Cap*

Henri Allorge. *The Great Cataclysm*

Guy d'Armen. *Doc Ardan: The City of Gold and Lepers; The Troglodytes of Mount Everest/The Giants of Black Lake; The Abominable Snowman*

G.-J. Arnaud. *The Ice Company*

André Arnyvelde. *The Ark; The Mutilated Bacchus*

Charles Asselineau. *The Double Life*

Henri Austruy. *The Eupantophone; The Olotelepan; The Petitpaon Era*

Barillet-Lagargousse. *The Final War*

Barbot de Villeneuve. *The Naiads/Beauty & The Beast*

Cyprien Bérard. *The Vampire Lord Ruthwen*

S. Henry Berthoud. *Martyrs of Science; The Angel Asrael*

Aloysius Bertrand. *Gaspard de la Nuit*

Richard Bessière. *The Gardens of the Apocalypse; The Masters of Silence*

Chevalier de Béthune. *The World of Mercury*

Albert Bleunard. *Ever Smaller*

Félix Bodin. *The Novel of the Future*

Pierre Boitard. *Journey to the Sun*

Louis Boussenard. *Monsieur Synthesis*

Alphonse Brown. *City of Glass; The Conquest of the Air*

Émile Calvet. *In a Thousand Years*

André Caroff. *The Terror of Madame Atomos; Miss Atomos; The Return of Madame Atomos; The Mistake of Madame Atomos; The Monsters of Madame Atomos; The Revenge of Madame Atomos; The Resurrection of Madame Atomos; The Mark of Madame Atomos; The Spheres of Madame Atomos; The Wrath of Madame Atomos* (w/M. & Sylvie Stéphan)

Jean Carrère. *The End of Atlantis*

Félicien Champsaur. *Homo-Deus; The Human Arrow; Nora, The Ape-Woman; Ouha, King of the Apes; Pharaoh's Wife*

Didier de Chousy. *Ignis*

Jules Clarétie. *Obsession*

Jacques Collin de Plancy. *Voyage to the Center of the Earth*

Michel Corday. *The Eternal Flame; The Lynx* (w/André Couvreur)
André Couvreur. *Caresco, Superman; The Exploits of Professor Tornada* (3 vols.); *The Necessary Evil*
Gaston Danville. *The Perfume of Lust*
Camille Debans. *The Misfortunes of John Bull*
Captain Danrit. *Undersea Odyssey*
C. I. Defontenay. *Star (Psi Cassiopeia)*
Charles Derennes. *The People of the Pole*
Georges Dodds (anthologist). *The Missing Link*
Charles Dodeman. *The Silent Bomb*
Harry Dickson. *The Heir of Dracula; Harry Dickson vs. The Spider*
Jules Dornay. *Lord Ruthven Begins*
Alfred Driou. *The Adventures of a Parisian Aeronaut*
Odette Dulac. *The War of the Sexes*
Alexandre Dumas. *The Return of Lord Ruthven; The Man who Married a Mermaid* (w/P. Lacroix)
Renée Dunan. *Baal; The Ultimate Pleasure*
J.-C. Dunyach. *The Night Orchid; The Thieves of Silence*
Henri Duvernois. *The Man Who Found Himself*
Achille Eyraud. *Voyage to Venus*
Henri Falk. *The Age of Lead*
Paul Féval. *Anne of the Isles; Knightshade; Revenants; Vampire City; The Vampire Countess; The Wandering Jew's Daughter*
Paul Féval, *fils. Felifax, the Tiger-Man*
Charles de Fieux. *Lamékis*
Fernand Fleuret. *Jim Click*
Charles-Marie Flor O'Squarr. *Phantoms*
Louis Forest. *Someone is Stealing Children in Paris*
Arnould Galopin. *Doctor Omega; Doctor Omega and the Shadowmen* (anthology)
Judith Gautier. *Isoline and the Serpent-Flower*
H. Gayar. *The Marvelous Adventures of Serge Myrandhal on Mars*
Louis Geoffroy. *The Apocryphal Napoleon*
G.L. Gick. *Harry Dickson and the Werewolf of Rutherford Grange*
Raoul Gineste. *The Second Life of Doctor Albin*
Delphine de Girardin. *Balzac's Cane*
Léon Gozlan. *The Vampire of the Val-de-Grâce*
Jules Gros. *The Fossil Man*
Jimmy Guieu. *The Polarian-Denebian War* (2 vols.)
Edmond Haraucourt. *Daah, the First Human; Illusions of Immortality*
Nathalie Henneberg. *The Green Gods*

Eugène Hennebert. *The Enchanted City*

Jules Hoche. *The Maker of Men and His Formula*

V. Hugo, P. Foucher & P. Meurice. *The Hunchback of Notre-Dame*

Romain d'Huissier. *Hexagon: Dark Matter*

Jules Janin. *The Magnetized Corpse*

Gustave Kahn. *The Tale of Gold and Silence*

Gérard Klein. *The Mote in Time's Eye*

Fernand Kolney. *Love in 5000 Years*

Paul Lacroix. *Danse Macabre; The Man who Married a Mermaid* (w/Alexandre Dumas)

Louis-Guillaume de La Follie. *The Unpretentious Philosopher*

Jean de La Hire. *The Fiery Wheel; Enter the Nyctalope; The Nyctalope on Mars; The Nyctalope vs. Lucifer; The Nyctalope Steps In; Night of the Nyctalope; Return of the Nyctalope*

Etienne-Léon de Lamothe-Langon. *The Virgin Vampire*

André Laurie. *Spiridon*

Gabriel de Lautrec. *The Vengeance of the Oval Portrait*

Alain le Drimeur. *The Future City*

Georges Le Faure & Henri de Graffigny. *The Extraordinary Adventures of a Russian Scientist Across the Solar System* (2 vols.)

Gustave Le Rouge. *The Dominion of the World* (w/Gustave Guitton) (4 vols.); *The Mysterious Doctor Cornelius* (3 vols.); *The Vampires of Mars*

Jules Lermina. *The Battle of Strasbourg; Mysteryville; Panic in Paris; The Secret of Zippelius; To-Ho and the Gold Destroyers*

Maurice Level. *The Gates of Hell*

André Lichtenberger. *The Centaurs; The Children of the Crab*

Maurice Limat. *Mephista*

Listonai. *The Philosophical Voyager*

Jean-Marc & Randy Lofficier. *Edgar Allan Poe on Mars; The Katrina Protocol; Pacifica 1, 2; Robonocchio; Return of the Nyctalope;* (anthologists) *Tales of the Shadowmen 1-13; The Vampire Almanac* (2 vols.)

Ch. Lomon & P.-B. Gheuzi. *The Last Days of Atlantis*

Maurice Magre. *The Marvelous Story of Claire d'Amour; The Call of the Beast*

Camille Mauclair. *The Virgin Orient*

Xavier Mauméjean. *The League of Heroes*

Joseph Méry. *The Tower of Destiny*

Hippolyte Mettais. *Paris Before the Deluge; The Year 5865*

Louise Michel. *The Human Microbes; The New World*

Tony Moilin. *Paris in the Year 2000*
Michael Moorcock's *Legends of the Multiverse*
José Moselli. *Illa's End*
John-Antoine Nau. *Enemy Force*
Marie Nizet. *Captain Vampire*
Charles Nodier. *Trilby and The Crumb Fairy*
C. Nodier, A. Beraud & Toussaint-Merle. *Frankenstein*
Henri de Parville. *An Inhabitant of the Planet Mars*
Gaston de Pawlowski. *Journey to the Land of the 4th Dimension*
Georges Pellerin. *The World in 2000 Years*
Ernest Pérochon. *The Frenetic People*
Pierre Pelot. *The Child Who Walked on the Sky*
Jean Petithuguenin. *An International Mission to the Moon*
J. Polidori, C. Nodier, E. Scribe. *Lord Ruthven the Vampire*
P.-A. Ponson du Terrail. *The Immortal Woman; The Vampire and the Devil's Son; The Police Agent*
Georges Price. *The Missing Men of the* Sirius
René Pujol. *The Chimerical Quest*
Edgar Quinet. *Ahasuerus; The Enchanter Merlin*
Jean Rameau. *Arrival; in the Stars*
Henri de Régnier. *A Surfeit of Mirrors*
Maurice Renard. *The Blue Peril; Doctor Lerne; The Doctored Man; A Man Among the Microbes; The Master of Light*
Restif de la Bretonne. *The Discovery of the Austral Continent by a Flying Man; Posthumous Correspondence* (3 vols.); *The Fay Ouroucoucou* (2 vols.)
Jean Richepin. *The Crazy Corner; The Wing*
Albert Robida. *The Adventures of Saturnin Farandoul; Chalet in the Sky; The Clock of the Centuries; The Electric Life; The Engineer Von Satanas*
J.-H. Rosny Aîné. *Helgvor of the Blue River; The Givreuse Enigma; The Mysterious Force; The Navigators of Space; Vamireh; The World of the Variants; The Young Vampire*
Marcel Rouff. *Journey to the Inverted World*
Marie-Anne de Roumier-Robert. *The Voyage of Lord Seaton to the Seven Planets*
Léonie Rouzade. *The World Turned Upside Down*
Han Ryner. *The Human Ant; The Superhumans*
Henri de Saint-Georges. *The Green Eyes*
Louis-Claude de Saint-Martin. *The Crocodile*

Frank Schildiner. *The Quest of Frankenstein; The Triumph of Frankenstein; Napoleon's Vampire Hunters*

Nicolas Ségur. *The Human Paradise*

Pierre de Selenes: *An Unknown World*

Norbert Sevestre. *Sâr Dubnotal: Vs. Jack the Ripper; The Astral Trail*

Angelo de Sorr. *The Vampires of London*

Brian Stableford. *The Empire of the Necromancers (1. The Shadow of Frankenstein; 2. Frankenstein and the Vampire Countess; 3. Frankenstein in London); The Wayward Muse; Eurydice's Lament; The Mirror of Dionysius; The New Faust at the Tragicomique; Sherlock Holmes and The Vampires of Eternity; The Stones of Camelot* (anthologist) *News from the Moon; The Germans on Venus; The Supreme Progress; The World Above the World; Nemoville; Investigations of the Future; The Conqueror of Death; The Revolt of the Machines; The Man With the Blue Face; The Aerial Valley; The New Moon; The Nickel Man; On the Brink of the World's End; The Mirror of Present Events; The Humanisphere*

Jacques Spitz. *The Eye of Purgatory*

Kurt Steiner. *Ortog*

Eugène Thébault. *Radio-Terror*

C.-F. Tiphaigne de La Roche. *Amilec*

Simon Tyssot de Patot. *The Strange Voyages of Jacques Massé and Pierre de Mésange*

Louis Ulbach. *Prince Bonifacio*

Théo Varlet. *The Castaways of Eros; The Golden Rock.; The Martian Epic* (w/Octave Joncquel); *Timeslip Troopers* (w/André Blandin); *The Xenobiotic Invasion*

Pierre Véron. *The Merchants of Health*

Paul Vibert. *The Mysterious Fluid*

Villiers de l'Isle-Adam. *The Scaffold; The Vampire Soul*

Gaston de Wailly. *The Murderer of the World*

Philippe Ward. *Artahe; Manhattan Ghost* (w/Mickael Laguerre); *The Song of Montségur* (w/Sylvie Miller)

Victor Margueritte. *The Bacheloress; The Companion; The Couple*